The Travel Auction

Mark Green

The Travel Auction is also available as an eBook from Amazon, (Kindle) Smashwords.com (all other eReaders) or iTunes, Sony, Kobo and Barnes & Noble websites.

www.markdavidgreen.co.uk

Acknowledgements

I owe a big thank you to a few special people who helped make the writing of this book possible:

To my mum and dad, Christine and Norman, for the extra tuition in my early years.

To my grandparents, Cliff and Irene, for helping me financially which allowed me valuable rewriting time.

To Sarah Butler, for her feedback on the early drafts.

To Jan and Gary Jones, for their kind gift of a travel journal which provided the backdrop for this story.

To the wonderful people I met in South America.

And to my wife, Nicola, for being my travel companion, book editor and first mate.

<u>One</u>

I felt my throat tighten and instantly knew that I'd made a terrible mistake. I glanced around the blurring party faces, difficult to recognise through my alcohol-induced haze. I gasped, fighting to breathe and instinctively patted myself down, frantically searching my pockets. I tried desperately to suck in more oxygen before I started to choke, my legs collapsed and I hit the floor hard, convulsing. Someone shouted, muffled and distant as panic set in around me.

"Shit! Where is it? Quick, find his..."
And that's the last thing I remember. Next thing I knew I was waking up in hospital with the hangover from hell.

"You look like crap, mate," said a voice I vaguely recognised.
"Kate?"

"Don't be daft. You're a free man now, remember?"
I groaned and tried to sit up as a shockwave of nausea washed over me. I managed to lean over the side of the bed, then threw up all over Justin's shoes.

I was still feeling rough on Monday morning, which made my telephone call to the travel company particularly difficult. I swore under my breath as I replaced the receiver and slumped over my desk. *What do I do now?*

"I guess I'll have to advertise," I said to Justin.

"So you'll put an advert on eBay for what? *Lady wanted: occasional nursemaid to needle-phobic thirty-something, for all expenses paid trip to South America. Oh, and must have the name Kate Thornly.*"
Justin sniggered. I gave him the finger and took a bite from my sandwich. His sarcasm annoyed me but I was also acutely aware of how much truth there was in it. I'd been dreaming of a trip like this for years, working up the courage to throw caution to the wind, give notice at work and just go.

"Actually..." I said between mouthfuls of sandwich, "...that's not a bad idea."

*Adventure of a Lifetime for **KATE THORNLY!***
Time Left 6 days 7 hours 32s
Bid History 0 bids
Starting bid £0.01
Reserve Not Met

Enter Maximum bid £

<u>Description</u>
Three-month trip around South America with thirty-something
male. The seller will meet all expenses. This is a genuine sale.
Bidders MUST be able to meet <u>all</u> of the following conditions:
1. Must be able to leave on 2<u>nd</u> October for three complete
months.
2. Must have all jabs up-to-date for South America. i.e.
Argentina, Peru, Bolivia, Paraguay and Brazil. (Injections -
polio, typhoid etc. but in particular yellow fever.)
3. Must be physically fit enough to complete 4-day Inca Trail.
4. Mustn't be squeamish and should be able to administer
emergency first aid and must be comfortable handling needles.
5. MUST have a full 10 year passport and MUST, MUST, MUST
*have a passport in the name of **KATE THORNLY** – this is*
essential – all bidders must e-mail a scanned copy of their
passport for verification prior to bidding.
6. Spanish speaker preferred.
7. Any bid must include a profile of you.
8. Please e-mail any questions before the deadline.

THIS IS AN UNUSUAL, BUT I GUARANTEE
COMPLETELY GENUINE OFFER. I HAVE AN ALLERGY
TO NUTS AND NEED A TRAVEL COMPANION WHO'S
ABLE TO ADMINISTER EMERGENCY ADRENALIN
SHOULD THE NEED ARISE.

Justin peered over my shoulder as I finished typing.
    "You're not serious?"

"Why not? Has to be worth a try. Kate and I had an agreement. I got a zero interest credit card to pay for the trip up front and she was supposed to pay me back in monthly instalments. Instead, she cancelled her standing order when she gave me the elbow. I rang the travel company; they can't refund me and won't change the name on her ticket. So, I either find another *Kate Thornly* to go with me, or I ditch the entire trip and lose all that money."

"All you need now is a guardian angel armed with adrenaline," said Justin, somewhat sarcastically.
I shrugged.

"She'll have a fantastic holiday out of it," I said, unsure whom I was trying to convince.

"What about a photo?" said Justin.
I considered this for a moment; it wasn't something I'd thought of.

"To be honest, looks aren't important. I just need a travel companion who can keep an eye on what I eat and to be there if I have another episode..."
Justin rolled his eyes.

"What?"

"A photo of you, dopey. These *Kate Thornlys* should know what they're getting into – you could be the elephant man!"

Kate Thornly (the 2ⁿᵈ)

Of course I'd heard about the eBay auction, who hadn't.
But luckily I'd avoided all the early attention from my mates because none of them knows me as *Kate Thornly*, to them I'm Angel.

I hate being called Kate. Have done all the way back to school. Kids can be so spiteful. *Katy the Cake* they'd taunted me, because I was a bit overweight back then.

So I decided to use my middle name, the one my dad had apparently insisted on shortly after I was born and he'd buggered off.

At the age of nine, I started telling mum I wanted to be called Angela. She didn't take the news well. It took several weeks for her to wheedle the reason out of me. I eventually told her one tearful afternoon at a friend's birthday party, where I'd insisted everyone call me by my new name. I think mum felt guilty, unaware I was being bullied. So we made a pact and from that day I was no longer Katy the Cake. Mum didn't like calling me Angela, so over time I became Angel. From then on without any 'Deed Poll' amateur dramatics and aside from occasionally having to use my real name for form filling or booking holidays, I more or less forgot that *Kate Thornly* had ever existed. Until that bloody eBay advertisement.

Me
Somehow, the advert on eBay got noticed, but a few of the replies weren't quite what I was expecting…

E-Mail From: Kate Thornly
To: Jonathan Cork
Sent: 26 September 08:26
Subject: South America

Surely you should be paying me to come with you to a continent where they eat guinea pigs and hate the English for reclaiming the Falkland Islands? My fee is one thousand pounds per month, plus all additional expenses.
(Mrs) Kate Thornly

E-Mail From: Kate Thornly
To: Jonathan Cork
Sent: 26 September 17:18
Subject: Holiday Travel

Dear Jonathan,
I would dearly love to accompany you on your Latin American adventure. I just have one query: can you send an itinerary of the trip advising when we'll be in a major city as I need to draw my pension every Thursday? I look forward to hearing from you.
Yours sincerely
Kate Thornly (divorced 1985)
PS. You look rather dashing in your photograph

E-Mail From: Mathew Tope
To: Jonathan Cork
Sent: 27 September 01:44
Subject: Holiday Travel

Hi Jonathan,
I'm not Kate Thornly yet, but I'm in the final stages of my gender
re-alignment surgery. I've still to officially change my name (my
new friends call me Mildred – unfortunately I've had to leave
many of the old ones behind for reasons of acceptance of my new
self) and Kate Thornly seems like a nice feminine name. I'm not
sure how long it takes to change a name by Deed Poll, or how
quickly I can get a new passport, but would you consider waiting
for me? You seem like a decent man who might be broadminded
enough to accept a new woman such as myself. Can't wait to
hear from you, I'll write again after my surgery this weekend.
Best wishes and new horizons
Mildred (soon to be Kate Thornly…?)

I wasn't prepared for the responses I got from the advertisement.
I heard a rumour that a web link to the advert was e-mailed from
company to company in most cities. I don't know if that's true,
but the 'hits' counter on my eBay page was up to 80,000 after
day two, nearly 300,000 by day three and as I sit here now it's
over 750,000. Surely there can't be that many Kate Thornlys in
the country?

Kate Thornly the 1st was not amused.

"I've been made a laughing stock," she moaned to me over
the phone.

"That wasn't my intention," I said, but I couldn't help a
private smile.

"But now someone else will get to go on *my* trip. I helped you
plan it, I've nurse-maided you all these years, and now another
me gets the benefit…"

"I'd stop there if I were you Kate. Aside from leaving me for
someone else, you've also left me with *your* debt. So I'm afraid
if you're looking for sympathy from me, you are…"
Click.

I lifted my head from my hands and glanced over at Justin.

"This is bonkers. Where the hell do I start?"

"How many have you got? We'll whittle them all down to a short list, like they do for job interviews.

"Five hundred and twelve," I replied, in a daze from sitting in front of the computer screen all day. Justin shook his head and grinned.

"What?" I said, from behind fingers still clasped across my face.

"You're an analyst, right? At most times as we have often speculated, a perfectly useless skill. But here's an opportunity to put that knowledge to some use."

I lifted my head from my hands.

"We set parameters, strip down the numbers according to your criteria…"

"Except that I don't really have any – I'm not looking for a girlfriend," I interrupted.

"Maybe not, but we have to be brutal with the raw data to crunch the numbers down. That's what we do, remember."

"Did," I corrected him, smiling for the first time that day. Handing in my notice to go off travelling had been a huge deal and I'd dithered for months before finally biting the bullet. But now, despite the small problem of recruiting a new travel companion, it was a huge relief to be leaving the office job I'd always hated.

"Okay, *did*. But let's use those skills before you leave them somewhere in darkest Peru, never to be seen again…"

I shrugged, glad someone else was huddled over my computer to help take some of the responsibility.

"Let's make a list. Top of the agenda – age. I assume you don't want to travel with a pensioner?"

"Nor a teenager," I said, remembering one of the e-mails.

"Er, no. Although…"

I rolled my eyes, tapping my keyboard, setting up a search programme. Justin winked at me then dropped his eyes to the pad.

"Twenty to thirty five?" he said, jotting down some notes.

"Twenty five to forty."

"Marital status. I'm assuming single?"

We spent several hours building our database and inputting information, applying parameters and arguing over my apparently 'conservative' choices.

"And finally, but most importantly, breast size?"

I closed my eyes in despair.

"Just kidding. Go for it."

I glanced up, attempted a half-hearted smile and then hit 'enter'. Justin pulled his chair nearer.

"How many?"

I stared at the big zero on the screen.

Kate Thornly (the 2nd)

I thought I'd just keep quiet, let it pass, but my friend Maria had other ideas. She'd booked a holiday for us last year and had been surprised at the name on my passport, so I'd had to explain. Maria has a good memory, so once the penny dropped that my name matched the ad, she started on at me and didn't let up.

"Think about it, three months all expenses paid. This is once-in-a- lifetime stuff, especially with your, well, you know…"

"Which is exactly why no one in their right mind would ever pick me to go with them…"

"Stop right there," Maria's stern voice interrupted.

I sighed, knowing I was in for one of her lectures.

"You are an intelligent, attractive woman. What have you got to lose?"

And that's how it started.

Two

Me

The auction deadline was looming and I was no closer to getting on a plane with a travel companion. Actually that sounds a bit defeatist. There were options, by that I mean a shortlist of three possible *Kate Thornlys*, but none of them filled me with much enthusiasm.

The first Kate (let's call her Kate 'A' for now, to save any confusion later) was twenty-five, just scrapping into my lower age range, not that age mattered anymore, I was getting desperate. The only problem was her looks. I don't mean she was unattractive, far from it. But she was the spitting image of Kate Thornly the 1st – not something I wanted to be reminded of every day for the next three months. Justin couldn't see the similarity, but I could.

Strike one.

Kate 'B' was at the higher end of the age range at forty-eight. I fleetingly considered her, but was put off by her gothic appearance. In her letter she seemed a little too interested in the Inca sacrificial sites and their whole 'offerings to the gods' philosophy. A pity, she would have been an interesting prospect, if I were in any way interested in the occult.

Strike two.

Talk about extremes. Kate 'C' was off the scale, but in a completely different way. I can't remember which church she was a member of, possibly one of those trendy Christian youth groups. But what really put me off were the references in her e-mail about how much charity work we could do in each country. That didn't fit into my agenda at all. I hadn't worked my arse off in the city, and slaved away for all those long hours to waste time working for other people, what was the point in that? Call me selfish and arrogant, but that's just the way it was.

Strike three.

Which left me with nothing. Zero. Diddlysquat.

Kate Thornly (the 2ⁿᵈ)

I no longer have a friend called Maria. No, never met her. Who? What a cow!

We'd had a good laugh speculating about what sort of person he'd end up with; it really was potluck wasn't it? I mean, he was tied to a *Kate Thornly* but had no say in what type of person she was. It was all just down to a name. Of course I didn't write in, despite Maria's insistence, I wasn't that stupid or easy to persuade. We Scots are stubborn to the last.

Do you know how far I went to avoid getting involved with that stupid advert? Knowing how conniving my friend can be, okay, her heart is in the right place and she always thinks she's doing things 'for my own good,' but knowing how mischievous she is, I actually hid my passport. As soon as she started to try and persuade me, I recognised the tremor of excitement in her voice and the alarm bells went off. I excused myself to go for a wee, nipped into the bathroom and tucked my passport behind the basin pedestal.

I thought I was one step ahead of her. Unfortunately, when we'd gone away on holiday last year we'd taken photocopies of our passports as a precaution against having them stolen. A very fine and sensible idea at the time, but Maria still had those photocopies tucked away in a drawer somewhere, gathering dust. Until now.

Picture me shaking my head at Maria as I write this. Thanks a bunch *amigo*.

Me

A rabbit appeared out of a very empty hat. Kate Thornly the 2ⁿᵈ dropped into my inbox just in the nick of time. And she seemed so, normal.

"Thirty two years old… trained nurse… up for a challenge… Bloody perfect," said Justin as he speed-read through her introduction letter.

"And the passport matches?"
I nodded, still a little shocked that I might actually have found someone.

"What about the photo?"

I double clicked on the attachment, which still managed to raise a smile even after several viewings. It had been Justin's idea to request all photos be taken with a newspaper. This was so that, in his words, I "wouldn't end up with someone who may have looked okay in a photo taken fifty years ago…" I had to hand it to him, it was a good idea, despite being a bit tacky.

"Bloody hell!"

Justin was staring at the screen. An attractive girl with mousy hair, probably around five feet four, slim but with partially visible curves, was standing in a shower cubicle, half turned towards the camera. She was naked, with cascading water frozen in mid-air around her. It was a stunning shot that grabbed my attention. The real genius however, was that the newspaper front and back pages opened across the middle part of the photograph, barely covering from the lower portion of her milky white breasts to just below the hemline of an imaginary mini skirt. The image was even more erotic because the expression on her face was quizzical yet warm and couldn't possibly have been posed for. It had been captured, almost as if she were unaware the photograph was being taken.

Justin was salivating as he studied every inch of the photograph.

"You lucky, lucky bastard! What the hell are you waiting for? Pick up the damn phone!"

Kate Thornly (the 2nd)

There was something odd in Maria's behaviour. She was desperately trying to conceal her excitement, so I asked her outright what was going on. I should have known she was up to something.

"I'm taking you shopping," she said.

"I don't need anything."

"I do. Come on, humour me, I value your opinion."

I shook my head and smiled. It was a private joke when we went shopping together. I'd sit by the fitting rooms and Maria would ask what I thought of the endless clothes she would try on. I'd agree or disagree with the fit, colour and suitability, etcetera, confusing the hell out of the shop assistant who was by then convinced I had absolutely no taste. Afterwards we'd have a coffee and laugh our heads off as Maria mimicked the reaction of the shop assistant to our double act.

Sitting in Maria's car, I was none the wiser. I heard the car boot open and then it slammed down again, rocking the car - something heavy having been thrown in. I turned to face Maria as she climbed into the driver's seat.

"Couple of bits for the journey," she said.

"Oh. We're not going local today then?"

"Not exactly."

I shrugged, it made no difference to me. I had the whole day and besides, I enjoyed our little adventures.

Me

"What about a contingency plan if..." I began.

"Relax. You spoke to her, right? And she didn't give any sign of backing out or being a loony, so it's all good, we have lift off. You're gonna have the most amazing time, forget all about the *other* Kate Thornly and it's happy days."

I took a deep calming breath. As if I wasn't nervous enough about the whole trip, I'd now be going with a complete stranger. Even so, it was exciting to take off travelling for three months. And her picture was dynamite!

Reading her letter again, seeing the photo and speaking to her on the phone had definitely fed my ego. I reckoned I was in for a raunchy trip and I was secretly rubbing my hands together. After all, any girl who was willing to send in that sort of photo had to be up for a good time...

Kate Thornly (the 2nd)

"You did what?!"

If I was expecting a sheepish apology, I was soon put right.

"Listen, you can do this. The man wants *you*. It's the adventure of a lifetime and don't you dare back out. What the hell else have you got planned for the next few months? You've been tiptoeing around life ever since... what I mean is, it's all organised. I've even found your passport, naughty minx - it took me ages. You've a backpack in the boot with all the essentials. So sweet pea, *you're* going to South America!"

I've no idea how long my jaw hung open, but it was long enough for Maria to reach across and gently push it back up.

"We're meeting him in an hour. Tomorrow morning you're getting on a plane. First stop is Argentina, then Peru, Bolivia and Brazil. You better get him to send back some pictures, the girls all clubbed together to make this happen and will want to hear how you're getting on. Angel, are you okay with this?"
I was unable to say anything for a long time. How do you react to something like that?

"YEEEEHHHARRRR!!!" I screamed out, a nervous reaction rather than an excited one, as a big knot formed in my stomach.

"WHOOPPPEEEE!!!" I shouted again, and then broke into a fit of giggles that quickly developed into tears. What sort of person wanted to go travelling with me? What use could I possibly be?

Maria screeched the car to a stop, undid her seat belt and reached over to hug me.

"You'll be okay, this is just what you need. You can do this," she repeated over and over as I cried into her shoulder.

Me

I woke abruptly, in a cold sweat. It was the same nightmare that had haunted me since mum died. Was it really a month ago? I shuddered and leant over to check the clock; 3:16am. I felt the familiar guilt well up. I hate hospitals, always have. And those last few visits to see mum were awful. I'd get hot, then feel sick and have to get out. It was the *smell,* clinical and desperate…

I screwed my eyes tightly shut, remembering my own recent stay in hospital. I don't remember much about the ambulance ride, only the expression on the paramedic's face.

"You had us worried there," she'd said, in a tone that was both concerned and disapproving. She didn't look me in the eye again.

What on earth had I been thinking? I wasn't a nutcase, I had a good job, career prospects and… I allowed myself a wry smile. *Nutcase.* Now there was an irony.

I took a deep calming breath and sank back into the pillow. In just a few hours I'd finally be leaving all that behind, flying away on an incredible adventure. There was just the small matter of meeting my new travel companion.

Kate Thornly (the 2nd)

As we got closer to the hotel I felt the butterflies in my tummy playing havoc and a mixture of nervous excitement flooded through me. I suddenly realised that Maria had been speed talking for the last half an hour, not unusual for her, but I wondered if it was something more than just being nervous on my behalf. Then it hit me. She was trying to stop me from thinking too much. I suddenly realised there were questions I needed answered.

"How did you get round the issue of a recent photo?"

"Oh, just a bit of clever desktop editing. Nearly there," Maria replied, a nervous twitch in her voice.

I wasn't convinced but was running out of time to interrogate her because she started slowing down.

"I don't believe you."

Maria made a left turn and stopped the car, remaining silent for a moment.

"I caught you unawares. I taped a newspaper across the frame of the bathroom door and took a photo of you in the shower. I got the headline and date in the foreground and you in the background."

"Hang on, that was the day you told me it was lightning outside. But it was the flash going off?"

"Erm, yes. Come on, let's not be late," said Maria, climbing out of the car. I followed her as she opened the boot and picked up the rucksack she'd brought.

"You haven't told him, have you?"

But my words were lost in the whirl of the revolving door and I suddenly found myself standing in the hotel lobby. I started to shake my head, and then couldn't help giggling. This was going to be the shortest blind travel date in history.

Me

I was quite taken with Kate Thornly the 2nd the first time I saw her. She stood in the lobby looking a bit lost, waiting for her red-faced friend to arrive heaving a huge backpack. Maria, I think

17

her name was. The first inkling that something wasn't quite right started to sink in as I approached Kate to shake her hand in a friendly, but business-like greeting.

"Hello there, you must be Kate Thornly. I'm Jonathan Cork." Kate smiled and offered her hand. I was so caught up in the nerves of meeting her that I didn't spot anything amiss.
Thud!
Maria dropped the pack off her shoulder next to Kate, puffing from the exertion.

"Good luck lugging that around South America. Right, that's me done. Gotta run. See ya."
I raised my eyebrows as Maria hugged her friend and whispered something in her ear. Then she grinned and winked at me, offering a passing comment as she turned and walked out of the hotel.

"Look after her, she's a real angel."
I frowned as I watched Maria scurry away. Something was niggling away at the back of my mind. There was an awkward pause as we both stood there.

"Right, well. Um, would you like a coffee, have you eaten?"

"Coffee would be great, thanks," she said, in a light Scottish accent.
I nodded, picked up the pack (which *was* bloody heavy) and walked over to the comfy sofas in the corner of the lobby. I set the pack down and turned to offer Kate the nearest seat, confused to see her still standing in the same spot. I walked back to her, a little sheepishly.

"Anything I should know?"

"Perhaps. Yes. Definitely. I didn't write the letter to you, or speak to you on the phone, my friend did. It was to broaden my horizons, bless her. The photo was also her doing," said Kate Thornly the 2nd.

"Oh."
We stood there like a couple of lemons as a couple leaving the hotel filtered past us, intrigued expressions on their faces.

"Shall we sit down, have a chat? I'm sure we can straighten things out. You have a backpack, so presumably you'd be willing to come along?"

"Why the hell not. Lead the way," she said, raising her elbow to form a gap between her body and arm.

"Of course," I said, then hesitated.

An amused smile broadened on her lips.

"The reason Maria applied for me is because I'm not the easiest of travel companions…"

"No? Why not…"

I still cringe when I think back. How could I have been so stupid not to realise?

There was a long pause.

"Because Jonathan, I'm blind."

<u>Three</u>

<u>Kate Thornly</u> (the 2nd)

"You're... blind?" said Jonathan, horrified.

You often hear people say *I wish I'd seen the look on their face...* But I think that every time I meet someone new. I could immediately tell from the tone of his voice that this situation was now a disaster. He couldn't possibly go travelling to South America with a blind companion.

I was convinced I'd be back with Maria in minutes. She'd whispered in my ear before she left that if it all went tits up, she'd wait for me in the car park for an hour. Which of course was bound to happen. There was no way I could go off travelling around South America with a complete stranger, I was blind, not stupid!

"I'm sorry you've had a wasted journey... couldn't possibly go with me... rugged terrain and, um... have enough trouble looking after myself... erm... have you come far...?"

I could hear him pacing as he rambled on.

"Jesus, I need a drink!" he muttered and walked away.

<u>Me</u>

I knocked back the large whisky in one, wincing as it burned its way down my throat. What the hell was I going to do now?

<u>Kate Thornly</u> (the 2nd)

I stood there for some time feeling ridiculous. Surely he'd be back, apologising for being so rude?

Nope.

Okay, sod you mate!

I had a vague idea which way the main entrance was, so I knelt down and felt for my rucksack. Having worked out where the straps were, I heaved it onto my back. Maria wasn't joking, it weighed a ton!

I could feel the occasional waft of fresh air from the revolving doors, which presented me with a bit of a problem. It's all down to timing, you see.

Chop, chop, chop. The doors whirled past the opening like an airplane propeller in slow motion. Now, which limb did I want to lose first?

Me

Thwack!

I lifted my head from my hands and opened my eyes, the noise just beat my conscience in pulling me back to reality. I twisted round in my seat to see Kate Thornly the 2nd standing by the revolving doors, her backpack wedged in them. I watched, bewildered, as she felt her way into a vacant segment of the doorway, stepped over the rucksack, then hauled it in after her. It took a moment for the penny to drop – she'd thrown the rucksack into the door to stop it spinning, clever girl! The middle-aged couple stuck in an opposite segment with their noses squashed against the glass weren't amused however and started banging on the glass.

I jumped up and rushed over, fighting the temptation to laugh.

Kate Thornly (the 2nd)

"Alright, keep your hair on!" I shouted, pushing against the revolving door with my forehead as I dragged the rucksack with my left hand and trailed my right against the curved glass, waiting for the gap.

There! go, go, go!

I leapt into fresh air, but wasn't quite fast enough yanking my rucksack out and I felt it jam against the next part of the door.

Bugger!

Me

The middle-aged couple were now banging furiously on the glass, trapped only a few inches from the hotel lobby.

Outside the hotel, an irate Kate Thornly the 2nd tried to heave her jammed rucksack out of the door, but it wouldn't budge. It took me a few seconds to realise that I had to push the door the opposite way to free the rucksack, so I attempted my best apologetic smile and pushed the door against the angry couple.

I heard a scream and saw Kate Thornly the 2nd tumble backwards, having put all her weight behind pulling the rucksack just as the door released it. The couple pushed past me, swearing. By the time I got to Kate Thornly the 2nd she was sprawled on the floor in a dishevelled heap.

"Kate, are you okay?" I said weakly.

"Piss off, you rude arrogant bastard!"

"It was just a shock, the blindness thing... here, let me help you up," I said, putting my hands under her arms to lift her up.

"Take your fucking hands off me!"

I stepped back as she stood up, dusted herself down and pulled sweaty hair out of her eyes.

"I'm not a cripple!"

"I'm sorry, I was just trying to help,"

"Then get my rucksack and buy me a sodding drink!" she said, wiping her tearful eyes.

Kate Thornly (the 2nd)

"I don't think I've ever been so humiliated," I said, taking a gulp from the glass of wine, banging it on the table.

"Your friend conned us both, so technically it wasn't my fault. You can't blame me for..."

"*Technically* you're a coward for running away!"

"It was a shock, alright! From your reply to the advert, I was expecting..."

"What, exactly? Someone *able-bodied*? Not *disabled*? Not a liability?" I shouted at him.

There was a long silence, during which I hoped he was squirming uncomfortably in his seat.

"Someone who matched the description given to me," he said quietly.

"Well boo-bloody-hoo! Have you never internet dated? People are never as they appear. It's all smoke and mirrors and bullshit self-marketing. Wake up to the real world Jonathan! Maria told me you were a decent guy who had integrity. So where's the match in *that* description?"

Me

What a complete and utter mess. I watched her sink back into the chair, arms folded, angry as hell. I wondered how quickly I could get rid of her without a big scene.

"Look, I'm sorry you feel deceived too, but she's *your* friend. You have to take some responsibility for Maria stitching us up."

"That's no excuse for your reaction!"

"Okay. I'm sorry. You've made a fair point. I didn't handle this meeting very well. But clearly this, us travelling together, isn't going to work. I apologise for wasting your time. I think its best we shake hands now and go our separate ways."

"You're not even prepared to give it a try?"

"How can I? If after a few days or weeks it's not working out, what then? I've already paid out a fortune. Not your fault I know, but the cost of your full fare back to England part way through the trip would be massive. And I don't have that sort of money. Do you?"

"No."

"Exactly. It's all or nothing. And let's face it, we've hardly got off on the right foot. So I can't take the risk. We need to cut our losses and go our separate ways."

That ought to do it, I thought, relaxing. I'd just have to adapt and muddle along as best as I could on my own. I stood and offered my hand.

"It was, um, an interesting experience, meeting you."

Kate Thornly (the 2nd)

I sat there for a moment, thinking.

The hell with it.

I stood up and offered my hand. Much as I hate to admit defeat, he was right. We couldn't possibly go travelling together, especially with no way out if we didn't get on. I felt him clasp my hand briefly, then pull away, in a hurry to send me on my way.

But in that split second I changed my mind. Why the hell shouldn't I have the same opportunities as any other girl? And I can be pretty determined when I want to be, or bloody-minded and stubborn, depending on your perspective. I gripped his reluctant hand and didn't let go.

"By the sound of your eBay advert, you *can't* go alone. That nut allergy will kill you if you don't have me with you."
Silence.
Good, keep going with both barrels.

"I was a nurse until three years ago. My eyesight hasn't gone completely, yet. I can see very close up, after a foot things get blurred, further than that, not much. I've got something called Retinitis Pigmentosa. It's hereditary and it's only going to get worse. There's no cure. But I still have my nursing skills. And you have a problem I can help with."
He may not want to take me with him, but I wasn't going to give up that easily. No way.

"Right, okay then. Good. The problem is still the same…"
I began sizing him up for my next move.

"Actually you've got two problems. One, you need someone to taste any food that might contain nuts. And two, you need someone who can act fast if you run into difficulty."

"Yes, but I'm not sure you're the right person… I mean you can test the food, sure, but if anything happens…"

"You carry adrenaline with you, right?"
I started to prepare myself.

"My old girlfriend used to…"
I mentally lined up where I thought he was relative to the table and sofa.

"Do you have any on you at the moment?"
Slight adjustment, five seconds…

"Yes, but…"
Three seconds…

"Where?"
Get ready.

"In the breast pocket of my jacket. I try to forget it's there because…"
Go!
I let go of his hand and propelled myself towards him, knocking the table aside as he fell back, my knee landing on the sofa between his legs. I found his shoulder, used it as a reference point and reached inside his jacket pocket. I grabbed the adrenaline 'pen' and ran my other hand down his chest, over his groin and located his thigh. I pressed my thumbnail into his leg.

24

"That quick enough?"

I stayed sitting astride him, listening to his rapid breathing and feeling the tension in his body.

"Take that bloody needle away!"

We held eye contact for a moment. I was close enough to see the hazy outline of his face.

"So I can come with you?"

"Jesus, yes! I've got the point okay, just take that bloody thing away…"

If I could have seen further than just in front of my nose, I'm sure I would have enjoyed seeing the other people in the lobby staring at us. I decided to let him live, for now.

"Good. Another glass of wine please, a large one this time."

I replaced the cap and pushed the pen into his jacket pocket. I felt the way back to my own sofa, leaving him breathing uneasily and sweating; I could feel the hot glow.

"Quickest draw in the west amigo. That's Spanish by the way. I've got a couple of those learn a new language in a week CDs!"

Me

She's a complete raving lunatic! I blame the National Health Service for breeding such aggressive nursing staff.

It took me quite a while to regain my composure after that. I just sat there breathing erratically as a waiter placed two glasses of wine in front of us, even dropping me a mischievous wink as he left.

What the hell had I got myself into?!

Kate Thornly (the 2nd)

I think Jonathan was pretty impressed with my demonstration, though he didn't actually say as much. In fact he was very quiet afterwards, perhaps that's just his way. But at least I'd proved my point, no helpless female here. Okay, I did slightly bully him, but it was for his own good. Anyway, it's too late for him to change his mind now; we're flying out in the morning, Jonathan Cork and a new and improved *Kate Thornly*.

It's weird to be called by my birth name again. It's even stranger to think that Jonathan will be calling me the same name as his ex. I wonder what went wrong between them?

25

Dinner that night was a strange affair.

"It'd be really helpful for me to understand your mood. So you need to talk to me," I said, when the silence finally became too much.

I sipped my soup and waited.

And waited.

"Have you abandoned me Jonathan?"

More silence.

"You're hardly being a gentleman," I said a little louder. Was that a sigh I heard? Difficult to say with all the background restaurant chatter.

"I'm still here."

"But you were thinking about doing a runner, right?"

"Maybe. How's the soup?"

I lifted the spoon to my mouth and slurped really loudly, like I was hunting down the last dregs of a McDonald's milkshake.

"Is that really necessary?"

I could hear the annoyance and embarrassment in his voice and it amused me. I guess I was just testing the water.

"Just making sure you're paying attention. Thing is, if you're not much of a talker, we need to work on that. If I can hear you then I know where you are, and in the unfortunate event of you chucking anything nut-related down your throat, I need to be close so I can get there quickly. I gauge distance by your voice, so you've got to talk to me, *a lot*."

"That may take a bit of getting used to," he said.

"And you need to be more expressive in how and what you say, I can't see body language, I can only listen or *touch* to find out what's really being said. That's something *I* have to get used to."

There was a long pause.

"I'll see what I can do."

Me

Still in a state of shock, it took me until coffee after the meal to broach the rather tricky subject of *boundaries*.

"This is a bit awkward, but we should probably talk about sleeping arrangements for the trip," I blurted out, somewhat clumsily.

"Are you going to be a gentleman and sleep on the floor?" she said, allowing a wry smile to creep across her lips.

"Um... well, three months is a long time and I've paid a lot of money... I was originally travelling with the *other* Kate, so sharing a bed would have been perfectly natural. Now things have changed, I don't have enough cash for separate rooms. So perhaps we should try and share, but without any, erm, well, you know, any..."

"Without any... *shenanigans?*"

I nodded, forgetting that body language was wasted on her.

"Probably best to keep everything on a business footing don't you think? Try to get through the trip without any complications."

"What is it Jonathan, worried you're not over Kate and won't be able to perform if I come on to you?" she said, in a playful voice.

I flinched as I felt her foot brush against my shin.

"Don't be stupid, it's not that at all..." I said indignantly.

She giggled, a wicked grin on her lips.

"You men are so predictable! Relax, I'm just teasing you."

At this point I should have conceded she'd wound me up a treat and retired gracefully from the conversation. But I was flustered and on full automatic pilot.

"Look, I just want to establish some boundaries early on, so there isn't any confusion..."

"Do you really think I'm the sort of girl who's going to leap on you and give you the best night's shag you've ever had, having met you less than two hours ago? You're not that charismatic!"

I just sat there, completely dumbfounded. What the hell could I say to that?

"A pact then," she said, draining her wine and offering her hand across the table.

"A pact?"

"Yup. Not to get sexually involved."

"Okay," I said meekly.

I gently squeezed her hand.

"That means no wandering hands in the middle of the night. We stay to our own side of the bed. Agreed?"

"Agreed. But I'm not that sort of bloke..."

"I was talking about me!"

I sat on my side of the bed, wondering how I'd ended up in this bizarre situation. This was supposed to be my big dream, the once-in-a-lifetime trip I'd been planning for the last fifteen years. But now here I was, about to be full-time carer for a disabled, sorry, *partially-sighted* person.

For the second time that day I thought about doing a runner. I'd sneak out of the room in the middle of the night and go on my own and just be really careful what I ate. But then, she played the oldest trick in the book and aroused my curiosity...

Kate Thornly (the 2nd)

I sat on the bath deep in thought. Jonathan was not the open-minded travel companion I'd been led to believe.
I guess Maria put an extra bit of spin on the telephone conversation she'd had with him. Even so, I was warming to the trip. Three months away would be one hell of an adventure. I just needed to get Jonathan to chill out. So I started to put together a cunning plan to ensure I was by his side at the airport check-in desk the next morning.

I stood up, took a deep breath and opened the door, pulling off my t-shirt as I left the bathroom.

"I thought we'd get this out of the way early on, so that we can stop tiptoeing around each other, being polite."
I knew he was still sitting on the far side of the bed because I could hear his faint breathing. I kicked off my shoes and unzipped my jeans, starting to wiggle them down over my hips.

"Forgive me for jumping to conclusions, but I'm sensing you still have some reservations about travelling with me, despite my earlier demo. So, here's a little test for you."
I stooped and pushed my jeans over each ankle.

"One advantage of being blind is that I won't laugh at your paunch, if you have one. But if I ask you to shut your eyes, because I sleep in the nude and am about to strip off, you have a choice. So, Jonathan - decide. Are you going to be a gentleman, or will your manly curiosity get the better of you?"

I reached behind my back and unhooked the clasp of my bra. Thank goodness I'd put on some reasonably nice underwear this morning, practical and comfortable, but with a bit of lace.

I wondered what he'd do.

"Ready? Shut your eyes... now."

I slipped my bra off, then in no particular hurry, eased my knickers down over my thighs. Then I felt my way to the head of the bed, pulled back the covers and climbed in.

"Did you peek?"

I know it was naughty, but what the hell, we needed an icebreaker.

"I'm a gentleman, there are rules about that sort of thing..."

He passed by the end of the bed on his way to the bathroom.

"Yeah, but did you look?"

I heard the bathroom door shut and grinned. I'd put him on the back foot, embarrassed him. Maybe I could have some fun on this trip after all...

Me

Jesus Christ!

I'm no prude and I admit I enjoy checking out the female body as much as the next man, but what are you supposed to do in that situation? Is it really bad etiquette to look, or is it rude *not* to?

I shook my head and sat down on the corner of the bath to think. My brain needed a moment to catch up with the madness of this crazy situation.

Once I'd got over my shock, I couldn't help smiling. Perhaps this trip wasn't going to be so bad after all.

But of course all this is irrelevant. What you really want to know is, did I look?

Well, what would *you* have done?!

Four

Kate Thornly (the 2nd)

I avoided the naked test the following morning by letting Jonathan go to the bathroom first. By the time he was done, I'd gathered up my clothes and got dressed, a little sheepishly if I'm honest. I think the wine might have had something to do with my reckless behaviour.

I mentally slapped myself on the wrist, then sat down to wait for my turn in the bathroom. My stomach was wrapping itself up in knots. South America here we come. Yippee!!

Me

Travelling with someone who has a disability is a completely new experience for me. You have to think about the really simple things in a completely new light. It's more than that of course, it forces you to see past your own hang-ups and reduces things down to a much simpler level. Right now I was having to make allowances that I'd never had to with *my Kate Thornly*. Not that she was mine anymore of course.

It had been laughable really. Like a bad porn movie where a pumped up workman, complete with a Freddie Mercury moustache arrives at the house of a damsel in distress.

"I've come to fix your fridge…" the workman would say, in a thick Norwegian accent.

The plumber from over the road was only supposed to service the boiler! Kate Thornly the 1st had kindly agreed to wait in at my house for him. She did shift work and was starting later in the day. I thought I'd surprise her with a spot of lunch; instead she surprised me by being straddled across Frank on the kitchen floor. Turns out she'd already eaten!

I dumped her on the spot. Well you would, wouldn't you? Despite being embarrassed at getting caught, she wasn't remotely remorseful.

"I'm sick of having to nursemaid you Jonny, real men see to *my* needs."

30

I didn't even bother asking how long it had been going on. What was the point?

There was something of an irony here I thought, as Kate Thornly the 2nd and I shuffled up to the check-in desk, her arm hooked in mine. I'd brought it all on myself, I decided, and this was my penance.

Kate Thornly (the 2nd)

So far Jonathan had been great at letting me hook my arm in his and guiding me around the airport, but I suspect it was more through a sense of duty than because he wanted to. He probably thought he'd drawn the short straw, ending up with me, but I'd soon show him he hadn't. He just needed educating in how to have a laugh...

"I could do with a wee," I said.

"Can't you wait until after check-in?" he said, a little sharply.

"That could take some time. Probably best I go now."

I heard an intake of breath and felt his arm stiffen around mine.

"Did you get out of the wrong side of bed this morning? You seem a little tense," I said.

"I'm fine. This way."

We picked up pace and I felt myself skipping along to try and keep up with him. It wasn't easy to co-ordinate my step with his and not being able to see changes of direction didn't help.

Trouble is, when I come up against this sort of insensitivity, I get annoyed and dig my heels in. So I decided to play up, just a little.

"Here we are," he said.

"Great, thanks."

I stood there waiting, having a secret smile at his expense.

"What's up?"

"You need to show me to a cubicle."

Kerclang! His jaw hit the ground.

"I can't go into the ladies, I'll get lynched."

I squeezed his arm, enjoying his discomfort.

"Then we'll have to go to the gents."

There was a silence as he considered this suggestion.

"It's not like I'm going to see anything, is it?" I added.

I decided to give him a little nudge and started walking, pulling him with me.

31

"Is it this way?"

"Bloody hell! Come on then."

He took up his normal stride and led me off to the right, slowing down as we manoeuvred through a door, which wasn't easy being so close to each other.

"Morning gentlemen please don't be alarmed. I can't see past my nose, so your vanity is safe with me…" I called out, laughing heartily inside. I guessed Jonathan's face was several shades of crimson by now.

"Can you tell me how close we are?"

I felt his arm disentangle itself and his hand grasped mine.

"Here, that's the door. The toilet is two steps straight ahead. The loo roll will be on your right when you sit down."

"Great, thanks. Won't be a mo."

I shut the cubicle door behind me and clamped my hand across my face to stop laughing out loud. It was his own stupid fault, if he'd been a bit nicer I wouldn't have put him through the mill. I finished up and felt for the door opening.

"All done Jonathan darling. Can you tell me where the flush is please?"

I felt him brush past me. A moment later I heard the water rushing through the system. I held my hands out.

"Sink?"

"Jesus!"

He clasped my elbow, walked me a few paces then pushed my hands under running water.

"Thanks babe," I said, sensing another man on the other side of me. I tipped my head in his direction as I rinsed my hands.

"That's lovely cologne. May I ask what it is?"

There was a pause long enough for a bemused expression – I'm guessing here, but men are predictable.

"Erm, thanks. I don't actually know. My wife bought it for me," he said, then scurried away. Was I really that frightening?!

Me

This was going to be a long three months.

It was embarrassing having to escort Kate Thornly the 2nd into the gents' toilets like a small child. I was shaking my head all the way back to the check-in desk. Humiliating, that's what it was.

Kate Thornly (the 2nd)

I was aware of the lady at the check-in desk, but I can only see vague facial expressions when I'm really close to someone and I mean nose to nose. Even so, I can detect sympathy in someone's tone of voice, and this was immediately evident as we handed over our passports and went through the usual security questions. They're sometimes a bit of a stumbling block, especially when it comes to the question of 'did you pack your own bag?' I have to rely on Maria to step in and say that she helped me, which normally satisfies the airport staff. In fact, it's worked every other time I've flown. Except today.

"I packed with the help of my boyfriend," I said, leaning towards Jonathan, smiling in the direction of the lady.

Me

I snapped out of my daze, vaguely aware of an expectant silence. I looked over at the check-in lady and raised my eyebrows.

"Sorry, miles away."

"Did you pack your girlfriend's bag sir?"

"No, of course not, we only met yesterday."

Oops.

Sometimes I'm just too honest. Clearly this was one of those situations where a small white lie would definitely have been the way to go.

The room was small and stuffy. I watched the two security staff sift through her clothes, presumably packed by her friend Maria, who clearly had a warped sense of humour. On the table was the usual assortment of stuff you'd expect; some summer dresses, shorts, jeans and fleeces for the colder climates. But there were also a few *other* items.

"Is there anything a bit, you know, racy?" said Kate, oblivious to the ridiculous scene of two middle-aged customs officers trying to hide their amusement at the sight of a skimpy studded leather thong. Its front pouch was clearly intended for the male gender, judging by the elephant trunk willy warmer. Next was *'Mr Stiffy penis-encouragement cream',* apparently made from an old family recipe. A large 'Sherlock Holmes' style magnifying glass also appeared.

"Does this stuff actually work sir?" asked one of the customs men. He was struggling to get the words out without bursting into laughter, whilst using the magnifying glass to zoom in and out of the small print on the *'rock hard'* pot of penis rub. A set of handcuffs followed, then finally a Superman outfit, tight blue and red Lycra complete with a large 'S' on the front. By this stage neither man was able to contain himself. They were howling with laughter.

"Did Maria have a little fun at our expense?" Kate said in an innocent voice.

"No. I really am an impotent, magnifying glass-toting Superman, who wears an elephant thong under his cape. Did I miss that off the advert? How careless of me. Bloody hell! Three months of this!"

My voice may have conveyed just a touch of sarcasm, can't think why.

"Hang on a minute, you're *Kate Thornly*," one of the customs men said.

Oh shit.

I knew what was coming next. I closed my eyes and dropped my head into my hands, not daring to peek out between my fingers.

"That's me," said Kate.

"*The* Kate Thornly. On eBay?"

One of them turned to me, struggling to get the words out between snorts of laughter.

"Got yourself a real handful here mate! Three months eh, good luck..." His voice tailed off, unable to finish his sentence as he turned to his colleague and tipped his head at the door.

"Bloody hell!" was all I could manage, making a mental note to try not to swear so much. But I knew this was probably going to be very difficult indeed.

Kate started to laugh, and despite my best efforts to stay angry, I just couldn't.

I started to chuckle as well, allowing myself to relax, getting rid of the tension. I laughed until I was struggling to catch my breath. Then, for some bizarre reason, I started to cry.

Five

Kate Thornly (the 2nd)

Jonathan thought I hadn't noticed, but when emotions switch like that, body language gives it away. I couldn't *see* the change, but when I reached out to hook his arm under mine, I felt the trembling and tension. It was awkward for a moment or two, standing by his side, realising he was upset, but not understanding why, or how best to comfort him.

"You okay Clark Kent?" I said, hoping to distract him from whatever it was that had upset him. I heard him sniff, trying to pull himself back together.

"It's just… a trigger. It happens sometimes."
I nodded and smiled at him as I squeezed his arm.

"Fancy a cup of kryptonite?" I said, this time feeling his arm relax a little. He laughed. I could just make out his blurry head shaking from side to side.

"This is totally bizarre. Us, here, what lies ahead…"

"Look at it this way, if you get bored of me, you can trade me in along the way for Catwoman. Deal?"
He sighed and I felt him relax a little.

"Deal," he said, easing his arm away to place his hand in mine. We shook, sealing the agreement, then started stuffing clothes back into our packs. I felt through my pile, tracing hemlines and stitching, mentally identifying the clothes Maria had packed for me. There were some new things here – thanks Maria, bless you. Doesn't mean I've forgiven you though…

Me

"You said there was a *trigger,* back in that room. Anything you want to talk about?" said KT2. (My new nickname for Kate Thornly the 2nd)
I sighed, toying with my cup of coffee. I'd already decided, before I even wrote the advert, that I wouldn't open up too much to the new Kate Thornly. But now I figured it probably wouldn't hurt, particularly given the Kate I'd ended up with. It may sound

weird, but because KT2 couldn't see, and we couldn't exchange eye contact, it made it easier for me to open up.

"My mum died a few weeks ago."

"I'm sorry," said KT2.

I nodded, forgetting that an unspoken acknowledgement was lost on her.

"She made me promise to book this trip six months ago, when she was first diagnosed…" I began, then stopped short.

Something was niggling at me. I froze, listening to the tannoy announcement, then glanced down at my watch.

"Shit! We've got to go. NOW!"

I started running, then stopped in mid-stride, taking a look over my shoulder back at the table. I dashed back, silently cursing KT2.

"Give me your hand. Let's go!"

I hurried KT2 along as best as I could, one hand clasped in hers, the other holding her elbow to try and give her some stability as I jogged beside her at an awkward angle.

It was a close call, but fortunately the departure gate was still open when we got there, breathing heavily and sweating. The airline staff frowned at us until they realised that KT2 was blind. As they checked our passports, there were also a few raised eyebrows and comments along the lines of "She's *that* Kate Thornly…" but we didn't waste any time and rushed past them towards the plane, where the Madrid-bound Brit-pack in the middle section slow-clapped us aboard. It wasn't the best of starts to our travels.

I sat back, shut my eyes and pushed my head into the seat.

"Did we make it?" KT2 asked, looking a bit flustered.

"Only just. Sorry, my fault," I said.

"Apology accepted. You are such a bad fiancé."

I snapped my eyes open. KT2 turned towards me and studied me with her blank eyes.

"Didn't Maria tell you? I've been looking for a husband for, oh, about a month now. Just woke up one morning, looked in the mirror and decided."

She turned and glanced across to her right where an overweight middle-aged man sat with a filthy look on his face.

"We're getting married, you know."

"Make sure you're not late that day," the man said as he turned away to look out of the window, clearly not happy we'd kept the plane waiting.

I nudged KT2 in the ribs.

"Married?"

"Yes, in Rio. Everyone wears white on the beach to see in the New Year. I just assumed, what with your advert and all, we'd be getting hitched. Isn't that what you were intending by ending up there? With the first Kate Thornly I mean. I don't mind taking her place. You'll have to do something about grinding your teeth though, terrible turn off when I'm, you know, getting in the mood..."

I felt my heart pound and all colour drained from my face.

KT2 leant forwards, felt her way up to my chin and gently pushed my lower jaw up. I pulled away from her, then stared into her eyes, which for obvious reasons, were impossible to read.

"You're joking," I said at last, relief pouring out of me. I half laughed, shaking my head as the plane started to creep backwards.

"Gotcha!" said KT2, grinning from ear to ear.

"Excuse me," said the man next to KT2.

"Are you *the* Kate Thornly?"

I groaned. The sooner we got away from the UK the better...

<u>Six</u>

<u>Buenos Aires, Argentina</u>
<u>Me</u>

I have a feeling it's going to take me several days to recover from the seventeen hour flight, plus transfers. All in all I reckon it was a good twenty-four hours non-stop travelling. Factor in having to escort KT2 everywhere and it's no wonder I was shattered when we arrived. It's hard having to keep up an almost constant running commentary when we're on the move; turn left here, speed up a little, stop. Yet another public toilet visit.

But, I'm getting the hang of it. Or I was before we left Madrid behind. That's when any chance of intercepting an English-speaking woman on her way into the ladies and asking her to escort KT2 disappeared. Perhaps I should have paid more attention to the Spanish lessons I'd had a few weeks before we left.

We left.

Now that's an odd thought. I'd closed myself off, there had been too much to think about - placing the ad and trawling through the replies. I hadn't had the time to think it through and come to terms with the break-up. But for the next three months I had all the thinking time in the world. No working twelve hours a day, no hectic weekend social life, no friends to distract me. I'd stepped out of my old life, a safe, cocoon-like existence and was now lying in a hotel bed at what, four o'clock in the morning, sharing a double bed with a blind girl...

"Are you asleep?" KT2 whispered, making me jump despite her soft voice. She'd interrupted my train of thought at the precise moment I'd started to think about her. Surreal, especially at this time in the morning, eight thousand miles from home and about eight million miles from reality.

"I was. How are you KT2?"

If she was surprised by her new name she didn't let on, and if she was mildly amused then I wasn't aware of it because our room was pitch black.

"Awake."

I chuckled.

"I'm not. I'm in a sleep-deprived dreamlike state with reality and fantasy merging together."

"Are you sober?"

I laughed and tilted my head towards her to see if I could make out her facial expression, but I could only just see the vague silhouette of her head.

"How can I be anything but? You've been with me constantly..." I stopped before my tone hinted annoyance at having to be by her side twenty-four seven.

"You could have a secret hip flask to dull the pain. Vodka, so I couldn't smell it on your breath..."

"I think you'd know," I interrupted, an amused smile twitching across
my lips. "But in answer to your question, yes I am sober. Are you?"

"Me? No. Three sheets to the wind. Absolutely plastered. It's the only way I can stand your damaged aura."

"My aura?!"

I had to laugh again. What a strange conversation. Must be the tiredness, making me soft in the head.

"Yes. Fixated, distracted and emotionally stunted. Special cosmic glue is required, aura-specific of course," said KT2, a playful tone in her voice.

"You're shaking your head, I can feel the sheets moving. Do I amuse you Jonny?"

"This situation is what amuses me. It's weird, don't you think?"

"Maybe. But this is only day three. Ask yourself the same question at the end of the trip. It'll be interesting to see if your view has changed."

"Do you have a prediction?"

"Oh yes."

"Care to share it with me?"

"Nope. Sleep tight Jonny."

And that was that. KT2 rolled over, pulling some of the duvet with her. We tugged it back and forth a few times, then both settled back into our pillows.

I couldn't help an amused smile as I drifted off to sleep, too tired to register that I don't normally settle that well with someone new lying next to me...

KT2

I'm pretty sure it wasn't Jonny who'd booked the hotel, it was far too chic and fashionable to have been chosen by a man. Not a straight one anyway! The Baucis Boutique Hotel was located in the fashionable and bohemian Palermo part of Hollywood, downtown Buenos Aires. A recently opened courtyard hotel, it was relatively small, but had tastefully decorated rooms that were both original and artistic. I'm relying on Jonny's description of course, but I think he was quite taken by our glamorous and heavily perfumed hostess, so he was unusually enthusiastic describing our surroundings.

The floor was rugged flagstones, there was a hint of gothic in the modern artwork on the walls and a minimalistic, ultra cool bathroom with a frosted glass partition. I liked the place, it was quirky. I didn't even mind there being no hot water. But Jonny complained about everything including freezing in the shower and having to pee in the dark because the light switch didn't work. I suggested he wear his head torch.

"Oh, good idea. I didn't think of that," he said.

Typical male office worker, I thought; not very resourceful and a bit of a whiner. I didn't mind the cold shower, it woke me up and was refreshing after the hot, muggy night.

"Whose big trip was this, yours or the first Kate's?" I asked as we sat eating breakfast.

Okay, it was a slightly loaded question, but I was curious about his relationship with the *other* Kate.

"It was always my idea. Actually that's not strictly true because my mum encouraged me and..."

He pulled himself up short. I waited patiently, feeling my way around the bread, cheeses and ham until I found my coffee cup. After a long silence I decided to press on.

"Is your dad still around? What does he think?"

"He died when I was twenty. Car crash."

Jonny sounded lost talking about his family. It must have been tough, losing both of them.

40

"What about you KT2, any family history you want to discuss?"

"Not right now. But maybe later, in the fullness of time…"

"You mean we need to become friends first," he said, a trace of irritation in his voice. I took my time before answering.

"Some things belong in the past."

Me

I was frustrated, I thought we were starting to get on okay, trust each other with personal information, but over breakfast we'd ground to a halt. So we spent the rest of the morning each doing our own thing. I read a forgettable paperback and KT2 listened to music and a talking book. I didn't ask her what book it was, I wasn't really interested in making an effort. What was the point? So long as we got along reasonably well and she was with me at meal times, then she was fulfilling her part of the arrangement. We didn't really need to communicate other than at these times.

With hindsight, this might have been a little selfish on my part. KT2 probably needed to hear me talk more, but that's just the way it was.

Later on I'd got over my grumpiness and suggested we go for a wonder around. Palermo is like an arty, fashionable part of London, a bit like Camden Market or Portobello Road in Notting Hill. Only it's a lot hotter with a European like cafe culture heavily influenced by its Spanish and Italian immigrants.

The Argentine people themselves are really friendly and inquisitive about the British, overturning my preconception that they might still feel hostile towards us over the Falklands. Leaving the Palermo district for the down town area however is much like any big city, although the traffic is different. There are lots of big American 1960s buses, which contrast with the smattering of smart modern buildings amongst the drab concrete.

After a reasonably pleasant and largely uneventful day that lacked any non-essential communication, I decided to try and break the slightly awkward atmosphere between us. I asked our voluptuous hotel glamour puss to recommend the best place for a steak dinner, which is how we found ourselves at Don Julio's, just a couple of blocks walk away. Any doubts about the quality of the establishment vanished as soon as we entered its bustling atmosphere. The two tier, split level wood-panelled restaurant was packed with happy diners and I did my best to describe the scene to KT2. There was an open plan kitchen area, which sizzled with dancing flames as the steaks were cooked. It smelt amazing. The walls were decorated with hundreds of empty wine bottles, crammed into every nook and cranny. They all had some sort of comment written on them with a thick black marker pen: celebrations, thank yous, birthday memories.

I'm a bit of a red wine enthusiast, so I felt right at home in the place. Not to the extent that I can name grape mixes or wax lyrical about the pedigree of specific vineyards, but I definitely know what I like and Argentina produces some of the world's finest red wines. So we had a bottle over dinner. Then what the hell, I ordered another. It would have been rude not to, it was so cheap.

Good job KT2 wasn't a vegetarian, (now that would have proved awkward, as she had to taste all *my* food first) she would have gone hungry in Argentina. The steak was so melt-in-the-mouth tender that they didn't even bother to set the table with steak knives, ordinary cutlery was sufficient. It was the best steak dinner I've ever had.

We sat in companionable silence, letting the background restaurant chatter wash over us. My mind started to wonder.

What was the other Kate Thornly doing? Did she regret not coming with me? Was she still seeing the plumber?

"I had a few weight issues, when I was younger," said KT2, a distant voice pulling me back.

"Issues?"

"Mmm. I was teased a lot as a kid. They used to call me Katie the Cake."

"But they couldn't say that anymore," I said, knowing that I should pay attention, gently encourage her to carry on.

"No. But… I went through a stage, in my teens. Went off the rails for a bit."

I nodded, too tipsy to realise my body language was lost on her.

"Was that when the RP started to damage your sight?" I asked.

KT2 nodded, but said nothing. Despite the wine haze, I made a mental note not to push too hard for information, that's when she'd dried up before. I decided to try a different approach.

"But you found your way back, onto the tracks."
She beamed and the furrowed lines on her forehead disappeared.

"That I did. I met Maria. Her friendship changed everything. She made me see the fun in life, whatever hand you're dealt.

"How did you meet?"

"At the eye hospital in London. Her son also has RP. Then she saw that ad on eBay and decided it would be good for me to go on an amazing trip around South America with a complete stranger. And the rest Jonny, is history."

"Perhaps by the end of this trip we'll be good friends," I said without thinking too much about what I meant.

"Perhaps. Do you think we'll finish the adventure together?" I hesitated over my answer.

"Of course. I'm not a complete arse. I won't leave you stranded…"

"This isn't about having a misplaced sense of duty. If we don't get on, or you have the opportunity to follow other *avenues,* you should take them. I'm a tough cookie."
The conversation was taking an unexpected turn and I wasn't sure how to respond. I decided to take a leaf out of KT2's book and try a little humour to diffuse things.

"So long as you're a nut-free cookie, then that's fine by me."
That brought a smile. She felt around her plate for her wine glass and raised it up.

"Nut-free guaranteed," she said, as we clinked glasses.

We walked back to the hotel arm in arm. It felt a bit weird, probably because I should have been here with Kate Thornly the 1st. I found it difficult to settle that night, thinking about the enormity of the travelling that lay ahead. I pondered whether going away without Kate Thornly the 1st was going to pay off.

KT2
I'm wondering if I should say something about where we're staying in Buenos Aires and the city itself, but I'm afraid the place holds no attraction for me. Not because I can't see, or the

people are unfriendly, but because for me cities are full of risk. Back home I've held off having a guide dog for as long as possible. But sooner or later it will happen. I doubt the dog would like cities any better though, too much noise and too many opportunities to get lost.

Palermo, the area our hotel was in, was nice. It felt safe and smelt leafy, despite the pollution – both cars and dogs. It sounded relaxed too, the pace was less hectic than the city centre and shop assistants didn't pounce and pester, they blended into the background, knowing their customers required rather more delicate treatment. Nearer the city centre however was a very different story. The pace increased dramatically, there was much more of a sense of *urgency*.

We did try to go uptown, but it wasn't a great success. I'm starting to suspect that Jonathan hates cities as much as I do, although he won't admit it. Little things have led me to this conclusion; the tension in his arm as he guided me and his awkwardness amongst the sheer mass of people.

Me
It's a city, much like any other. But why, having lived and worked in London for many years, did I suddenly feel so *claustrophobic* and overwhelmed by Buenos Aires? It wasn't a threatening place. In fact it had a relaxed, bohemian feel about it, but I couldn't wait to move on. According to my distorted logic, it couldn't be me who was stressing, it had to be KT2. So I blamed her for my anxiety. Only real men act like that. Big of me, eh?

I can't remember how the argument developed, but it was almost certainly started by me, probably getting frustrated at having to escort KT2 through the crowds. After a stressful morning I was desperate to escape the chaos, so I steered us to the steps of a monument and sat down. I wondered how I would cope with the rest of the trip if I was struggling this much in the first week. I leant forwards and rested my head in my hands.

"Jonny?" KT2 said, a trace of apprehension in her voice. I ignored her, not to be nasty, but just because I wanted a few quiet moments thinking space.

"Jonathan?" she said, louder this time. I glanced up, squinting in the sunshine. KT2 was standing above me, reaching out in an awkward way, grabbing at thin air. Perhaps I'd been daydreaming, because it took me a moment or two to register that KT2 didn't know I'd sat down. She probably thought I'd abandoned her. I know it was mean, perverse even, but I just sat there watching her, intrigued as to what she would do next.

"Are you there Jonathan?"

I watched her drop her hands onto her hips. What scared me about the situation was not how much she relied on me, but how much *control* I had over her. It wasn't pleasant watching someone suffer because of my lack of attention. Was this part of the reason I was in this situation in the first place? Did Kate Thornly the 1st despise me enough to go off with someone else because I was too controlling? Now that was a mind-spinning thought. I opened my mouth to put KT2 out of her misery...

"Yeeowww!" I shouted out and doubled up as KT2 removed her foot from my crotch, then slowly lowered herself to squat in front of me.

"There you are Jonny. Did I step on you? Silly me, I must remember to change my contact lenses."

"I sat down to escape the bloody crowds. I was just about to say something..."

"Something like, *see ya later Kate,* as you legged it? "

"No, of course not. I don't think I'm good with crowds, it's so chaotic here. I just needed to sit down, take it all in."

"You're a Londoner, all this is second nature!"

I sighed, knowing she was right.

"It should be, but I'm struggling at the moment," I said, reaching out to take her hand, which she pulled away.

"It's a bit odd to just sit down in the street though, don't you think?"

"I'm perched on the steps of a monument. I was so wrapped up in my own thoughts that I forgot you couldn't see me sit down. I'm sorry, I just forgot, okay? Come on, take a seat."

I reached out again and this time she allowed me to guide her fingers to touch the edge of the step.

We sat there for several minutes in silence, letting the bustle of city life hurry by. I started to feel better watching, away from the crowds, constantly jostling each other for a position on the pavement.

"Do you miss her?"

Now there was a question to make me really think. There was a long pause before I answered.

"It's strange because I miss the familiarity. If I'm completely honest, I'm struggling with the concept that someone needs *me*. I relied on Kate too much and got complacent. Now the tables are turned it's a big learning curve for me to adjust to. Does that make sense?"

KT2

For the first time I started to wonder if it had been such a great idea to come away on this trip. Actually that's not strictly true. I'd probably questioned being here most days, but not this seriously. Today had scared me, because I was so reliant on Jonny and that was only going to increase as the trip progressed and we got off the beaten track. He'd talked about the jungle for Christ's sake! But listening to his explanation, I began to relax slightly. I felt a bit stupid too, accusing him of planning to abandon me, but sometimes I can't help feeling paranoid. Standing there, calling out his name, I felt vulnerable.

"Is it actually worth your while adjusting? What you're getting out of this arrangement seems pretty small by comparison," I said.

"That thought has crossed my mind, but ending up in hospital a couple of weeks ago was a bit of a wake up call. Kate Thornly the 1st probably saved my life a couple of times over the years, so no, yours is not a small contribution. I can't do this trip without you."

It was a start, but I wasn't totally convinced.

"It may never happen. You'll drag me around with you, begrudgingly for three months when we could both just call it now and probably be happier because of it," I said.

He considered this for a moment.

"That's a possibility. It may be I have nothing to worry about, but you're here as an insurance policy. One I hope I never need to cash in, but I picked *you,* remember? So I'd better honour my undertaking. I promise I'll never deliberately leave you anywhere on this trip."

I have to say I was impressed by his climb-down. It was probably one of the nicest apologies I've had. To be honest, I felt for him. Maria and I had misled him. His trip of a lifetime with his long-term girlfriend had vaporised and I was not the rescue package he'd had in mind.

We sat there for a while in silence, but it felt comfortable this time, like we both needed a moment to let the words sink in and *breathe*... like a good red wine.

Me

After a while watching the world hurry by, I glanced across at KT2, trying to gauge her mood.

"The big adventure starts this afternoon. Together, if you're up for it?" I said.

She smiled and turned to face me, her eyes off-centre to mine.

"You have to promise to talk to me more when we're somewhere new, describe what you can see, so I know you're close by."

"Okay."

"And I don't want you to think of me as a pain in the arse. I can sense it and it's unsettling. We need each other, remember that. But being blind doesn't mean life around me has to be boring. We can be friends, we'll have a laugh. Just try to be more patient with me."

"Agreed. Perhaps we could both open up a bit more, as we become friends."

"I'll wake up the skeletons and spring-clean the wardrobe, but you mustn't judge me," she said.

"That works both ways."

I watched her relax and smile.

"I think we have a deal," she said, offering her hand, which I squeezed in a gentle handshake.

"So, city boy, are you ready for the adventure of a lifetime?"

Seven

Out of the Smoke
Me

For the first time since we'd arrived in Argentina, I felt my heart pounding and butterflies in my stomach. It was as though the last few days had been a warm-up. Buenos Aires was safe with its large quantity of English speakers, but now the hardcore travelling was really about to begin.

We climbed out of the taxi at the main bus station with no atmosphere between us, only a sense of excitement. I helped KT2 with her pack and paid the taxi driver.

"Let's go find a bus!" I said, grinning from ear to ear. KT2 offered her elbow and I linked my arm in hers and led her through the entrance.

"It sounds busy. What do you see Jonny?" said KT2, reminding me of my end of the bargain.

"It's massive, like a huge aircraft hanger with two levels. Upstairs are maybe two hundred ticket booths, each with their own bright colour neon advertising signs. On our level are loads of shops built into the alcoves, stacked with everything from electrical goods to snacks, magazines and vegetables. It's like an indoor market spilling out onto the concourse. There are loads of people milling about and it's quite clean but a bit chaotic. Can you hear the TVs? They're in bars, cafés and ticket booths, all showing Spanish-speaking soap operas. How's that for now?"

"Perfect. Thank you," she said as I led her towards the bustling escalator. I guided her on first, talking her through when to lift her feet onto the moving steps.

"Wow, the size of this place is staggering! There are brightly lit ticket counters as far as the eye can see."

We searched for the bus company that would take us on a twelve hour overnight journey to Carmen de Patagones, but it wasn't where the sign said it should be. I started to get a bit frustrated at this point because my pack was heavy and I'm not the fittest person in the world - that's working in an office for you.

"Perhaps the numbering system has changed," she said.
I sighed, my legs were aching already under the weight of the backpack.

"Okay. We'll dump the packs. You can stay with them while I scoot around the entire floor...

"I'm quite happy to come with you, I'm enjoying stretching my legs after the taxi ride."
Damn. This meant I'd have to carry on lugging the pack around. I thought about arguing, but it wasn't really in the spirit of co-operation we'd agreed on.

"Straight on. We'll do a complete circuit, but I doubt we'll find it..."

"Don't be negative Jonny, it's always worth a second look." And so off we went.

Bollocks. She was right. I stopped opposite the correct bus company, which had a completely different number to the location sign by the entrance.

"Is this it?" she said.

"Yup. Guess you were right."
The old man behind the counter was friendly and helpful, pointing to his computer screen for the location and type of seats that were available. We ended up with a 'suite' which was two fully reclining 'bed' seats next to each other, right at the front of the top deck. Despite these being the most expensive seats on the bus, a twelve hour journey was only twenty quid each, a bargain!

As I sorted out paying, I noticed the ticket man glancing over my shoulder at KT2. I turned to follow his eyes, wondering what he was thinking. Had he worked out that KT2 was blind? Or was he just appreciating a pretty girl? I frowned, was I really so wrapped up in myself that I'd forgotten the most basic of male instincts? Justin would have me shot for such treason!

"Stop staring, it's rude," she said.

"You can see that?"

"Nope, just fishing. Gotcha!"
I smiled and turned back to the ticket clerk. He raised his eyebrows in KT2's direction and winked at me - *Lucky you.* I nodded at him, collected my receipt and steered KT2 away from the counter.

"Do you feel more vulnerable, not being able to see? Around men I mean. You're an attractive girl and… well, you know."

"Where did that come from?"

"I just wondered. The ticket man winked at me after looking at you," I said.

"Was he a looker? Maybe I should check him out…"
She half turned as if to walk back towards the counter.

"Not your type. Do you feel vulnerable?"
KT2 shrugged.

"Occasionally. If I'm being talked *at* by someone. I can't see escape routes obviously, so I'd have to talk my way out of a situation. But what I can't see doesn't necessarily worry me. The biggest problem I have is recognising the signs. I've learned to listen very carefully to voice tone and I rely heavily on instinct. I'm lucky really, it's better to have *lost* your sight than to never have had it at all."

I was pretty quiet then until we got on the bus. It was already becoming obvious that this trip was going to be humbling in many ways. I thought back over some of the many opportunities I'd had in my life and passed up. I found myself feeling slightly ashamed.

"Wow, this is fantastic!" said KT2, sitting in the big comfortable seat. She felt her way around the width until she found a lever which when pulled, dropped the seat right back, fully horizontal. She lay there giggling at the novelty.

"Lift your feet up," I said, as I raised the bottom of her seat to complete the bed. I guided her boots onto my lap so I could unlace them.

I felt the distant rumble of the engine starting and looked out of the window as we crept out of the huge bus depot, past at least fifty other busses arriving, departing and loading up. I realised how claustrophobic I'd been feeling since we'd arrived, compounded by the sight of a shanty town of corrugated tin roofs that seemed to stretch to the horizon. How lucky we were to have stayed in such an upmarket, affluent part of town. I felt a pang of guilt and I realised how necessary this trip was for me.

I glanced over at KT2, knowing I should relay to her what I could see, but she was snoring lightly. I smiled, then my eyes drifted back to the slum city that backed onto the main railway lines.

It's probably not that bad, I thought, immediately checking myself – was that 'London logic' still? I realised I'd have to work hard to lose that narrow- minded perspective.

We began to leave the corrugated roofs behind. The taller affluent city centre buildings beyond, merged into the smog and gradually the frequency of buildings lessened. Night soon fell and the open road stretched out across an increasingly barren, dusty Patagonia.

I woke KT2 when the elderly male steward brought food. It seemed we were in first class, because three full courses were delivered to us. Cold meats, cheese and crackers to start with, then a hot minced meat pie and a fruit salad to finish – it was fantastic! As soon as dinner had been cleared away, the television screen overhead flickered into life. It tickled me to watch Helen Mirren in *The Queen* with Spanish subtitles – quite surreal given we were on a bus in Argentina!

KT2 made it past the opening credits, then dropped off again. I eased her seat down and lay a blanket over her. Something was niggling at the back of my mind as I tucked the blanket in, but I couldn't pin it down. I carried on watching the film, puzzled as to what it was. Of course! My travel partner hadn't moaned about anything. Kate Thornly the 1st would have found something to complain about. I chuckled. Perhaps there were some advantages to travelling with a blind companion after all.

KT2

I don't think Jonny was too upset at me for falling asleep. I was knackered and the seat was really comfy. It was definitely the best night's sleep I've had so far and it was on a bus. How mad is that?

I was vaguely aware of a couple of stops in the night, but I quickly drifted off again. The next thing I knew, Jonny was shaking me. We were early arriving in Carmen de Patagones and had about a minute to get our stuff together and get going!

We both stumbled off the bus bleary-eyed with loose shoelaces. Jonny left me on a bench, clutching our day bags, while he went to get the main rucksacks. I shivered in the early morning chill as the bus rumbled away, leaving us at the small bus station, which sounded pretty deserted.

"Are we the only passengers to get off?"

"Yup. Looks like a bit of a ghost town. You okay here for a moment? I'll go and check out a street map for hostels."
I nodded, shivering again, wondering where I'd put my fleece.

"Here," he said, draping the warm fabric across my shoulders, "I grabbed it off the bus."
I smiled, wondering if he could see me doing so. Sometimes I forget to be more vocal with my own pleasantries.

"I'm smiling my thanks, in case you didn't see," I called out, aware of his disappearing footsteps.

"I know," I heard him call out faintly.
I wondered what sort of place we were in. The air smelt fresh and clean, not like the exhaust fumes and pollution of Buenos Aires. I heard footsteps behind me and turned towards him.

"We're only a few blocks from the hotels mentioned in the Lonely Planet. Shall we walk or cab it?"

"I'll always walk given the choice!" I said, pushing myself up.

"Give me a hand with my pack."

"You sure? It's pretty heavy…"

"C'mon Sinbad, load me up."
There was a pause, then I heard a grunt as he lifted the straps over my shoulders. I adjusted my footing, then held out my hands for my day pack.

"I'm ready. Which way Captain?"

Me
It was a beautiful early morning, around seven thirty I think and I was only too happy to describe the small brick houses we were passing as we followed the narrow dusty lane from the bus station. There was more greenery here than in most of the barren towns we'd passed through, but it was still pretty desolate. Several dogs opened a sleepy eye as we walked past, enjoying a Sunday morning lie-in in the sun.

We'd taken to holding hands because being linked arm in arm with big packs meant we kept bumping into each other. I couldn't help comparing KT2 with Kate Thornly the 1st, who would have been moaning her head off if she'd had to carry her backpack more than a few steps. I really did admire KT2's determination to lead as ordinary a life as possible.

Extraordinary, I corrected myself.

"You've gone quiet Jonny. What can you see?" said KT2, not annoyed, just inquisitive.

"As you can probably hear, it's pretty deserted. We're walking along a track behind the back gardens to a row of weathered terraced houses. There are wispy plants being blown across the dusty road. It wouldn't surprise me if a leathery old gunslinger walked out of a pair of saloon doors, spurs chinking, chewing a manky cigar. It feels... empty. Ah, here we are at the main high street. It's getting more built up now. To the left looks like the town square, *Platha,* I think in Spanish. There's a bandstand with intricate wrought iron handrails in the middle. Along one side of the square is an impressive gothic looking building standing tall and proud. There are also a few trees dotted around. The surrounding buildings are mostly rendered concrete with faded red or blue window shutters. They have an old style colonial feel and look a bit tatty. I'm guessing the weather here in winter is pretty unforgiving. I reckon some buildings were probably quite elegant once."

We walked on for a moment, KT2 seemed to be digesting my descriptions, placing the layout and surroundings in her mind.

"Sorry about forgetting the commentary. You're quite..."

"Independent?" she said, a playful tone in her voice.

"Yes, despite... you know."

"Once you get past all the negative thoughts, you just learn to get on with it."

"How hard was it to accept, in the beginning?"

KT2 slowed, turning her head towards me.

"It was hell Jonny," she said, a dull edge to her voice.

I squeezed her hand, waiting a respectful moment or two before I spoke again.

"Nearly there. The first hotel is to the right, probably another hundred metres. You okay with your pack?"

KT2 nodded, walking on in silence. I hoped I hadn't overstepped the mark, or been insensitive.

"Okay. It should be right... here. Oh. That's odd. The numbers jump up. Yet logically eleven forty should be here..."

"Logic probably goes out the window in South America. What year is your guide book?"

"Two thousand and three," I said, checking the inside cover.

"Perhaps it's out of date. The hotel may have shut down or moved. Remember the bus station ticket booths?"
KT2 had a point. Instead we set off for Hotel Percaz, which according to the guide book had 'less musty rooms' so it was probably a better bet anyway.
The once grand building was on a corner, giving it a presence over the other terraced buildings.

We were lucky to find anyone on the reception desk this early, but fortunately a family was leaving, so out came the phrase book.

It didn't go well. I made a reasonably good effort at asking for a room, but I couldn't understand the lady's reply. I was left wondering whether they actually had any rooms, because she seemed to be trying to tell me the time. Fortunately the travel gods were smiling on us. Another lady approached the desk and translated in perfect English. It seemed there was a room available, but it needed cleaning and the sheets changing (it was only just after eight on a Sunday morning, after all…) so if we could come back in a couple of hours or so, it would be ready. I assumed she was part of the hotel's management, but it turned out the lady, her husband and young daughter, were guests at the hotel. She introduced herself as Linda and told us that before her daughter was born she'd studied at university to be a translator. I introduced her to KT2, who smiled and offered her hand. Linda registered straightaway that KT2 was different. I was wondering whether I should explain or point to my eyes or something, but KT2 beat me to it.

"Hi Linda, my friends call me Angel. I can't see very well, but I sense you are a nice person. Thank you so much for helping us."
Wow, what a perfect introduction. I watched them shake hands, aware that some sort of unspoken understanding had taken place. With Linda's help, we were able to leave our packs with the hotel. This done, we thanked her and made our way out into the morning sunshine to explore.

KT2

We found our way to the Platha, which was only a couple of blocks away. The stone and grassy area was apparently neat and minimalist, with perimeter benches and the bandstand a central feature. Most of the benches were still in shadow, so Jonathan guided us to the steps of an impressive building that I think was the town hall, or church.

We sat down on towels and soaked up the warmth of the morning sun as Jonny described the rest of our surroundings. The river was half a mile or so down a steep hill, wide and fast flowing, across which was the larger, richer town of Viedma.

I heard a car draw up near to the foot of the steps and recognised Linda's voice calling from the road, asking us if we wanted a tour of the town.

"What do you think? Could be a bit dodgy," Jonny whispered to me. I sensed he was going to politely decline their kind offer, so I reached out and touched his arm.

"I think it's very sweet. It's not like we've got anything to do for a while."

"Are you sure? I'm not that street-wise so perhaps we should be cautious…"

"My instinct says its fine. And I've learnt to trust it over the years. Thank you Linda, we'd love to," I said, offering my hand so I could be guided down the steps to the car, a hazy blob that sharpened up only slightly as we got closer.

The little fiat was a snug fit! After a quick bit of rearranging, we climbed in behind the front seats and sat squashed together. Linda started to tell us the town's history, making a particular effort to describe the relevant buildings or locations in great detail. I wondered if this impromptu kindness and hospitality would ever happen back home. Probably not, I decided.

Being blind can make you invisible. Perhaps the reason is embarrassment or awkwardness, so people often say nothing. It can make for a lonely existence. Perhaps that's why I sometimes play for a reaction. That way any attention you draw to yourself, positive or negative is a good thing, because it punctures that invisibility bubble.

As the little car trundled through Carmen de Patagones, Linda's passionate descriptions of growing up there brought the sleepy town to life. All I ever seemed to hear at home was people moaning.

We drove to a viewing area on top of hill with a large monument overlooking the town, which had an impressive history. A couple of hundred years ago, the neighbouring town of Viedma assembled forces to attack the smaller town of Carmen de Patagones. With only seven men on horses, the town stood little chance of protecting their homes and families against a force of over a hundred. So a bit of improvisation and ingenuity was called for. The seven men from Carmen de Patagones rode their horses round in a big circle on the top of the hill we were now standing on. The longer they did this, the more dust the horses kicked up. This gave the illusion that a far greater force had gathered to defend the town. The brilliant, audacious scam worked and the invaders called off their attack. The seven horsemen were hailed as heroes and immortalised by the monument.

"It just shows what can be achieved with a bit of lateral thinking and plenty of bullshit," I said without thinking, quite overwhelmed with the sheer brilliance of the ruse.

"Bullshit?" said Linda.

"It means, erm a clever lie," said Jonny, squeezing my hand to tick me off for landing him with an awkward explanation.

We drove over the river via a disused railway bridge which had been tarmaced over, but the heat had distorted the surface, making for a bumpy ride into Viedma.

"We go for *mate* now. Please, we will not be disappointed if you do not like," said Linda.

I vaguely recalled hearing something about this popular 'ritual,' not unlike our own national obsession with drinking tea. So we sat on the grass in the sunshine next to the river while the *mate* was prepared. Jonathan described what was happening.

"There's a kind of large egg-cup shaped mug that's been carved out of wood. Inside it has a silver straw, with a wire filter at one end to prevent the *mate* herbs travelling up the spout when you drink from it. Linda's husband is pouring what looks like a coarse concoction of chopped leaves, twigs and bark into the cup. He's adding liquid sugar and some hot water from a flask."

The concoction was passed around for us to drink and each time the hot water was topped up. The flavour was so strong that it made me cough, no wonder Linda suggested we line our stomachs with some small cakes. Although we didn't realise it at the time, Jonathan has since read in the Lonely Planet, that being invited to share *mate* is a great honour in South America.

After we'd finished the *tea break*, we squeezed back into the Fiat and headed back over the bumpy railway line to Carmen de Patagones. Back at the hotel, I offered to buy our hosts a cup of coffee, but Linda gracefully declined. So we exchanged addresses and promised to send them a postcard from each of the other countries we hoped to visit on our trip. Waving goodbye to our new friends, I started to realise what travelling was all about. But why had it taken me so many long years in a city job I'd hated to find out?

Eight

Me

The guidebook was right, Hotel Percaz's rooms were a bit musty smelling. We joked it was probably the town's best hotel and was unlikely to be the worst room we'd stay in during the trip.

"How many days do you think we'll be here for?" KT2 asked as she sat down on the bed.

"Probably a couple, enough time to look around."

"Cool. And the river that we drove over, was there a path alongside it?"

I frowned, not sure of the relevance.

"Think so. Why?"

When she told me, I thought she had to be winding me up.

"A run? You mean as in jogging, for fun?!"

KT2 was nodding vigorously as she felt her way around her rucksack and started unclipping buckles and opening compartments.

"The very same," she said, producing a very smart pair of trainers. I was stunned. I remembered seeing them on the table during the customs check, but hadn't thought much about it. Never in a million years would I have thought she actually intended going running in them.

"You've got to be kidding?!"

She wasn't.

"How the hell are you going to manage not to break your neck..."

She was grinning at me, then winked, quite an odd mannerism given that she couldn't see me.

The penny started to drop.

"No. Not me. I can't run, I'm hopeless..."

"We're a team, remember. Just think of it as training for the Inca Trail."

KT2 started rummaging in her pack for a pair of shorts and tee shirt. Up until this point I'd been convinced she was teasing me.

"I don't have any trainers."

58

"Then wear boots."

"They're too heavy."

"Good resistance training."

"I'll look stupid."

"Then shut your eyes. It's amazing how much vanity it takes away."

"You have an answer for everything!"

"Aye. You've got two minutes to get ready, then I'm going on my own. And I'm sure you don't want that on your conscience…"

I sighed deeply, cursed, then reluctantly unzipped the legs of my travel trousers to make them into shorts.

"You're certifiable."

"No, I just refuse to be beaten by something I can do nothing about."

"What about just accepting that's the way things are and…"

KT2 leaned forwards and held her face close to mine. There was a glimmer of anger in her deadpan eyes.

"That would be defeatist."

KT2 handed me what looked like a dog's lead, a two metre long webbing with a clasp on each end.

"Screw lying down to die."

"Okay," I said meekly.

She's bloody crazy!

I struggled along beside KT2, clumping along awkwardly in my walking boots, trying to keep up. Oh, did I mention that whilst struggling for breath, close to my first heart attack, I was also supposed to be directing her around lamp posts, trees, curbs and other pedestrians? We had a few close calls I can tell you! Oh, mustn't forget dodging dogs being walked – ten at a time – aarhh!

I would have laughed at the irony, if I'd had the energy. Tied to KT2 with a lead, I was her bitch.

I wouldn't have believed it possible that a blind woman had the confidence to run, let alone the faith in *me* to guide her at this breakneck speed. Was she completely out of her mind?!

Finally she started to slow down, allowing me a moment to catch my breath, or rather allowing me to double up on the pavement, gasping for air.

"How are you getting on with those lightweight boots?" she asked.

I'm sure she was laughing at me, but I couldn't physically raise my head to look at her.

"Ready to run back now?"

I shook my head vigorously, you can be sure I found the energy for that.

"Let's go, I'm getting hungry," she said, and started jogging back the way we'd come, tugging on the lead. I cursed through gritted teeth.

"Language like that will mean we go for longer next time."

"Next time?!" I spluttered, as I tried to control my erratic breathing.

"Of course. Three months is far too long to not work out. I get grouchy if I don't exercise."

If I could have caught up with her to strangle her, I would have. As it was, all I could do was struggle along behind. But it wasn't just my aching limbs and raw chest that was painful, my pride was badly bruised. How could I have let myself go to such an extent that a blind woman was running me ragged? It wasn't right, I was supposed to be the strong one. I gritted my teeth and held on. If I stopped now, I'd never forgive myself. I might die trying, but she wasn't going to humiliate me like this. No way.

We finally got back to the hotel after a long hard slog up the steep hill. I slumped down onto my hands and knees, exhausted, gasping for air, my eyes screwed tightly shut, blanking out the pain in my lungs.

"Thanks Jonny, I needed that. Same time tomorrow?"

If she had a playful tone to her voice, it was completely lost on me.

"Sod off!" was all I could manage, spitting the words out. It was hardly my finest hour.

KT2

I think Jonny enjoyed our little run, although I was a bit concerned at how long it took him to recover. I must have stood next to him on the pavement for at least fifteen minutes before he stood up. He didn't sound good. What was he going to be like at altitude? I have to confess to a wicked smile at this thought. Who had the *condition* now?!

Me

It's been several days since my *first* run with KT2 and I ache in just about every muscle in my wretched body. We're only exercising every other day at the moment to 'allow the body to recover.' Wonderful.

I even have a pair of proper running shoes, bought in our next port of call, the small city of Puerto Madryn, half way down the east coast of Argentina. I wasn't given much choice, KT2 had been adamant that she was (a) going running regularly and (b) actually thought she was doing me a favour taking me along with her. Even stepping off the coach was painful – I feel like I've aged thirty years!

The first thing I noticed as we arrived in Puerto Madryn, was how much colder it was now we were another six hours further south thanks to a pleasant bus ride. We were around nine hundred kilometres from Buenos Aires, which explained the cooler climate. I dithered a bit over selecting a hotel when we arrived at the bus station, there were so many tourist touts. One advertising sign declared "we speak English fluently" which was a blatant lie! But the official tourist office lady was very helpful and issued us with a map, approximate hotel prices and locations.

KT2

After an amusing half an hour fending off offers for various hotels, we set off on foot, with Jonny providing a mix of his usual commentary and snippets from the guide book.

"Puerta Madryn is located on Peninsula Valdes, a spit of land on the East Atlantic coast which is a haven for sea life. The town is a mixture of industrial fishing port and a relatively new tourist resort. The old town centre was probably in the fish processing factory area, but it's now shifted along the coast where there's a sandy bay, promenade and hotels and restaurants. The concave shaped beach has a long concrete pier at the end nearest us, which actually serves as a neat dividing line between industry and tourism."

There was apparently a big difference between our 2003 Lonely Planet Guide and the up-to-date tourist map that showed a rapid expansion of tourist hotels, shops and restaurants. This was matched by the changing *smell* of Puerta Madryn as we walked from the bus station, through the fishing industry part of town to our hostel in the newer, glitzy tourist district. Metallic fish processing plant fumes subsided, leaving a fresh, salty, damp sea smell, which was carried on a bone chilling wind. Time to layer up with more fleeces, hat and gloves!

Jonny had great fun describing our room at the Vaskonia hostel, because each wall was painted a different pastel colour; green, pink, blue and beige. The bedding was apparently a scary 1970s patterned mix that wasn't to be faced after too many beers! At $80 pesos a night, it was at the bargain end of town, this being a popular tourist spot, so we did well finding it with vacancies. Despite the dubious colour scheme, it was clean, with fresh bedding and plenty of blankets, wasn't too musty and had hot water – a bonus!

After a fantastic BBQ buffet dinner at the Brahma Chop restaurant, which looked out over the bay, we both started yawning and voted for an early night. Back at the hotel, sleep wasn't easy coming however, due to the constantly banging doors in the courtyard and the exaggerated erotic sound effects from someone banging the local prostitute! Either some gal was having extra large size portions of manhood – for over an hour – or there were some over enthusiastic theatrics in order to tout for repeat business! The screaming and loud panting echoing across the hall was extreme to the point of being comical. We lay in bed laughing and curiously I didn't feel too subconscious any more about having a stranger in my bed. I was getting used to knowing Jonny was lying by my side.

Me

I lay awake listening to the hilarious sexual antics and wondered how different the trip would have been with Kate Thornly the 1st. Easier in many respects, of course, but, there are some things that I've been pleasantly surprised by with KT2. It's weird, but being more vocal, having to describe where we are, the people we meet, isn't actually as much of a pain as I'd initially thought. It makes me think about what I'm seeing and forces me to register everything, rather than just letting the important bits pass me by.

One really odd realisation I've had, is that there's less chance of an argument between KT2 and me. It was a bit weird at first, getting used to this. It was as though I had all the power because what I can see is never up for scrutiny or discussion.

Lately though I've come to realise that my preoccupation with 'control' is misplaced, because it's not that at all. It's actually all about *trust*. KT2 has faith in me to accurately describe the countries and cultures we're passing through without exaggeration or misrepresentation.

I've never had that much trust invested in me. You know what? It's a pretty good feeling.

But it wasn't just what I could see that KT2 trusted me with, it was also what I could *read*.

E-Mail From: Maria Stockton
To: Jonathan Cork
Subject: Msg for Angel (Kate Thornly)

Hi Jonathan,
I wonder how far you'll both have travelled by the time you get this e-mail? I'm sure by now you've got over any initial reservations and are realising what an energetic and easy-going travel companion Angel is. (Has she told you why we all call her Angel rather than Kate?)

I'm hoping you're able to read this message out to Angel, for obvious reasons I need your help on this.

I sat facing the screen in an internet café and read the message again, wondering whether I could bring myself to read the message aloud to KT2.

"Is it embarrassing to read out?" she said, from the low stool behind me. I decided to be brave and bite the bullet.

"Erm, no, well yes, in a way. It's just that I'm not used to reading my own messages aloud, let alone someone else's..."

"Just give it a go. If I laugh it won't be at you, Maria sometimes has a blunt instrument sort of approach, which is usually amusing."

"Okay. Here goes."

Hi Angel,

Whoopee!!! (make sure Jonathan does my Whooppeee!!! justice) You are now 7,000 miles away on your trip of a lifetime! Are you still in Argentina, have you learnt how to tango yet?! How are you both getting on? All the girls send their love and would like scores out of ten for conversational ability, fancy footwork and bedtime linguistic skills…

Love ya

Mim

"I think you can do better with your 'Whooppeee!!!' You're not putting your heart and soul into it, are you?" said KT2 in a playful voice.

I turned round to glance at her over my shoulder.

"I'm shy."

"Think of the café orgasm scene in the film *When Harry Met Sally*. You have to lose your inhibitions and just go for it."

I started to protest when she let out a loud "WHOOPPEEE!!!" and punched her fist in the air, narrowly missing me. I felt my face turn bright red, aware that everyone in the busy internet café was now staring at us.

"See, that's how you do it. Don't be scared, just imagine we're in an empty room, block everyone else out and…"

I'd had enough. I got up and walked out.

Nine

Me

I stood outside in the cold with my hands clasped on my head.

Damn woman.

My mind was jumbled with all sorts of stuff.

*Kate Thornly the 1ˢᵗ would never have embarrassed me like that.
Why the hell didn't I come on my own? But at least the trip
wasn't going to be boring and why the hell was I so cold?*

I swore out loud, then checked myself, aware that I'd attracted a
few disapproving glances from passers-by. There are some swear
words everyone in the world knows.

What was going on in my head?

Did I deliberately storm out leaving my jacket inside, so I'd have
to go back in? Was I sinking into madness at constantly having
to speak aloud all the time? Or were my eyes being opened to the
real world?

God knows.

One thing was for sure, I'd have to go back in or freeze my
goolies off out here. I decided that despite being overweight, my
genitals were not that well insulated. I shook my head and
laughed at myself. Time to eat some humble pie.

I went back inside.

"Hi. Sorry. Had to get some air, got a bit claustrophobic," I
said, instinctively placing a hand on her shoulder for a brief
moment. KT2 squeezed my fingers gently, her touch light but
lingering. It must have been the stress of the situation and the
warmth inside the café, but I felt a tingle as our hands parted,
something… and then the moment was gone.

KT2 leant forwards over the desk, felt for the computer screen
and blocked it with her hands.

"Just give me a moment to finish off," she said.

I frowned, confused.

"You can see the screen?"

"Not really, no. It's a haze, even up close, but I can touch type. There are mistakes that I can't see to correct, obviously, but my friends can usually interpret what I mean."

"Oh. What about reading incoming messages, if you're on your own?"

"At home I have a speaking programme. It sounds like Stephen Hawkins, but it does the job."

"Right. I'll grab another terminal. Let me know when you're done."

It was naughty of me I know, personal space and all that, but I was intrigued to see what KT2 was saying in her return message. I guess her reliance on me only extended so far. But having had so much faith put in me up until now, her perfectly reasonable request knocked me back a bit.

KT2

I signed off my e-mail with the parting comment *not such a dead duck* and pressed the send key. I eased back from the keyboard, checking myself as I remembered there was no back to the low stool.

A wicked thought flashed through my mind that I could try another one of Maria's 'Whooppeee!!!' shouts, but I thought better of it, Jonny was clearly still traumatised. When I'd had my sight I was a bit of a handful, as several ex-boyfriends will testify. At least I hadn't completely lost my sense of mischief.

I called out to Jonny that I was finished and sat waiting, amusing myself by recalling the message I'd sent back to Maria, knowing she'd have a laugh at my adventures so far.

"Are you English?" said the voice to my side. The pronunciation was slightly accented, but I couldn't quite put my finger on where he was from.

"Scottish. Similar, but better," I said, shuffling round on the stool to face the voice.

"Better how?"

"In every way. Tougher, friendlier, wilder."

I was particularity pleased with my last description, and the voice sounded youngish, so why not flirt a little?

"Ah. Sean Connery tough and William Wallace wild?"

66

I couldn't help giggling, the voice was educated and had a sense of humour. I heard Maria's advice in my ear: *Quick, get his phone number!*

"I can't quite place your accent..." I said, expecting him to volunteer where he was from.

"So guess."

Bugger! He wanted to play, tease me a little. *Alright mister.*

"I'm tempted to say German, but your tone is softer, not nasal enough. Hmm. Dutch?"

"Like the little boy with his finger in the dyke?"

I'd not heard Jonny appear at my side. He didn't sound very happy.

"You done? I'll just go and pay," he said, breezing past.

"Your friend is not Scottish," said the voice, quieter this time, presumably because Jonny was still in earshot.

I offered my hand.

"I'm Kate, but my friends call me Angel."

I felt his small hand in mine, cold and clammy, like a wet fish.

"I'm Freddy," he said, trying to hold onto my hand a little longer than I felt comfortable with.

"There's something different about you. A sparkle in your eyes. They would shine even more over a candlelit dinner..."

I cringed. Anyone unobservant enough not to notice that my eyes were cloudy and vacant at that close range, clearly wasn't taking that much interest in *me.* I withdrew my hand, surprising myself by wishing Jonny was at my side.

"We could go Dutch, after, if you like..."

That was it, time for me to go. I pushed the stool back and stood up, but felt a hand clasp mine. I flinched, ready to pull back, shout out, but something was different, the hand was warm and vaguely familiar.

"Sorry for keeping you waiting darling. Ready? Or would you like to stay and entertain your new friend?"

I grinned at Jonny's reassuring voice.

"I'm ready. Goodbye Freddy."

I leant forwards a little, dropped my voice.

"Your technique needs a little more work and your breath would benefit from a couple of gallons of mouthwash."

Jonny took his cue and led me out of the café, picking his way around the other customers. I flinched as the cold air hit my face and rushed into my lungs, but it couldn't stop a big grin spreading across my face.

Me

Okay, I'll admit it, I'd been a bit mean to KT2 in the internet café, but there was a valid reason. I had an e-mail from Kate Thornly the 1st and it had caught me by surprise, spooked me. I don't know what the real motivation behind her message was, but reading between the lines I think she couldn't believe I'd actually gone without her. I think she expected me to be pining for her at home, wallowing in self-pity rather than getting on with my life. The tone of her message was mixed. There was regret that we'd not parted on good terms, but as usual with Kate, there was a sting in the tail. Something about a rumour she'd heard that my travel companion was blind – was this really such a wise idea with my *condition,* she'd asked?

I don't consider myself a vindictive person, but I definitely felt slightly smug when I read that – if she wasn't jealous, then why contact me at all?

KT2

"I've still got it," I said, in the mood to tease him.

"He wasn't your type," said Jonny.

"How do you know, office boy?"

He didn't like that. And he couldn't help his response, but it still stung.

"I can see…" his voice trailed off, but I was already too many steps ahead. He didn't stand a chance.

"So I'm irrelevant, my opinion has no value?"

"I didn't say that…"

"I'm blind, not stupid. Got it?"

"Okay right. A visually impaired, all-seeing, all-knowing, bloody-minded woman."

"Last time I felt around down there, yeah!"

"And you women just love to mess us up!"

"Oh we do, do we? So on that basis you'll be better off without me!"

68

"Probably!"

"Fine! And just for the record, I may have the same name as your ex-girlfriend, BUT I AM NOT HER! Bugger you to hell and back Jonathan Cork, you spoilt little shit!"

The walk back to the hotel was frosty, but a welcome escape from the argument. We both maintained a stony silence, taking a rough grip of the other through linked arms. He steered me through the hotel entrance, then with barely a word, he left me in the room on my own.

Unfortunately my passport was in his money belt. Otherwise I'd have taken off for the nearest airport. Bastard!

Ten

Me

I stood in the street outside the hotel and ran through some bullet points that summed up my life; I had no job to go back to. No long-term girlfriend. I was in a foreign place thousands of miles from home. I was with a girl I didn't know. She was blind. My mum had recently died. What a complete mess!

I glanced each way. Where to now?

KT2

After a couple of hours I got bored of the hotel room and needed a change of scenery. I know that must sound odd, but what I really mean is that I needed background noise, to hear other people around me.

Because Jonathan had been trying to describe each new place we stayed in, I was able to form a basic map of the area inside my head. Three paces to the door, left hand opening. One step out into the corridor, left, then twelve paces to the stairs. I located the hand rail and eased myself down the steps. At this point I had no plan other than to get out for some fresh air and be around other people. I was starting to realise how claustrophobic travelling with one person could be...

Once I cleared the bottom step (there were twenty-two) I extended my travel cane. I don't often use it as I prefer to go out with other people and I'm a bit out of practice, but when needs must, it does the job.

And so off I went, through the small reception, helped at the door by the receptionist, who must have been surprised to see that I was blind. I thought about leaving a note, but where would I say I'd gone?

The air on the street had a chilly bite to it, but it was fresh and I felt I could breathe again. I tried to place myself on an imaginary map and plotted out previous journeys as best as I could. There was one street with several bars that we'd been to for a snack. They had to be livelier than a lonely multicoloured hostel room.

But which way? I mentally tossed a coin in my head and decided.

Left.

The stick pattered on the pavement as blurry figures diverted around it, giving me a wide berth. It felt good to be out!

Me

I sunk my second drink and toyed with the glass, wondering what Kate Thornly the 1st was doing.

The waiter arrived with my order. I'd not eaten for hours and I was starving. As I munched away, my hearing homed in on a familiar voice behind me. I turned to see KT2 arm in arm with a tall Argentinean man, probably ten years younger than me. She had a white cane in her hand but didn't need to use it. She'd clearly found an escort to the door. I almost called out to let her know I was here, but a pang of jealousy stopped me.

I turned back to my fish and chip dinner and shovelled another forkful into my mouth and frowned. Something wasn't quite right…

KT2

It was really sweet of Lucho to help me at the door, he was probably worried I'd start crashing into things. *Blind drunk* took on a whole new meaning where I was concerned! I could feel the draft and sensed the cool outside air just as I caught the faintest smell of a deodorant I recognised. I slowed my step and was turning towards the source when I heard him start to struggle to breathe. His hoarse, desperate attempts to suck in enough oxygen stopped me dead in my tracks. Then I heard the crash of china and cutlery and a dull thud as a body rolled off its seat and hit the floor.

My heart started pounding. There was a collective gasp and I knew I didn't have much time. I shouted out that I was his friend and I felt Lucho yank my arm through the gathering crowd, then guide my hands down onto Jonny's convulsing body. He was fighting to draw breath. I frantically patted him down, searching for the adrenaline pen. It wasn't in its usual place.

Shit! Where was it?!

"Coat?" I shouted out, miming putting on a jacket. Someone grabbed my hand and thrust padded material into it. I searched through the pockets and finally found the adrenaline. Then I hesitated, despite the urgency of the situation. I leaned down close to his face.

"Guess you need me now, don't you Jonny! "

"Hhhhwwwwghhh!..."

"You'll have to speak up, I can't hear you!"

"Ggysshhss!..."

"What's that? You're sorry for being an arsehole and you'll treat me with a bit more respect?"

"Arrggg!"

"Good answer laddie!"

I jabbed the adrenaline into his thigh.

The sharp intake of breath as he sucked in oxygen was the best sound I've ever heard. I sat back on the floor, exhausted from the frantic effort, but grinning that I'd brought him back from the brink.

The next thing I heard was applause. I guessed there must have been a group of twenty or so people who had gathered round. Someone helped me to my feet and guided me to a chair.

Me

"Bloody hell..." I managed in a gravelly voice, which didn't sound like mine. I sat back and flinched. There was no back to this chair, then I realised I was sitting on the floor. I glanced round the anxious faces, their clapping dying away. My throat felt raw and tight, but at least it wasn't constricting my breathing, squeezing the life out of me. I stood shakily, then slumped down at the table and stared at the unfinished plate of food in front of me. I nearly threw up.

I pushed the plate away and sunk my head down onto the table, supporting it with my crossed arms. How had I been so stupid? I turned and saw KT2. She looked as white as a sheet. I shuffled my chair over to her.

"Thanks," was all I could manage, my throat was still feeling as though I'd swallowed a red hot poker. I watched KT2 adjust her lifeless eyes towards me. Only this time, they were alive. And angry.

"If you ever treat me like that again, I will leave you. I may be blind, but I'm not a fucking doormat," she said as she lifted my money belt into view, then tossed it on the floor between us. In her other hand she held her passport.

"I'm looking after this from now on, with my own money and credit card. That way I can walk away anytime I want. And just for the record, you ignoring me makes me feel unwanted and unappreciated. I'm this close to heading home. Mistreat me again and I'm gone."

I felt my shoulders slump as the effects of the adrenaline shot started to subside. I reached down and picked up the money belt and sheepishly stuffed it into my pocket.

"I'm sorry. I saw you on the arm of that bloke and..."

"I can't hear you," she said, not letting me off the hook.
I sighed and lifted my voice above a mumble.

"I got jealous, I'm sorry. This isn't easy for me. I know we have a business arrangement, but it was as though Kate Thornly the 1st was still rubbing my nose in it..."

"By me accepting a guiding hand from the manager who didn't want a blind person drinking in his bar?"
I stared at her.

"You were being thrown out?"
Now I was the one feeling anger.

"No, I wasn't. But it's nice to hear some passion in your voice. You see what difference a bit of mutual respect makes? It makes me feel part of the adventure rather than a pain in the arse you can't wait to ditch."
I didn't have the energy or the right to respond to a dressing-down like that. I dropped my head, exhausted after the trauma.

"What did you eat?" she said at last, breaking a long silence.

"Fish and chips. I fancied a taste of home."

"Fish in batter, fried in nut oil?" she said.

"It seems likely, don't you think?" I said, allowing sarcasm to creep into my voice. I glanced over in time to catch a small smile on her lips.

"Unless that's a special blend of peanut butter beer you're drinking..."

"They don't have the brand I like."

This time she chuckled, shaking her head.

"You silly bastard."

"Stroppy cow," I replied.

I started to laugh, more a release of nervous energy than anything, but it felt good to let it go. It had been a very close call and I was lucky KT2 happened to be in the same bar.

"I need a drink. Let me re-phrase that. I *owe you* a drink KT2."

I stood, my legs felt like jelly.

"That would be grand. Pint of Guinness. Failing that, large whisky, the best you can find. Or if you're feeling particularly grateful to be alive, both."

I couldn't help smiling at her cheek.

"Don't just stand there, I'm getting thirsty!"

KT2

Today was a turning point. It's taken a couple of weeks, but what a difference it's made. I'd proved my worth and Jonny finally accepted that he couldn't do this trip without me.

"There's something that's been puzzling me. How did you manage to let the others in the bar know that you could help me? I mean with the language barrier?"

I polished off my pint of Guinness and picked up the whisky glass.

"I took a few Spanish lessons for a trip to Barcelona last summer. But it's all in the visuals Jonny."

"So when we leave Argentina and get more off the beaten track, you could be a useful person to have around?"

"Yup. Semi-bilingual and life-saving. Quite an asset I reckon."

He 'chinked' his glass against mine.

"How's your throat?"

"Very sore. But this has to be the best kind of post-trauma care. I hate hospitals. Seen too many of them over the years and they've never been a pleasant experience."

I nodded, remembering my own spate of visits over the years. I felt myself go cold, the blood draining from my face. Some memories belong buried deep in the past. I shuddered and reached out a shaky hand for the near-empty whisky glass, unable to find it.

"You okay, KT2?"

I felt a warm hand guide mine to the glass which I hurriedly pressed to my lips, determined to extract every last drop.

"Someone just walk over your grave?" he said in a concerned voice.

"A reminder, of darker days. A long time ago," I said, mentally kicking myself for even acknowledging there was something wrong.

"Want to talk about it?"

"Nope."

Me

It was one of those evenings when you seem to lose time. When we rolled out of the bar it had been dark for quite awhile. I'm guessing it was around ten. God knows where the time went. We certainly covered some ground that day. It's amazing how a near-death experience can transform your outlook on life!

I suppose it was bound to happen sooner or later. No matter how careful I was with my food, there was always this risk. It was a lot easier to manage in the UK of course, but out here I needed to be extra careful.

The lesson for me to learn (yet again!) was that like it or not, KT2 and I needed each other. No matter how much I might bang on about wanting my own space, out here we were effectively one. We had to be, just to survive each day. A bit melodramatic perhaps, but we were stuck with each other. So I decided I might as well get used to the idea. Anyway, it was a cracking excuse to get absolutely plastered.

My god, I'm rambling. Alcohol does that to me.

KT2

I stood there wondering what I'd forgotten that was stopping me from taking myself off to the toilets.

Where were they? – oh yeah, that would be it.

"I can't remember the layout in here… can you show me the way please Jonny?"

"Of course. Follow me my lady. I am your knighty in shining armour," said Jonny, stumbling against the table as he linked his arm in mine. It was difficult to tell who was leaning on the other more. There was the distinct possibility that we may have had too much to drink…

I heard Jonny mutter apologies in slurred pigeon Spanish as we bumped into tables and people on our way to the toilets.

"Don't mention the war, or Maggie Thatcher…" he whispered to me, which triggered a fit of giggles.

"Through this door, then you're on your own. For obvious reasons I haven't checked it out, being the ladies and everything," said Jonny, swaying against me.

"Right. Are you prepared to come in and rescue me if I haven't returned in five minutes?"

"Into the ladies? No way! They lynch people here for that sort of thing, don't they?

"Best use the gents then," I said, squeezing his arm.
So off we went, through a couple of doors, until I smelt the unmistakable aroma of stale urine. Yuk. This wasn't going to be a pleasant experience.

"Um, just hang on there a moment KT2, I'd better just sort things out…"

"The toilet seat?"

"Mmm. It's not good. Two seconds. Okay?"
I heard the toilet roll spinning as he yanked off enough to do the job. I started to relax in the knowledge that within about thirty seconds I'd avoid peeing my pants. But then there was a gruff voice behind us, and we were off, backing away from the disgusting smelling toilet as one of the bar staff shooed us out of the bar. Our jackets were thrust into our hands as the icy blast of air hit my lungs, the door shutting firmly behind us.

Jonny tried not to laugh.

"Can you wait until we get back to the hotel?"

"Not really, situation critical," I said, emphasising my plight with a sort of pathetic cross-legged hopping.

"The beach?" he suggested.

Me
Bloody hell it was cold! I stood on the beach near the water's

edge, as far away from the promenade and the streetlights as we could get. Even so it wasn't quite dark enough, so I held my jacket out to shield KT2 from any passers-by. The wind was freezing, I could feel my nipples rock hard and sore through my shirt.

"Hurry up KT2, or I'll turn into an ice sculpture!"

"Shh! Stop talking. Can't go…"

Jesus! I started to dance a jig to try and keep myself warm, relieved to hear a gushing sound that went on for ages.

"Blimey, where did all that come from?"

"I'd already had a few before you decided to try and die on me…"

"Just a couple eh? Jesus it's cold."

"You try sticking your privates out in this wind, then you'll really know how cold it is. Not that there would be much hanging out there in this temperature, I'm sure."

I pulled a face that of course she couldn't see. Then at last she stood up, wriggling her hips back into her jeans. I took this as my cue and pulled my jacket away, unintentionally catching a glimpse of her underwear as she zipped up her jeans.

"I think you may have been a bit premature there Jonny. See anything you like or were you just window shopping?" she said, wobbling on her feet before falling over. I hauled her up and we started walking briskly towards the lights and activity of the promenade. But we were stopped short by a dazzling torch light.

Whatever he said to us was fast, loud and in Spanish, obviously. I'm ashamed to say we just giggled as we were frog marched swiftly back to the hotel by a local policeman. He was not a happy chappie. And that's where my memory fades. I can't remember walking through the hotel lobby, the stairs to our room, or collapsing into bed, fully clothed.

Eleven

KT2

The last place in the world I wanted to be the next morning was sitting on a bloody boat rolling on the swell looking for whales. It's not that I'm uninterested in wildlife (despite not being able to see it) but timing has to play a part here, and this wasn't the best of hangover cures.

Fellow passengers had exchanged pleasantries and it was a nice day, very bright. Spirits on board were high and there was a lot of excitement at seeing the whales in their natural habitat, but Jonny and I were both very quiet. People probably thought we were rude. I expect Jonny was wearing his dark glasses too, so we must have appeared to be ignoring people. Oh well. It was one of the few benefits of losing my sight. What facial expressions I couldn't see, wouldn't upset me.

Jonny did his best to describe our surroundings, despite being hung-over. The boat held about a hundred people and was launched from a small beach within a rugged cove. The sand was dark brown and the surrounding landscape faintly lunar. We were now probably a couple of miles off land and the water was choppy and grey.

I felt the boat lurch which caught us off guard. Jonny had been holding onto me, but he'd let go to blow his nose and I tumbled into the person next to me. He was an older chap judging by the tone of voice and posh accent.

"Good grief, watch what you're doing. Are you blind?" I apologised, obviously, but he wasn't in the mood to accept it.

"Is that alcohol on your breath? At this time of the day. Disgraceful!"

He turned away, muttering under his breath, making it difficult to hear any more, except for the word "common."

"Excuse me, Captain Peacock. My friend actually *is* blind. An apology's in order."

I placed a hand on Jonny's arm, it wasn't worth it. The way I was feeling, I couldn't be bothered wasting our energy.

"Don't worry, pricks like that always get what's coming to them," I said.

Jonny guided my hands onto the guard rail, which I gripped tightly. We'd not seen any whales yet, but I could sense the concentration of everyone scanning the horizon.

Even so I felt a bit low. This was a fantastic trip, but part of me questioned what I was doing on the boat? I wasn't going to be able to see anything.

I felt the boat lurch as the group moved over to the opposite side, but it appeared to be a false alarm. By this point the Captain had the engines on tickover and we were drifting on the tide and wind, waiting for our first sighting. I allowed my thoughts to wander and started to question, *why me*? I hadn't had a particularly extravagant or outrageous life before my sight started to deteriorate, nor had I been a bad person.

I was about to sink further into self-pity when I stopped dead. What had I just heard? With the boat still heeling over as everyone stood on the opposite side, Jonny and I were alone.

"Never again KT2. I drank far too…"

"Shh!"

I stood and leant over the edge of the boat, listening intently. The whale was surfacing right beside us! I grasped Jonny's hand, whispering urgently to him. We both leaned further over, I heard the water below us rush and bubble as the whale broke the surface.

"Wow! It's gorgeous KT2, what an incredible creature," whispered Jonny. For a magical few seconds he described the long slippery body and the barnacle-encrusted snout, while I listened to the beautiful sound of air being expelled from her huge lungs. Of course the moment she blew water vapour, it alerted everyone else and they all scrambled over to our side of the boat to get a closer look.

"She has a calf KT2! Right by her side," said Jonny, his voice loud and excited. I grinned, all my negative thoughts evaporating.

"Well done you!" Jonny said as he squeezed my arm. The whale blew more air and water high over our heads, the smell fishy and stale, but alive and real.

Then two things happened almost in unison. I heard that voice again, the one with plumy accent. And I started to feel very sick.

"Bloody hell I've got whale spit all over me! I know this trip is for you darling, but in my day we'd harpoon the bloody things…"

The voice was close. I had a rough idea of where, but needed more specific targeting information. I tugged on Jonny's arm, knowing I didn't have much time, feeling my stomach start to wrench.

"Upper class prick. Distance and direction? Quick!"

Fortunately Jonathan caught on pretty fast, either that or his reply was instinctive.

"Two metres, nine o'clock…"

He'd barely finished as I felt the convulsions rising to the back of my throat. I positioned myself and threw up, spewing warm putrid liquid towards the posh git. The amusing part was the way he screamed, not manly at all. Jonny immediately came to my aid, as much to drag me away from the man as to make sure I didn't lose my footing and go over the side. There were shocked gasps, followed by stifled laughter as the man was ushered away to get cleaned up.

We used to get his type in the hospital all the time, but they soon quietened down after a hearty dose of 'nurse justice.'

Me

I struggled not to laugh. Someone being sick on you is disgusting, but since he'd made such a penis of himself, it was hilarious! Does laughing at him make me a bad person?

I was feeling a strange sense of connection to KT2 after the last two days. A woman of many talents I decided. If nothing else, this trip promised to be far from boring. Perhaps because I was having to describe our surroundings I was taking in more. Becoming more relaxed.

As the boat headed home, I could see the rugged barren coastline and the strange mix of tourist resort stretching out along the peninsula and nearby fishing community. There was a clear separation between the old traditional working town and the bright lights and glitz put on for the tourists. Funny what you start to notice when you start lifting your head from the sand…

KT2

We finished off the day back in Puerto Madryn with a bracing walk along the substantial concrete pier, which stretched a long way out to sea. During our walk, Jonny pointed out two seals basking in the sun on the back of a Navy patrol boat. According to the guide book extract Jonny read out, January and February see Orcas killer whales surfing up the beach to snatch seals in a spectacular display of survival of the fittest. I shuddered, it didn't seem like a fair fight.

We strolled on, comfortable with each other. I had the occasional flashback to my earlier vomiting episode and cringed, it wasn't my finest hour!

Me

We had a laugh about the last twenty-four hours over an early dinner. But that's as far as the evening went. We were both still wiped out from the drinking session the night before and were in bed by nine. Tomorrow we'd bus it back to Viedma to catch the sleeper train and cross the width of Patagonia to Bariloche, Argentina's Lake District. We're hoping to go white water rafting there, although I'm a little concerned at how KT2 will cope. I'll have to make sure I'm out of the firing line if she gets a bit queasy!

I turned out the light, shook my head, then smiled, still amused.

KT2

It was bound to happen sooner or later, this time it was Jonny's turn. Whatever it was he'd eaten, was making a hasty exit. He wouldn't have appreciated being heard, so I turned over and let him get on with it. He'd be less self-conscious that way.

In the morning I thought about teasing him. I'd had a reasonable night's sleep and was feeling quite chirpy, but hearing him groan made me think twice. I guessed he'd been up most of the night, judging by the rank smell drifting out from the bathroom, so I attempted a more sympathetic approach.

"Are you going to be okay on the train?" I asked, rolling over to face him.

"I think so. As long as they have a toilet on board."

"I guess this is all part of travelling eh?" I said and reached out to place a reassuring hand on his shoulder. I felt him flinch and pull back as he struggled out of bed and made a dash for the loo. There wasn't much I could do, so I snuggled deeper under the covers.

I'm not sure whether Jonny enjoyed the train journey very much. It can't have been much fun feeling as rough as he did. But all credit to him, he still managed to describe our surroundings.

"Imagine an old style train. Think Miss Marple and black and white films. Our individual sleeping compartment is a bench seat by day, transformed into two fold down bunk beds by night. There are other sleeping compartments along one side of the train, whilst on the other, a long corridor connects the carriages. Towards the forward part of the train is a buffet car. The tables aren't fixed, they're a rather quaint English tea room-style with pretty cotton tablecloths. The food is beautifully presented and delivered to each table on an ornate trolley by smartly dressed waiters who seem very comfortable with the rocking motion of the train. They're serving the food without spilling any and appear to be able to anticipate the train's every movement. Looking out of the window, we're travelling across vast stretches of dusty open land, desert-like, but with boulders rather than sand. There are random small settlements. Some of the ramshackle buildings are white walled and others a terracotta colour. It's a wonder how a community can survive out here, there's very little vegetation. It must be a hard life."

The best bit of the train journey for me was the cinema. Although I couldn't see the film, I could get a gist of the story by listening. But this was no ordinary cinema. It was in the last carriage of the train, which made sense because you wouldn't want people passing through as you were watching the film. As it got underway the carriage rocked and bounced around, which Jonny found highly amusing. He described how the action sequences had been filmed on a steadycam, making the images jerky and disorientating. But, this was countered by the train's own swaying, juddering motion, making the frantic action on the screen appear almost static. Probably not what the director was intending!

When we came back from the cinema, our cabin had been converted into a cosy sleeping compartment. Normally I'd have opted for the bottom bunk in case I got disoriented or forgot about the height, but it seemed likely that Jonny might need to get up in the night to dash to the loo.

He helped me up the short ladder into my bunk, making sure I could get under the tightly prepared covers, then climbed into his own bed below. It felt strange, lying there on my own. We'd been travelling together for over two weeks and during that time we'd always shared a bed. I lay there gently rocking with the train's motion, trying to pinpoint what I was feeling.

Lonely, I decided.

Me

I withdrew into my shell a bit for those couple of days. Although I wasn't the fittest of people, (the first jogging session with KT2 had proved that) I still wasn't used to being so unwell. To be honest, I think the indignity of it all was the worst bit. Sharing a single room (and bathroom) with me can't have been very pleasant, it's not like you can have diarrhoea quietly. I started to question the wisdom of travelling when I felt so ill. Only I wasn't really *ill* was I? It was only an upset tummy for goodness sake.

It's a shame I wasn't feeling great, because the train journey was fantastic. We left the flat barren dustbowl of Patagonia at six in the evening and by late morning the following day we were gently chugging towards Bariloche. Outside, the train was surrounded by snow-capped mountains on one side and lush forests on the other. We could have been in a European ski resort.

My spirits were lifted by the clean, fresh air and this amazing scenery. It was still on the cool side, but warmer than Puerto Madryn.

I guess the cold Atlantic wind was missing here.

We lugged our rucksacks off the train and headed for tourist information.

"And how long are you staying in Bariloche?" asked the English-speaking lady at the information desk.

Now there was a question I hadn't actually thought about. We were winging it. The only date we had to hit was the Inca trail in a couple of weeks' time. That had been pre-booked for ages.

"Erm, three, maybe four days," I volunteered, not entirely sure myself.

Something Kate Thornly the 1st and I had agreed on when planning this trip, was that when possible, we would try to find self-catering places to stay. This would give us a bit more space and freedom, but more importantly it would allow us to cook for ourselves and be certain that there were no nuts in any of the meals.

And that was how we found ourselves at the fantastic Cabanas Vientos del Sur, in our very own ski chalet high up on the far side of town. The views from the lounge window were magnificent. Lush greenery and the glistening lake with pine trees along the far shore beneath snow topped mountains. The wood-clad chalet was completely self-contained, with two bedrooms, a huge living room come kitchen and two bathrooms! (How sad am I to be excited about two bathrooms?!) And get this, all for only twenty quid a night! As luck would have it, the ski season had finished the previous week, so the price had dropped massively.

Such luxurious home comforts were in stark contrast to the endless bland hotel rooms we'd been staying in.

That evening we cooked a superb steak dinner after a leisurely trip downhill to the local supermarket. Even that was an adventure as we'd eaten out every day since starting the trip. I'm not the best cook in the world, but I know how to do steak – rare with a little seasoning, mashed potato and vegetables. It was fantastic!

It wasn't until the end of a very pleasant evening sitting 'watching' TV, that I wondered what the protocol would be at bedtime. Up until now we'd always shared a room and had developed a nice little routine to circumnavigate the undressing and dressing *thing*. Typically, I would go to the bathroom first, allowing KT2 to change into her night wear – usually a long tee-shirt and men's boxer shorts. It didn't matter of course if I wasn't dressed by the time she returned as she couldn't see if I was naked. That took a bit of getting used to…

But, I had a dilemma now there were two bedrooms. Did we have one each or continue to share? The owner of the cabins had assumed, as one would, that we were *together* in every sense and so only the main double bed had been made up.

Would it be rude of me to suggest we had separate rooms or chivalrous? I contemplated this for some time. We both started to yawn, yet neither one of us wanted to broach the subject.

"Um, I was going to offer you the double bed, and I'll have one of the singles next door. I know how you like to stretch out…" I said, trying to make light of my dilemma.

"Oh, right. I guess I did wonder about that. Makes sense I suppose."

There was an awkward moment or two.

"Did they make the bed next door then?" said KT2.

"No, I'll use my sleeping bag."

"Okay. I guess I'll see you in the morning then."

It seemed strange parting company for the night, retiring to our separate rooms. I had to chuckle at the irony. For the last two weeks I'd been overly conscious of not stretching out so I didn't inadvertently touch KT2. I'd learned to sleep almost rigid, barely moving throughout the night, which was unusual for me.

Kate Thornly the 1st had often complained that I was a fidget who wanted the whole bed. Yet here I was perfectly content in my sleeping bag, but missing the fact that I didn't have to worry about bumping into someone else. Was there something developing here that I needed to be aware of?

No, I decided. KT2 and I were polar opposites. Although I admired her attitude to life, this was a business arrangement, nothing more.

KT2

It was one of those awkward situations where you wonder about the best approach. But because you don't express a view either way it just sort of bumbles along and is never discussed. Neither person is brave enough to say, *actually I'll miss you if we have separate rooms. And it's a cold night. There's nothing more in it than that, but do you mind if we just snuggle up in here together?*

It felt lonely in the double bed on my own, despite being nice to stretch out. I couldn't hear Jonny close by and that was a bit unsettling. I suppose I'd got used to having him next to me. What had seemed awkward the first few days - sharing a bed with a complete stranger in a foreign country thousands of miles from home – was now perfectly natural.

I wondered how Jonny was getting on next door. Perhaps he was oblivious, he had suggested this after all. But then, knowing there was two separate bedrooms he might not have wanted to presume we'd still sleep in the same bed. Perhaps he'd felt duty bound to suggest sleeping apart. I shook my head and turned over.

Who knows…

Twelve

KT2

"Your boyfriend is very sweet, looking after you," said the soft English accent next to me. Her comment took me by surprise, it had never occurred to me that I'd ever be taken for Jonny's girlfriend.

"Yes, he is, isn't he," I said, feeling a bit self-conscious as I pulled the tight wetsuit over my calves and rolled it up my thighs, wobbling on my feet as I stood up.

"You all right there, need a hand?" said Sandra, my new found friend. She'd kindly escorted me to the small woodland cabin which served as the ladies' changing room.

"I'm okay thanks, just feeling my way round this rubber suit. Do we get a whip and stilettos too?"
Sandra laughed, then I felt her fingers against the small of my back, helping to unravel the neoprene.

"Here, it's all bunched up," she said.
I tensed up. I don't really like being touched without warning. That might sound odd as I'm always offering a hand or arm to whoever is around to help guide me, but I always know that contact is coming. It wasn't Sandra's fault. She could obviously see me struggling and was just trying to help.

"Can I ask you an odd question?" I said, slipping my other arm under the tight shoulder strap as she zipped the back of my wetsuit up.

"Sure."

"Can you describe Jonny to me?"
There was a pause while Sandra considered my request.

"He's about six two or three. A big guy, not fat especially, but a bit overweight. His face is slightly chubby, but round and jolly looking. He has a few days stubble but judging by the way he rubs his chin, he's probably normally clean-shaven. So, you're not actually together then?"

I smiled, shaking my head, but strangely I wondered whether Sandra was a potential threat. I checked myself. Threat to *whom* exactly?

"I don't suppose you remember seeing an advert a few weeks ago, on eBay?"

"You're *that* Kate? Wow! And you're blind too, how did that go down?"
I started to relax. I was interested that her description of Jonny was different to Maria's. Although I suppose it was bound to be. Maria just wanted me to go off on an adventure. What did it matter what Jonny looked like?

"I guess you could say it was an eye-opener!" I said, giggling. Sandra burst out laughing, maybe a little too enthusiastically. I felt her hand on mine. I flinched again.

"If I can help with anything at all, I'm your gal," she said, her breath very close to my cheek.

"Oh, thanks. Perhaps you could just show me to the door please?" I stammered, as I offered my elbow and she clasped my hand instead.

Me

I'd only been waiting for a few minutes, having been fairly quick getting into the wetsuit, which definitely wasn't the most comfortable thing I've ever worn. I'm a fairly big bloke and despite the young grinning instructor's claim that I had an 'XL' suit, I reckon it was a case of one size fits all. That's okay if you don't mind doing a contorted dance whilst trying to get your undercarriage comfy. But as soon as you try to straighten up again, your shoulders stretch the suit upwards and you're forced to wince and realign everything. So I was a bit pre-occupied when KT2 was escorted out of the changing hut by another English girl. I didn't pick up on anything out of place. Perhaps I should have led her down to the river myself, but she seemed happy enough.

"If my voice shoots up a couple of octaves KT2, don't worry. I've just signed up to a new government initiative to curb world overpopulation by volunteering to strangle my genitals. You okay?"

"I'm fine."

I glanced up and thought she looked relieved to hear my voice, but I still wasn't picking up on anything else going on.

"I'm looking forward to getting wet, to cool me down. These suits are hot, eh?" said the softly spoken English girl, which immediately pulled my attention away from adjusting my crown jewels.

"Thanks for taking care of Kate, I'm Jonathan," I said. I offered my hand, which without me realising gave KT2 the chance to latch onto me as Sandra released her.

"Hi. I'm Sandra. So you found another *Kate Thornly*. Good choice."

KT2 located my free arm and clung onto me, hugging the gap under my elbow with both hands. It was affectionate and I felt my body start to react to having these two pretty women in close proximity. They were a turn-on, but not in a pleasant way. Growing interest *down below* meant I was tightly trapped in the tangled confines of the suit.

"I think they need us by the boats," I stammered, as KT2 and I picked our way through the trees, down to the shore.

Sandra stuck to us like glue. It wasn't until we were sitting in the rubber dingy floating down river, that KT2 whispered in my ear and I finally understood what was going on.

"Help! I think she's hitting on me…"
I was a bit taken aback. Stupidly I thought Sandra was interested in me. Amazing how the male ego can be blind to the obvious.

"Are you sure? She seems nice enough."

"A bit too nice, if you know what I…"
The rest of her sentence was lost in the shout from our enthusiastic French instructor, followed by the roar of rushing water.

"Left side over!"
The four rafters opposite us pulled their paddles into the dingy, then leapt over towards us as a wave tried to lift our side of the boat and flip us over. Thankfully their shift in body weight did the trick and the boat stayed upright. I was still digesting KT2's observation about Sandra and frankly dismissing it. Surely Sandra had to be interested in me, right?

Wrong.

I looked at KT2, only to see Sandra grinning up at me, her hands on KT2's thighs.

"Sorry bout that, didn't know where to grab!" said Sandra, adrenaline heightening the tone of her voice.

I felt KT2 stiffen beside me. Fortunately there wasn't much time to worry or analyse how I felt about an attractive *woman* flirting with KT2, because it was our turn to dive over to the opposite side as the dingy spun round into the next wave.

"Right side over!" shouted the instructor as we all scrambled to shift our weight to the appropriate position. I went to lunge over, but felt KT2 hesitate. I grabbed her around the waist and pulled her with me to make sure she stayed in the boat. I tried to avoid the waiting arms of Sandra, but she seemed determined to gather KT2 towards her.

"Hell of a place to pull a dyke!" KT2 whispered as we waited on our side for the next command from the instructor. He was loving every minute of riding bronco at the back.

"Don't worry, I'll protect you. She's probably only trying to get to me through you anyway," I added.

I took the opportunity of a distraction during a flat section of the river and started a nervous, excited running commentary of our descent through the rapids.

"The water is white, frothing and wild! There are tall jagged rocky cliffs about fifty feet high on each side. To our left is Argentina, on our right, Chile. There are two other rafts ahead of us and more instructors in kayaks shooting the rapids with us. Ahead is a huge roller coaster wall of green, blue and white water. I can see the raft ahead of us dip down, it's lifting high now and, oh my god, here we go..."
I held KT2 tightly as we dropped down into a deep trough.

"Wave coming in, right side!" I shouted in KT2's ear, as a wall of water hit us side on. The dingy stalled, bent at forty-five degrees until it was spat out of the trough and sent us hurtling into the next roller coaster rapid.

"Whooopppeee!!!! shouted KT2, scaring the life out of me.

"This is bloody amazing!…"
Another wave rushed over our heads, smothering us in freezing water.

"Yeeehhhaaaa!!!!"

KT2

That was the biggest adrenaline rush of my life! I sat beside the river at the end of the rafting session listening to the water gurgle past, grateful for the warm clothes as I gradually came down from the excitement. I think Jonny must have had a word with someone, because in the changing room two other girls, a brummie and a French girl introduced themselves and asked if I needed any help getting changed. They seemed to understand my unease as they chatted happily about their boyfriends. I guess they wanted to reassure me that their attention was well-meant and genuine. I heard Sandra's voice behind them, but they'd escorted me into a corner of the room where they could protect me from any unwanted advances. They did a great job of handing stuff to me without touching me needlessly. How ironic that of all the situations in which to feel vulnerable and not sure quite to handle myself, it was in a ladies' changing room!

I thanked my new guardians as I sipped hot sweet tea with them, happy when the French girl whispered what a nice boyfriend I had. Their names were Dominique and Becky and they were staying at the same hostel as us.

"Is it true that you're *the* Kate Thornly? We heard about you in France!" said Dominique.

I chuckled and nodded my head. It was a new experience for me, being famous.

"What's he like in bed?" said Becky, loud enough so Jonny might have heard. I smiled as I pondered the question.

"A gentleman," I said, with a tinge of sadness.

Me

I was relieved to see Becky and Dominique take care of KT2. It was a strange feeling, being jealous of a *girl* who was making a move on someone I wasn't even with! During a few quiet minutes on the journey back into town I wondered why I felt like that – was I just being protective towards KT2 in a brotherly kind of way, or was there something more?

KT2

E-Mail From: Kate Thornly
To: Maria

Hey Mim,
I've attached a photograph of me in a wetsuit white-water
rafting! Apparently Jonny and I are in the top left of the picture,
you can just see me my terrified face through the spray. Who
would have thought I'd ever get a chance to do that eh?!

We're staying in a ski lodge and it's great to have our own place
for a few days. We're getting along fine, but to be honest it's
pretty easy travelling at the moment. I have a feeling that when
we leave Argentina in a few days it's going to get tougher. The
language barrier could be a problem, everyone speaks pretty
good English here, but that's going to change when we get to
Peru and Bolivia. There's so much to tell you already. We've had
a few ups and downs but for a complete stranger, I could have
done much worse. The weird thing is, everyone and I do mean
the WHOLE WORLD seems to know about us because of the
advert on eBay. "You're that Kate Thornly" everyone says and
they all want to know how it's going and what Jonathan's like in
bed! I know you're going to ask the same question and since
Jonny has to read out my incoming messages, I'd rather pre-
empt you so you can tone down your next e-mail accordingly.
(please!)

Nothing has been going on. But, the burning question is – do I
actually fancy him?

The simple answer is I don't know. He can be a bit dull at times,
you know, a bit corporate and conventional, but he's definitely
relaxing into the travel thing. I guess he's here, escaping London
life, so there's hope for him!

Love to all back home (except you know who – has he been
round hassling you?) and I promise to report in again soon,
depending on how many internet cafes there are in deepest
darkest Peru...
KT2

*Damn! That bloody man's got me signing my name KT2 now –
he calls me that all the time, and it really winds me up!*

I changed my name to Angel and sent the message.

Me
E-Mail From: Jonathan Cork
To: Justin
Subject: This is the life…

*We are now in Bariloche, the Argentinean Lake District. This
place is beautiful. Our cabin looks out over a lake that's
surrounded by snow-capped mountains. The air is cool and
crisp, but it's warm in the sunshine. We've been white-water
rafting, which was a challenge for KT2 (shorthand for Kate
Thornly the 2nd) especially as one of the other girls took quite a
fancy to her!*

*We're getting along okay, although I'm starting to wonder how
Kate Thornly the 1ˢᵗ is. Has she been in contact? It's strange,
thinking how different this trip would have been, if she'd have
been with me.*

*Ironically, I'm finding that travelling with KT2 has had the effect
of opening my own eyes. Does that sound odd? It does to me, but
it's true. I've always had to count on others in case I had an
attack and I was too reliant on the other Kate. I suppose I got
complacent. I can see that now someone has to rely on me.*

*We need each other, that seems to be the bottom line. Tomorrow
we leave for Cusco, Peru, where we'll join our group for the
Inca Trail. It'll be a challenging and testing time, so my next e-
mail to you might not be so positive!*
Jonathan.

Thirteen

Me

KT2's tee shirt had been bugging me all morning. I fanned
through my phrase book during our cab ride to the airport, but I
couldn't translate it. Maybe it was just me, but I'm sure I saw
people react as they read it. Unfortunately the language barrier
prevented me from asking them outright. I wondered if KT2 was
aware of the wording, but judging by our experience at Heathrow
airport, it wasn't very likely.

What the hell did it say?

After another ten minutes watching the green forests and snow-
capped mountains, I'd finally had enough.

"That's a nice tee shirt KT2, have you had it long?"

She turned to me, a shocked expression on her face.

"Has it got writing on it?" she said, her voice nervous.

As I watched her reaction, I started to realise that this had all the
hallmarks of another Maria stitch-up. I mentally kicked myself.
Perhaps I shouldn't have said anything, just ignored the sniggers
and amused looks. I'd not given it a thought at the ski chalet, I
suppose the usual rush to pack and check out meant I'd barely
noticed.

"I wasn't going to bring it up, but it's in Spanish and we're
getting some strange looks. Actually people are laughing and
pointing at us."

"Oh. I think Maria may still be having some fun at our
expense. Can you translate it with the phase book?"

"Some. *Amigo* means friend, and I think one of the other
words means *small*."

"Right. That's not good. I'll change at the airport. Or cover
up."

I frowned, wondering if KT2 had been on the receiving end of a
similar joke before.

"You know what it says, don't you."

There was a pause. Was that a smile twitching across her lips?

"I've a pretty good idea."

I waited for more, but that was it.

"And?"

"If it's the same as the English version last time we went out in a group, it loosely translates as *my friend is gay and has a small penis, but I'm available.*"

I spluttered, wanting to laugh, but the joke was on me. I noticed the taxi driver glancing in the rear view mirror, trying to read the tee shirt and I realised I could take this one of two ways. Perhaps it was time for me to lighten up a bit.

"Jonny, are you okay? Maria was just having a laugh..."

I allowed myself to grin, then laughed.

"Then there's only one thing to do."

I started to take my own top off, a smart travel shirt that was probably way too formal for our onwards journey anyway.

"What are you doing?" said KT2, hearing my movement.

"Let's swap."

"Swap what?"

"Tops. Turn the joke around."

By this time I was pulling my shirt off. We were about to give the taxi driver something even more interesting to look at.

"Here?" said KT2, an amused tinge to her voice.

"Hey, you're the one who's fearless in social situations."

"Yes, but... oh what the hell!" she said, giggling as she pulled the tee shirt over her head, revealing the outline of her pale breasts cupped in a black bra. I handed her my shirt, my eyes resting on her a second or two longer than was polite. I looked away as her cheeks flushed slightly and I caught eye contact with the taxi driver in the rear view mirror. He looked away and I slipped KT2's tee shirt over my head.

"There. Now we'll really give them something to laugh about," I said, pulling the tee shirt out and peering down at my chest so I could get a good look at the writing. KT2 giggled next to me and I glanced over to see her struggling with the buttons, which of course were the opposite way round to what she was used to. I almost reached across to lend a hand, but then remembered the unwanted help from Sandra at the rafting day.

"Want a hand?" I said, sheepishly as her eyes looked up into mine and she caught me enjoying her curves that the shirt provocatively hid. But of course she hadn't caught me, our eye contact wasn't real. But I suspected she knew anyway and I felt embarrassed.

"The buttons are all out of kilter. Normally I'm quite capable."

"I know. You're a very capable woman, KT2."

"You looking at me disrupts my concentration."

I laughed, sitting back, turning away to look out of the window at the passing houses, snow drenched trees and glimpses of the sparkling lake beyond. What an amazing place to live…

"Okay. I'm struggling. Would you mind giving me a hand please Jonny?"

I turned to face her, noting her frustrated expression and realised this wasn't a case of scoring points.

"You sure?"

"It's either you or the cabbie and I'm pretty sure you'll be careful with your hands and discrete with your eyes."

"Okay."

I reached forwards, starting from the bottom button, pretty sure that the taxi driver would be more than happy to oblige, given half a chance. Fortunately being a fairly big guy my shirt was loose on her, allowing me plenty of slack to work with. I tried to avoid brushing my fingers over the bare flesh of her tummy as I worked my way up.

KT2

Maria, you bugger! I'm going to strangle you when we get back! But we're on to you now, and as soon as we land we'll go through every item of my clothing and Jonny will vet it. (I'm sure he'll enjoy rummaging through my underwear!)

Embarrassment aside, I was pleasantly surprised at the playful attitude Jonny adopted towards Maria's prank. On second thoughts, that could have been so he could have a good look at my boobs!

It was a strange taxi ride because of the tee shirt swapping thing. Jonny, bless him, must have been aware of my discomfort at being touched without warning. So he was very careful and gently pulled the shirt away from my skin as he buttoned me up. I went quiet the further up he got until he asked me how many buttons I wanted showing. I reached up to feel where the last one had been buttoned and reckoned I could get away with one less. For some reason the simple *undoing* of a button got my heart beating a notch faster. Maybe it was because I knew he was close. I felt the gentle tickling of his breath on my face, could sense that his fingers were hovering close to my skin. It triggered something inside.

"There, all done," he said, his face still close to mine.
What was supposed to happen now?

We sat there like that for a second. I had no way of knowing what was going through his head. Was he having the same thoughts as me?

I felt the taxi slow and pull into a parking space. Then the driver's door opened.

"Here we are," Jonny said.

His voice became more distant as he opened his door and stepped out of the taxi. It left me wondering w*hat was going through his head?*

Me

I stood in the airport check-in queue and entertained myself for a few moments by wondering what would have happened if the journey had lasted a few minutes more. I dismissed the thought. *Face value,* I decided. Maria had stitched us up again and an unplanned but very nice view of KT2's cleavage had been the reward. I didn't feel guilty any more for catching an eyeful, it wasn't like I was being sneaky or lecherous. It just happened.

"Do you think Maria's tee-shirt is attracting more or less attention now you're wearing it?" said KT2, squeezing my arm, which was hooked back under her elbow in a now familiar position.

"I'll gauge the ticket lady's response. But I'm not sure how we'll compare reactions. Should I give a score out of ten?"

"Yes, definitely. Based on shock value, amusement and embarrassment," said KT2, giggling.

After a few minutes we stepped up to the counter and I handed over our documents, watching the woman's eyes as she checked our passports. She glanced up, her eyes instinctively drawn to the Spanish writing on my chest. She dropped her gaze to her computer screen, then did a double take. Her eyes widened as she tried desperately not to laugh.

"What's the verdict?" KT2 whispered.

"Looks like an eight for shock, nine for amusement and six for embarrassment. This lady has a sense of humour."

The check-in lady slid our boarding passes and passports back to us, but was unable to make eye contact. Instead she looked away quickly and rolled her eyes at a male colleague to check out my tee-shirt before we moved on.

"I win this round, far more shocking on me..." I said as I steered us away from the desk. It was weird, but having set aside feeling self-conscious, this new 'me' felt strangely liberated to know I was being laughed at. Something that would never have happened a few weeks ago...

Fourteen

Peru
KT2
Neither of us were that fussed about seeing Lima, it held the same frustrations and stress as Buenos Aires, so having arrived late in the evening, we'd arranged to fly out again the following morning. I think we spent less than seven hours there.

Walking out of the arrivals hall in Cusco, we were bombarded by sales pitches for accommodation from several 'official' tourist offices, all with their own hotel *recommendations.* Jonny was drawn to the offer of a map from a friendly sales desk and we had our hotel sorted.

Me
The square at the centre of Cusco's tourist area was very pretty, with precisely manicured flowerbeds set in neat lush grass, surrounded by immaculate wide stone paths and green cast iron bench seats. Block paved roads around the perimeter were busy with tiny Fiat 500 sized taxis, all in a hurry and driving erratically. White walled buildings with terracotta slate roofs had ornate wooden balconies. These were dotted with tourists of all nationalities eating, drinking and relaxing. At the top of the square was a very grand building with two tall Gothic-style square towers and a hugely imposing arched entrance door. Countless small spires sat on the top of the walls, all reaching upwards, tall and proud.

I stood in the centre of the impressive square and studied the tourist map to find our hotel.
We later found out we'd ended up in 'Gringo Alley', a narrow cobbled street off the main square crammed with colonial style courtyard hotels and restaurants. Although not threatening, locals lurked in the dark archways, ready to sell virtually anything you might want.

"...hey man, you like girls?... Want to smoke? Need cocaine?..."

After a while I found the best way to avoid being approached was to say nothing and just walk on past – a polite 'no thanks' gave them a nationality and language to latch onto and continue pestering. But with so many tourists to approach, they weren't too persistent.

KT2

The interesting thing about Peru other than the culture was that neither of us could see the altitude, but we both felt it. It was one of the few things on the trip so far that was a great leveller.

In those first couple of days it wasn't walking up the steep streets on the edge of Cusco that caught you out, it was at night when you were relaxing and not thinking about taking regular deep breaths. Sometimes I'd wake abruptly, struggling to breathe.

The other thing I found strange, was that it didn't seem to matter how fit you were, altitude sickness didn't discriminate; at times I suffered as much as Jonny. Although his fitness was improving thanks to our now regular runs.

"You awake Jonny?" I whispered.

There was a mumbled acknowledgement and I felt the bed creak as he turned to face me.

"You found yourself catching your breath yet?"

"I have, it's weird. I struggled a bit today walking around town."

"Me too."

We lay there in the dark in companionable silence.

"Is your trip meeting expectations Jonny?"

"I think so. But it's your trip too, we're in this together."

"Like business partners?"

He laughed.

"You could say that. So partner, how's your trip going? Are you glad Maria stitched you up with me?"

"Nah. I think she could have done a bit better in the looks department. I mean, from what I can see, you're a bit of a caveman!"

I felt a finger poke me in the ribs and I yelped, which just made us laugh more.

"Are you still clean-shaven Jonny? I only ask because I fear smooth office worker skin might not be good for my image."

"Your image? As what?"

"A traveller Jonny. I want us to fit in, absorb ourselves in these different cultures."

"Oh. Okay. I've been toying with just letting it all go wild, but I only manage a few days at a time before I start to feel a bit scraggly and end up shaving. But I could be persuaded."

"It's not like I can see you looking scraggly."

"True. The first Kate hated it if I didn't shave for a few days. She said it scratched her skin when we kissed. That was less of a problem towards the end, obviously."

"Obviously?"

"She was seeing the plumber by then."

"Ah hah. Shagging a bit of rough."

"Something like that."

The silence fell again for a couple of minutes.

"Well I think I'd prefer it if you grew a beard. This is your time to really relax, let your hair down. It'll be good for the soul."

"If I can get through the itchy stage I'll give it a go…"

"It's not like you've a girlfriend to snog now, is it."

"No. Thanks for that."

Oops.

I didn't mean that to come out the way it did. I tried another approach before an uncomfortable silence got a grip.

"Then to give you an incentive, I challenge you. No shaving for the rest of the trip. Are you man enough?"

"I'll give it a go."

"No cheating. I'll check up."

I slowly eased my hand over towards him.

"Stay still and shut your eyes for a moment so I don't poke you. Let's get a starting point here."

My fingers felt his head, I'd aimed a little high, so I carefully traced the outline of his ear down towards his chin.

"That tickles."

"Shhh. Let me concentrate…"

Me

Wow. Talk about erotic. Bloody hell!

KT2 gently traced the outline of my face with her cool slim fingers. In a way it was agonising, a huge turn on. We couldn't see each other, which was just as well, because KT2 might have guessed what my reaction would be. Until I did or said something, she couldn't be sure. I was really struggling to know what appropriate behaviour was. Should I reach out and touch her back? I wanted to.

"I feel stubble Jonny. What would the first Kate Thornly have to say about that?"

"She's not here."

"You must be pretty glad about that after the way she treated you."

I wondered if KT2 was aware that she might have gone a bit far, crossed the line? Just when we'd started to relax and enjoy each other's company as mates, she was now really turning me on.

"I'll check again in a week's time," she said, pulling her fingers away.

"Don't stop, that feels nice…"

The fingers touched me again, carried on caressing my face, circling my nose, then pinched it.

"HOONNKK!" she shouted, pulling back and laughing wickedly.

"Yeeooww! What was that for?"

"Those dirty thoughts! Wash your mind out with soapy water."

I exhaled in a sort of agitated sigh but found myself struggling for breath. I swore and turned over, in a huff.

I lay facing away from her, calming down but shocked at the electricity pulsating through me. *What the hell was she doing to me?*

KT2

Oh God what had I done? I'd played a dangerous game and had pushed him a bit too far. But it was unintentional. Or at least I think it was.

I lay there facing his back, trying to make sense of how I felt. But what was *he* thinking?

You're a tease KT2, probably. And right now I would agree with him. What was I doing?

"I'm sorry," I said, waiting for a reply that didn't come. The uneasy atmosphere was still floating around at breakfast, despite finding the best cafe in Cusco, "The Real McCoy." We sat on the balcony after an amazing full English cooked breakfast and tip-toed around *last night.*

Wondering how to spend the day, we got talking to the English cafe owners, who suggested a trip to Pisac market, a mini-adventure which turned out to be an excellent distraction.

Rather than join an organised whistle stop tourist bus excursion, we caught the local bus for less than a pound each and spent over five hours wondering amongst the endless sea of brightly coloured market stalls. Jonny was suitably amazed by the size and energy of the market to enthusiastically describe everything he could see.

Me

I'd not been thrilled at the thought of a day traipsing around market stalls, but that started to change as soon as we climbed aboard the rickety old bus, crammed with Peruvians all on their way to the market. I smiled at a toothless lady in a brightly coloured skirt and bowler hat as we sat down, wondering about the fate of the two chickens perched on her lap in a wicker cage.

The twisting hairpin road was not for the faint hearted; it felt like we were on a Dakar rally stage! As we clung on, KT2 leant over towards me.

"A roller coaster ride too, bonus!"

Our sense of excitement grew as we followed the crowd through the uneven cobbled street until a sea of vibrant colours opened up. The market must have been the size of five football pitches! I decided we should ease ourselves in gently and led KT2 up to a cafe balcony for a cup of coca tea so I could describe the scene from a suitable vantage point.

These stalls were selling almost anything you could think of. All of them had brightly coloured produce with canopies over the stalls. Vegetables, spices, clothes dye, fresh meat, flowers, beans, clothes... everything you could possibly want was all here. There was no way I could do justice to the incredible sea of colour, but

I gave it my best shot, acutely aware of how much KT2 was missing out on.

KT2

Jonny did a brilliant job of describing the visuals, but it was also the sounds and smells that impressed on me the scale of the market. Happy, vibrant haggling, sales pitches, hard bargaining, yet all carried out enthusiastically, without any hostility.

After a couple of hours wondering from stall to stall through the crowds, my stomach was rumbling. Mesmerised by a fantastic food smell, I tugged on Jonny's arm.

"What's that stall cooking? It smells amazing!"

"Looks like chicken, potato and vegetable stew. Its bubbling away in a huge cooking pot. There's about a dozen people on benches tucking in."

"Fantastic, lets give it a go!" I said.

Jonny wasn't keen at first, I think he was worried about food poisoning, but my nose and tummy decided it smelt too good not to risk it. I'm so glad I managed to persuade Jonny to give it a go, although he waited for me to taste it first, just to make sure it was nut free. He told me later it was the best meal of the trip so far!"

By the time we finally tore ourselves away from the market and caught the bus home we were exhausted from such a brilliant day out. I even managed to fall asleep on Jonny's shoulder for some of the roller coaster bus drive home!

Me

After a perfectly nice dinner that was still no match for the market stall chicken stew, we headed back to the hotel, deviating slightly to buy some bottled water. I was about to lead KT2 away from the shop by the square, but I was intrigued by the gathering crowd. They were watching tall rickety wood climbing frame structures being wheeled into position beside the grand town hall building.

The precarious structures were around thirty feet high and looked like they'd been constructed out of giant lolly sticks, wired together with an impossible amount of fireworks; fountains, Catherine wheels, spark spraying spinning merry-go-rounds, rockets exploding overhead and showers of bright sparks. It seemed each firework tower had been built by rival groups, all vying for the enthusiastic handclapping and cheering appreciation of the large crowd, many of them far too close to the exploding towers of fire! The flimsy structures twisted and bent with the energy of the fireworks. One frame even caught fire!

What an incredible way to finish a brilliant day! I felt the excitement drain away as we wondered back to the hotel and reality took a grip once more. We'd had a fantastic day and it had served to mask *other* issues.

I glanced over at KT2, smiling happily on my arm. I wondered how she felt about last night. We were due to start the Inca Trail in a couple of days time and I wanted to make an effort to enjoy it with a positive attitude. But that meant either facing up to my feelings and discussing them with KT2 in a mature, *cards on the table* kind of way, or ducking the issue completely and withdrawing into myself.

Like a coward, I chose the second option.

Fifteen

KT2

The next day we sat in an internet café catching up with the folks back home. I still didn't know how to start *the conversation* with Jonny. It was driving me crazy, not knowing how to broach the subject. So I plugged into my music and stuck my head deep into the sand.

His silence was the worst punishment. I wondered how long it would last. What if there wasn't good news in the e-mails?

I racked my brain, trying to think what I could do to ease the tension between us.

And then I knew. I fumbled around with the MP3 player controls and turned it off – dance music isn't the easiest to sing along to. Despite being blind, I still find I need to close my eyes to concentrate, so I did. Now, how did the song go?

"Deep down in Louisiana close to New Orleans, way back up in the woods among the evergreens, there stood a log cabin made of earth and wood, where lived a city boy named Jonny be good…"

Me

I turned and looked over my shoulder at KT2, along with every other person in the café. For a moment I was confused, then uncomfortable and finally embarrassed. But then I found myself relaxing and I broke into a grin. Instinct told me to get up and steer her out onto the street, but I didn't. For some inexplicable reason I joined in, impromptu karaoke style.

"…go, Jonny go, go…go, Jonny be good…" we sang. God we were terrible, but if KT2 didn't care, why should I? I saw her grinning between the pauses where normally the music would have carried the song. I quickly shut my computer down and wandered over to her, ignoring the bewildered faces of other travellers. I was about to break into another chorus when I felt KT2's hand on my arm.

"I think that will do Jonny, we've made our point."

"That we can't sing?"

"No, stupid. That it's beer time."

"Right."

I suddenly became self-conscious as the moment ended and we were left standing there surrounded by inquisitive faces.

"Should we wait for applause?" I said, starting to chuckle nervously. I was strangely stuck there, like a rabbit mesmerised by approaching headlights.

"Do they look like they are an adoring crowd?" KT2 asked, starting to flush slightly. It was the first time I'd seen her embarrassed.

"Not exactly."

I snapped out of my frozen state and clasped KT2's hand.

"Ready for a hasty exit?"

I rummaged in my pocket and dropped a larger than necessary note on the counter and led us through the bemused silence.

Once safely outside in the narrow alleyway, we both broke into laughter, snorting for breath as we tried to reprise our duet, without much success.

How do you describe *Mama Africa?* A dinghy first floor terrace bar overlooking the square? Better I think to let the people sum it up. The Russian toilet 'attendant' – "twenty Soles a tab, good shit man"... the cocktail juggling barman who also did a turn strutting his *Ricky Martin* stuff on the bar with his impossibly quick hipped *Coyote Ugly* female dance partner. The mix of drinkers was vast. Young hip Peruvians, international travellers, a few older hippy types, all getting wasted. There were open dope deals on the balcony, local prostitutes draped over the bar trying to catch the eye of the tourists, lethal pisco sour cocktails and an eclectic mix of 70's, 80's and 90's world music intercut with pulsating Spanish numbers, all pounding out to the delight of the hard partying travellers.

"Are we sure this is a good idea, mixing alcohol and altitude?" I shouted over the music, toying with the pisco sour.

"We'll just have the one," KT2, shouted back.

I shrugged my shoulders and touched my glass against hers, then took a gulp. The atmosphere in Mama Africa was vibrant, in your face and kicking every living moment out of life. It was definitely preferable to awkward silences.

KT2

"What time is our alarm call in the morning?" I said during a brief lull in
the music.

"Five, sorry. *Cinco.*"

"We'd better get our drinking in early then."
I took a slug at the cocktail, then relaxed back, a thought occurring to me.

"I think we need a strategy. For toilet stops."
I heard him chuckling from across the table.

"I'm serious. Fail to plan, plan to fail and all that. Now, I reckon we need to rely on people's good nature, take some pressure off you. I know about your perversions towards ladies toilets! So I propose letting Henry give us a hand."

"Henry being your imaginary friend?" said Jonny.
I reached down and rummaged in my bag, producing a bundle of white rods about the length of a ruler.

"Meet Henry Fonda, my magic wanda."
His chuckle developed into a deep belly laugh, drowned out by the loud intro to a recent number one, accompanied by cheers from the dance floor. I felt around the edge of the table with my free hand, then traced an arc below with my foot and flicked my wrist, feeling Henry unravel to a full length white stick.

"I thought I'd left Henry behind, but it turns out Maria isn't a complete sadist after all," I shouted across the table at Jonny.
I tapped the end of Henry around the table, scoping out the immediate surrounding area.

"People react differently to me, because I'm much more obviously in need of assistance, whether I want it or not. So the first time I need the *banos,* you show me the way. Next time, Henry will find me some help. It's amazing, he pulls every time."

"Not bad for a little fella," said Jonny.

"He does better than you, I'm sure," I said, cringing as I realised what I'd said, but I heard Jonny laugh over the music.

Me

I had to hand it to KT2, she was a resourceful, gutsy girl. Full of mischief too. She'd snapped me out of my mood and despite my reluctance, she'd achieved it so easily. Kate Thornly the 1st would simply have lost her temper.

Predictably, one drink turned into two, then three and many more. The more we drank, the more we got into the music and atmosphere and laughed at my descriptions of this crazy bar. There was no po-faced *I think you've had enough, you're becoming loud and are making an arse of yourself* expression to hold me back. We just went with the good humour between us, carried along with the infectious buzz from everyone around us. It was effortless. And so far we'd managed to avoid having *that* conversation.

I can't remember much of our stagger back to the hotel, just snippets; the rush of fresh air outside the bar, tripping on the cobbled pavement and almost pulling KT2 with me, warding off the local drug dealers in Gringo Alley and finally collapsing on top of the bed, staying awake long enough to say what a great evening I'd had.

The next thing I remember was the bloody phone SCREAMING next to me, its ring vibrating on the wooden table, a sledge hammer POUNDING on my temples. I heard KT2 groan beside me as I rolled over and scrabbled to answer it.

"Buenos dias Senor…"

The rest of the receptionist's greeting was lost in an early morning haze of dehydration and hangover. I think I managed a gruff "Gracias" before replacing the phone and sinking back under the covers, groaning.

"You awake KT2?"

"Mmm. Perhaps beer time wasn't such a great idea," she said, pushing herself up in bed.

I managed a mumbled reply, sleep was drawing me back and I was losing my struggle to stay awake.

"Um, Jonny? I don't want to freak you out, but you know we still need to pack, and if that was a five o'clock alarm call, then we only have half an hour to be ready for the Inca Trail, and that's without breakfast…"

Shit!

My eyes opened wide and I sat bolt upright.

Talk about speed packing! I'm afraid we weren't the quietest of hotel guests that morning, it was just a case of grab whatever we could, stuff it into our packs and hurry out as fast as possible.

Thirty minutes later we were standing outside in the square, waiting for the coach to arrive. I glanced around me, pie-eyed. All the amazing architecture was lost on me. I winced as a dull ache developed behind my eyes.

It had been a mad dash to get here. We were dressed in long hiking trousers, the type with the zip removable legs and several thin breathable tops. Oh, and a hat each. KT2 looked quite attractive in hers, in a schoolgirl kind of way. But that's as far as that train of thought went. It was approaching five forty-five in the morning, it was chilly and I was red-eyed and seriously hungover. It was hardly the time to be considering why I hadn't made a pass at my travel companion. But then again...

"You still there Jonny? Are you sleeping on your feet?"

"I feel like terrible."

"I know, you look like shit! I'm not sure if I can bear to share a bed with you again..."

I had to laugh. KT2 must be feeling as rough as me, yet she still had her sense of humour. I was about to reply when I heard the rumble of an ancient diesel engine and our bus rounded a tight corner.

"We go, the adventure begins!" said Bob, our 'Peru Treks' guide. He was a stocky, powerfully built Peruvian chap in his mid to late thirties who had a permanently happy smile on his face. He'd apparently been named by his parents after Bob Hope, the American comic.

I remembered to hook my arm around KT2's to help her on board the coach, much to Bob's amusement.

"Big night before Inca Trail eh? Tough later my friends."

Bob was grinning, he must have seen this so many times before, gringos overdoing the grog, then paying for it later on the trail. I couldn't sum up the energy to explain, so I just pointed to my eyes, then pointed at KT2 and shook my head.

"Ah, okay I understand. Miss Katie, I look after you, please put your arm in mine," said Bob, gently guiding KT2 towards the coach door and up the steps. I smiled my thanks at him and he clapped me on the shoulder. I liked him immediately.

KT2

My head was pounding! The hangover from hell and altitude are not the best mix. On the plus side, the mood between Jonny and I had improved and we seemed to be back to normal, as things had been before *that* night.

I felt better sitting still on the coach, but then we set off through the narrow twisting cobbled streets of Cusco and onto the winding gravel mountain roads. I started to feel sick. This wasn't the time or place for a repeat of the whale watching episode, so I closed my eyes and sank back into the seat, concentrating on not throwing my guts up.

"You're quiet, are you okay?" Jonny said after half an hour or so.

I woke up from my dozing – that sort of sporadic sleep where your head lurches forwards and you jerk yourself awake after what seems like only a few seconds.

"Felt pretty rough for a while back there," I said, attempting a smile.

"Take some layers off. Might make you feel better."

I nodded and started to shrug my jacket off, not easy in the confined space of our seats. I felt Jonny's hands helping me, gently tugging my arms out of the sleeves. It didn't feel odd or intrusive.

"Better?" he said as the last fleece came off over my tee-shirt and I felt my breathing become easier.

"Much, thank you Jonny."

I smiled and patted his thigh, then glanced to my left towards the brightness that I guessed had to be the window.

"What's it like out there, is it a nice day?" I said, wishing for the millionth time that I could see the countryside whizzing past. I missed colours the most and I wondered how pretty this foreign land really was.

"It's a beautiful day."

I waited for more, but that was all he was going to say. I felt a little disappointed, but then I remembered he was still hungover too.

"Would you describe it for me? Please," I said, preparing myself to mentally sketch a picture as he spoke.

"Of course. Sorry, I'm a bit vacant this morning. We're on a gravelly mountain road. The landscape is pretty barren, but green in places, if that makes sense. We've just passed a small town far below with a terrific little football pitch right in the middle of it. Now we're losing sight of it as we descend through the mist. I can see endless fields, some with green coca crops, others partially harvested. I can see a father and son work their plough behind some sort of cow…"

"That sounds like hard work," I said as I stared out of the window, drawing my own picture from Jonny's vivid descriptions.

"In the distance everything looks more extreme; greener fields, higher mountains, deeper valleys with dense, lush forest. Mist lingers in patches, it looks slightly eerie, but more mysterious than scary, the promise of the unknown. It feels like we're about to explore a new uncharted land for the first time…"

I felt myself smiling as his running commentary continued, despite feeling some sadness that I couldn't see these wonderful things. But who was I to complain? It beat the socks off sitting at home listening to endless talking books and dreaming of faraway places. Here I was doing it for real.

"Occasionally we pass through a small village. The houses are earth clad, with timber and thatch roofs. There are lots of people in traditional dress, loose ponchos for the men and brightly coloured dresses for the women, blue, yellow and gold. The ladies are wearing tall top hats, like a London city gent circa the 1800s…"

"Jonny, can I ask you a serious question?"

His commentary stopped and there was silence for a moment.

"Of course," he said, a little hesitantly.

"Did you bring your Superman outfit?"

I heard him laugh.

"I'm saving it for a special occasion."

"Good, then we're on level ground for the trek. Can't have you surging ahead with your superpowers. You will stick with me, won't you? On the trail I mean. I'm not worried about my fitness, but the walking might be difficult for me. You know, steep and slippery in places. I don't want to be a pain in the arse, but I'm saying I'll need your help even more than normal."

Me

I studied KT2's eyes. What was it I sensed?

Vulnerability. I reached forwards and gently touched her arm.

"Hey, this is a joint effort. We both signed up to this when we met in the hotel lobby, remember?"

I watched her lips break into a lovely smile.

"You were looking for the fire escape."

"I was a bit shocked. But I stuck around, didn't I?"

"Why? Can't be much fun for you."

I took a deep breath as I pondered the question, but my train of thought was interrupted by Bob standing at the front of the coach, grinning like a Cheshire cat.

"Friends, good morning. I am Bob, your guide. Welcome to the magical four day trek to the unforgettable Machu Picchu. The first day we say is easy. The second, challenging. The third day is rewarding and the fourth, unique. Sixteen of you brave and adventurous souls have gathered together to enjoy this experience. So, who do we have with us and where are you all from?"

Bob looked at the front seat where I could just see the heads of a young couple.

"Matthew and Samantha, from England."

Bob nodded and smiled at each person as he worked his way around the coach.

"Nudge me when it's my turn," KT2 whispered as the roll call got closer to our seats at the back of the coach.

"Okay, not long," I whispered back, wondering if it might be easier for me to introduce us both. There was a pause and I glanced up to see Bob grinning at me.

"Jonathan and Kate, from England," I said, a little flustered.

"Scotland for me! And my friends call me Angel," KT2 called out, to the amusement of Bob and the others on board. They all looked round at the couple who didn't really know each other. It wasn't the best of starts to our integration into the group.

"Okay, good. Lots of different nationalities; English, French, Spanish, Australian and Scottish. Friends, we are going to have a great time. You will be looked after by a big group of porters, who are selected from two local villages. They all know each other and you will see their sense of fun on this trip. They work hard, but they're able to provide a good standard of living for their families. I will introduce you to them later this evening...." Bob carried on with his description of the discovery of Machu Picchu in 1911 and the unusual fact that the Inca civilisation wrote nothing down about its way of life. No hieroglyphics or diaries or writings of any kind describe their community. As I listened, it occurred to me that I should probably apologise to KT2.

"Sorry for stepping on your toes. It's a bit like being back at school on the first day and having to stand up and say your name..."

"No it's not. It's a nice way to break the ice and welcome us all aboard. The sooner we get to know people the better. And by the way, I'm only half Scottish, but don't let on, I have my pride!"

KT2 always seemed able to diffuse any social awkwardness with her relaxed nature and her ability to poke fun at herself. I sat back thinking that Kate Thornly the 1st would never have been this at ease at the start of such a trip. I allowed myself a grin as I realised I was here, living in the moment, whilst she was stuck back at home.

Silly cow.

Well-hung plumber or not, who was having more fun right now?

"You're smiling," said KT2.

"You can't possibly know that," I said indignantly.

"I heard your wrinkles creaking!"

I tickled her mercilessly, making her yelp, which soon turned into a wicked laugh. KT2 pushed my hands away - our fingers parted and I felt a tingling sensation. I felt my chest tighten and my stomach churn. I looked away, but then stole a sideways glance at her.

It can't be *that*, I reasoned, confused as to what I might be starting to feel. My thoughts were cut short as the coach drew to a stop. I looked up and saw that we were in a small stony car park, jam packed with coaches from other tour companies. Everyone was busying themselves with unpacking their gear and preparing for the trek.

KT2

I couldn't see where we were of course, but I could hear the bustle and sense the excitement as we stepped out of the coach into the bright sunshine.

"Lots of people KT2, all sorting out their gear, buying waterproof ponchos and walking sticks from little Peruvian ladies in brightly coloured skirts. We're in a valley. There's a river running through it and I can just make out a steel rope bridge at the end of a track. On the opposite side of the bridge there's a large sign marking the start of the Inca Trail. Around us are maybe five or six different travel companies. Our porters are loading up with amazing amounts of equipment. Think two dustbin size bundles of equipment strapped to their backs. Many of them are wearing just sandals or plimsolls on their feet…"
Jonny was doing a great job with his enthusiastic commentary, quite some progress compared to the start of our trip.

The air smelt fresh up here, but despite a few days spent acclimatising, the reduced oxygen still caught me out.

"This'll do for a hangover cure Jonny," I said, unable to stop smiling.

"Want some water?" he said, guiding a plastic bottle into my fingers.

"Thank you."

"No problem. You all set?"

"I mean thank you, for this experience. I'd never have thought I could ever be here, travelling like this."
As he gently took the bottle off me I lunged forwards on impulse and wrapped my arms around his neck and hugged him tightly. I felt the initial tension in his body subside, then I checked myself and released him, not sure that this was the time or the place.

"Put him down, you don't know where he's been," said a cheerful voice I vaguely recognised from the introductions on the coach.

"I'm Barry, from Oz. But my girlfriend insists on calling me Bozzer. Something to do with your nation's strange sense of humour. She's a bit daft, but hey, she rolls a mean joint."

"We all have some redeeming features," said a girl's voice, with the hint of a West Country accent.

"I'm Madge, short for Madeline, Bozzer's long suffering bird."

I grinned and offered my hand.

"I'm Angel to my mates, and I'm almost totally blind. Which obviously explains how I ended up with Jonny, who looks like the back of a bus. But I'm told he's a man of action between the sheets, so I guess that's his redeeming feature…"

I leant forwards and lowered my voice.

"…as yet untested…"

I gave an exaggerated wink and grinned at their laughter. I felt two different hands shake mine, then stood there waiting for Jonny to introduce himself.

"I'm Jonathan. And I'll be returning Angel here to the loony bin after the trek. She doesn't have any redeeming features, but she can drink anyone under the table, as I found out last night." We all chuckled, and prompted by a rallying call from Bob, we joined our group and the growing throng of travellers heading down to the start of the trail. Or, as it was to turn out for us, Inca *Trial…*

Sixteen

Me

It was one of those weird moments when you shudder and you can't put your finger on the reason why. *Something* you can't understand. A sort of subconscious warning that takes you back to *that* day.

"You've gone really tense Jonny. Someone walk across your grave?" said KT2, rousing me from my darkest thoughts.

I'd forgotten that day so easily, since you.

But of course I didn't say that to her. How could I? Some skeletons were meant to stay under lock and key for eternity, especially when the rattling was still so fresh in the mind...

"Something like that. Maybe this place," I said.

I was looking up at a tomb in the side of the mountain that Bob had just explained was part of the ancient Inca tradition. There were several entrances cut into the rock about a hundred metres above the stone path. Patches of mist lingered and the sun had just dipped below a cloud as a light drizzle descended. I shivered and looked away from the tomb.

"I can sense it too. The spirits are restless Jonny. But don't worry, there's no Kryptonite being mined in them there hills..."

I tickled her, making her jump and giggle, but I had to grab her arm to stop her tripping over on the uneven path.

"If you want to bump me off you could at least wait until the sacrificial altar stone!" she said, grinning as she tried to return the tickle.

"I would, but I don't reckon offering you would appease the gods much, what with you being only *half* Scottish!"

And that's pretty much how the first day went.

Bob was right. It was fairly easy walking, the incline steady. Far below on the edge of the river, the tourist train between Cusco and Machu Picchu made easy work of the journey. But those day trippers were missing out on the real experience as they sped past unseen Inca forts and lookout points alongside the river. All of them perfectly constructed from stone blocks, all following natural contours of the land, in harmony with nature.

We struck camp in the early afternoon on a gently sloping grass field tucked into the side of a mountain. It had fantastic views across the valley below.

The other travellers were the sort of like-minded people you'd expect to meet on an adventure holiday like this. Chilled out, hardy types. Some had well-paid jobs and were taking their annual leave, others were travelling for a much longer period on tighter budgets. But up here, two miles vertically from the sea, (a mind boggling thought) we were all on a level playing field. What we did for a living had no bearing on completing the trek, or the reasons we were all here.

We sat on the groundsheet and sipped the coca leaf tea that Bob had brought round to our tents. I looked out over the valley and attempted to describe its magical beauty.
I couldn't do it justice of course.

"It seems so, out of this world. The mountains are rugged, barren, like the moon. All the shrubs seem robust, not delicate like garden plants back home. Here they're wiry and stout. I guess it's not mist that swirls around the mountain peaks and lingers in the valleys at this altitude, it's cloud..."

"Makes me feel lucky to be alive," said KT2.
Coming from a blind girl, her words tugged at my heart strings. How did she stay so positive when she couldn't *see*?

"It's because you're my eyes Jonny, in answer to the question you're pondering over. Just think how difficult this would be for you to explain, and for me to understand, if I'd been born blind."

I turned to stare at her, surprised to see tears trickling down her cheeks. I opened my mouth to ask if she was all right, but it didn't seem appropriate. So I pulled a packet of Kleenex from my pocket and gently placed a tissue in her hand. She nodded her thanks and silently dabbed her eyes.

"When did you first know? If it's okay to ask..." I said, wondering if I was pushing a bit too far, delving into her past without invitation.

"It's okay. Perhaps we should both open up a bit."

I wasn't sure if this was a question or statement.

"Yes, of course. Superman can always use another friend. He doesn't have many from this world..." I said.

She nodded, vacantly.

"I was nursing. I began making mistakes, misreading the chart, things like that. I was afraid to get my eyes tested. I knew it was a possibility, it was in the family. But I loved my job and never wanted to give it up, so I stuck my head in the sand, until it became clear I couldn't go on."

I offered KT2 a bottle of water and we sat there for several minutes. I looked out over the misty valley as the sun started to drift down towards the horizon.

"The day I left was awful. Work colleagues, some of them *friends,* were disappointed in me. I lost lots of mates that year..."

"Why? Wouldn't they have done the same, if they were in your position? What about these surgeons who have hepatitis or HIV operating on people, there was a case a few months back..."

KT2 was shaking her head.

"I nearly killed a patient Jonny. I misread the medication. It was a close call. I got a massive bollocking and had to confess to the ward sister I was having problems. She arranged for me to get my eyes checked out and I was told my sight would keep deteriorating. And that was my nursing career finished."

"But surely with all the knowledge you have there was still a chance of a job in nursing, at the end of a telephone for example..." I stopped as I noticed more tears streaming down her face.

"What is it?"

I wasn't sure if I should reach out and hug her, offer some comfort. But I decided to air on the side of caution and just sat there awkwardly.

"I was unwell for a while, afterwards."

She dropped her head forwards over her hunched up legs, wiping her eyes with the sleeve of her fleece. I couldn't watch her get more and more distressed. So I placed my arm over her shoulder and held her, feeling her lean into me, burying her head into my chest.

"That's perfectly understandable..." I offered, but she just shook her head.

"You don't understand."

In that pause where she might have said more, Bob appeared from behind the dining shelter, cupped his hands to his mouth and announced dinner was ready.

"Perfect timing" she said, lifting her head, hurriedly wiping the tears away.

Seventeen

Me

The camping set-up was like something out of the days of the Raj. When we'd arrived that afternoon all eight guest tents were already pitched and the porters were busy preparing the evening meal. Sixteen multi-national trekkers sat around a fold out table under a long narrow dining shelter. Everyone glanced around at each other, smiling politely, not sure exactly what to expect in the way of food. I think it's fair to say we were all pleasantly surprised.

KT2 and I were sitting in the middle of the group. Bozzer and Madge were a couple of places along to our right. Next to them were two French Canadian girls who constantly switched between their mother tongue and English, so it was difficult to follow their conversation. Bob and his second in command, Julia, a Peruvian woman in her thirties, sat at the opposite end of the table, smiling enthusiastically as the food was passed around. I noticed that they both dropped small samples of each course of food on the floor – a thank you to the gods for the meal they were about to eat. Perhaps because I was becoming generally more aware, I realised that people were curious about KT2. Of course that curiosity had always been there, but I'd not noticed it as much before. I had to admire her for introducing herself unprompted.

"I'm Kate, but my friends call me Angel. You'll have to forgive me if I'm a bit clumsy at the table, I'm virtually blind. Next to me is Jonny, " she said, in a conversational tone of voice, that was perfectly pitched not to draw unnecessary attention to herself, but clear enough to invite a response.

I guess not being able to hold eye contact, meant she didn't know who might be interested in chatting to her. Brave girl, making the first move.

I did my bit by glancing around the table at several pairs of interested eyes, nodding a greeting as my smile was returned. I was secretly impressed that KT2 hadn't gone for shock tactics in her introduction – perhaps that would come later…

"Hi Angel. I'm Susan. My boyfriend to your right is Rodney. Nice to meet you," said the girl opposite, smiling at me for KT2's benefit.

"Nice to meet you guys. I'm trying to place your accent and am going to go with New Zealand. Am I right or have I just insulted your heritage?" KT2 asked, looking over in Susan's general direction.

And that's how it went. Dinner wasn't a problem, not for us at least. I could see one or two people trying to get to grips with KT2's blindness. But only because they found the lack of eye contact difficult to get used to. Most wondered how a blind girl could ever consider walking the Inca Trail and I suspect they were both humbled and amazed at her achievement.

It was a polite and relaxed atmosphere. The soup bowls were gathered up and big industrial size serving plates arrived, filled with a delicious smelling stew with rice and vegetables. We'd obviously mentioned my allergy to the trekking company, who'd assured us there wouldn't be any nuts in the dishes, but even so KT2 tried my food first. It must have seemed quite an odd process to watch – me serving out food for both of us and then waiting until KT2 tasted it. Unfortunately our peaceful little ritual was soon interrupted.

Mikey, as he liked to be known, was your standard loud-mouthed yank. He was sitting at the far end of the table with his Dutch girlfriend, Anna, who he'd hooked up with while travelling. Anna gave the impression that whatever they had was a temporary thing.

"Hey Angel dust, what happened to your eyes?" said Mikey from the other end of the table. I caught a look from Anna. She rolled her eyes apologetically for her partner. Mikey's question was loud enough for everyone to stop their polite exchanges and listen in, their curiosity aroused. Unfortunately, and I don't say this about many people, I took an instant dislike to the guy. Maybe he was just trying to make conversation and his direct, brash approach just rubbed me up the wrong way. Perhaps I should have accepted it was just 'his way'. But no. The guy was an idiot, simple as that.

The silence around the table had been going for a few seconds by now. I must have had a pretty angry expression on my face, because I caught an apologetic glance from Bob. Mikey meanwhile was polishing off the rest of his dinner and seemed completely oblivious. I could feel myself getting more angry, but I felt KT2's calming hand on my knee.

"I lost my sight a few years ago, fighting dragons in Glencoe with my spiritual brother, Connor McCloud, of the McCloud clan."

What on earth could he say to that? Nothing remotely interesting or witty, that was for sure.

"Huh?"

Silence, it seems can be a very powerful tool, if used to your advantage. KT2 picked up her fork and scrapped it across her plate to mop up the last of her dinner, then passed her plate down the table where Bob collected them into a stack. Mikey was staring at KT2, trying to decide what to say next. She'd turned the tables back on him – why waste her time responding to his insensitive questioning? Nice one!

"Dragon? That's dumb ass bullshit…" he finally said, unable to decide if the conversation was over or whether he was being ignored. KT2 quickly cut him off.

"Dragons. *Plural.* I slaughtered them both in an epic battle. Their fiery breath scorched my face, burnt my eyes out. But what was taken from me, was replaced tenfold with other much more interesting senses. My telepathic skills were reactivated after years of inactivity. That means I have to tell you, as a fellow Inca traveller, the next thing you're about to say won't endear you to the group, so it's probably best to keep your nightly masturbation ritual to yourself."

There were a few slack jaws around the table, go KT2! Bob was fighting hard to stop giggling. He made a *please excuse me* type gesture as he collected the pile of plates, then ducked out under the tent flaps and was heard stifling a laugh as he walked away.

Mikey looked like he was playing back KT2's words in his head to see if there was anything he could respond to, but he couldn't. So he just sat there looking vacant. I was mentally

preparing myself in case he got nasty, but Bozzer quickly
defused the situation by clapping Mikey on the back.

"I guess that's you told mate! Give us a grin, tomorrow's
another day," he said in his broad Aussie accent.
Mikey eventually shrugged his shoulders, allowing a murmur of
conversation to resume around the table. Bob arrived shortly
after that with dessert, by which time the group were back to
their *getting to know each other* conversations.

I'd been unable to stop grinning since KT2's verbal play fight.
I leaned in towards her.

"It's going to be handbags at dawn..." I whispered.
She grinned wickedly.

"I bet he was furious," she said in a low voice.

"Yup. But he was unable to think exactly why he should be,
or what he could do about it – you being a famous dragon slayer
and all."

"One of my many hidden talents, amigo."

KT2

I lay in our tent that night and grinned for a long time before I
allowed myself to fall asleep. I wanted to savour and immerse
myself in the moment. I was here, in Peru, seven thousand miles
from my safe existence at home, a blind girl walking the Inca
Trail and loving it.

My fight and passion for squeezing everything I could out of
life hadn't deserted me, despite losing my sight. Today I'd felt
the most exhilarating sensations I'd had for a long, long time.

I thought back to when I'd found out I was losing my sight
and mentally kicked myself for not doing stuff like this while I
could still see something, *anything* of the colours and rugged
scenery we were walking through... But back then I was
struggling with other *issues*.

After a moment or two reflecting, I sniggered at how I'd
knocked Mikey down a peg or two.

"You're still thinking about dinner," mumbled Jonny from the
depths of his sleeping bag.

"Good guess. Did you have your head in your hands,
embarrassed at me making a scene?"

"A little. But Connor McCloud, from the film *Highlander*, now that's inspired. Christopher Lambert would have been proud."

We both giggled, careful to keep our voices low due to the closeness of the other tents and our fellow trekkers trying to sleep.

"Even immortals masturbate," said KT2.

"Probably quite a lot over several lifetimes!"

We both stifled our laughter. I bit my sleeping bag to try and suppress the noise. By the time we calmed ourselves down and stopped giggling, my face was aching from smiling and laughing so much.

Eighteen

Me

It's strange looking back to think there was no *physical* contact between us, but in every other way our relationship was going really well. I woke up the next morning facing KT2, who was snoring lightly from the depths of her sleeping bag. I crawled to the tent entrance, unzipped it enough to poke my head out and drank in the cold morning air. Wisps of cloud lingered in the valley, shrouding the campsite in a mysterious blanket that the early morning sun was just starting to break through.

I smiled at the sight of Bob in shorts, tee shirt and hiking boots accompanied by a porter carrying a tray. They were doing the rounds at each tent and handing out steaming cups of coca tea – now that was room service in style!

I watched Bob and the steaming teapot slowly advance towards us as bleary-eyed trekkers accepted the tea and exchanged a few words with Bob. True to form he was grinning from ear to ear.

I retreated back into the tent and let KT2 know that tea was on its way. She mumbled and rolled over, then sat up in her sleeping bag, stretching. There was something different about her this morning, I decided, a light dancing in her eyes, an enhanced energy. I wondered if I was being rude or voyeuristic, studying her features.

"What's it like out there?" she asked.

"Come and see for yourself," I said instinctively, then cringed, kicking myself.

"Breathe in the morning air KT2 and I'll describe it to you," I said quickly. She shuffled her sleeping bag towards me, feeling her way to the door by running her hand lightly over my back and shoulders. I unzipped the flap some more to let her put her head out.

"Morning handsome," she said, blowing a plume of vapour into the air.

"Morning gorgeous."

She turned to me and smiled, a slightly awkward *what happens next* expression on her face.

"How much of me can you see, at this distance?" I said, more to break the moment than out of curiosity. A smile twitched across her lips and she wriggled towards me until our noses were an inch apart.

"I can see you need a shave Jonny, but you have a nice smile, so I'll forgive you. Oh dear, that's not good."

"What?"

"Looks like you're heading for a really bad hair day."
She started to snigger, so I reached out of the sleeping bag and tickled her in the side, making her screech and roll away, laughing.

"She's right mate..." said Bozzer from the tent to my right. I turned to glance over at his grinning face as he accepted two cups from Bob.

"You wanna get a new wig."
I pulled a face, then dug KT2 in the ribs again, trying to 'shush' her giggling.

"No time for that, challenging day ahead," said Bob, as he knelt by our tent and passed me a cup of coca tea.
Does he ever stop smiling? I wondered as I accepted the tin cup. I placed the tea on the ground, guiding KT2's fingers into the handle. We both thanked Bob and the porter and lay there enjoying the slightly bitter but not unpleasant taste.

"Lots of steps today Angel, we'll be your eyes sometimes, okay?" said Bob, nodding to me before he moved onto the next tent.

"He's quite inspiring isn't he," said KT2, as I watched Bob pouring tea outside the next tent.

"Yes. I like his enthusiasm, it's infectious."

"Tough day today, city boy. Are you up to it?" she said, turning to face me, our noses close once more.

"Normally, no. But my personal trainer has prepared me well."
I watched a smile developing across her lips.

"Although she can be quite demanding. Actually I think she might be a closet dominatrix."
We both giggled as we sipped our tea.

"You talking handcuffs, PVC and thigh high boots, mate?" said Bozzer, climbing out of his tent and stretching, kicking his sleeping bag back inside.

"And I thought you Brits had no sense of adventure."

"Oy, watch who you're insulting mister. No shagging if you keep that up," shouted Madge from within the depths of their tent. I grinned at Bozzer, who winked at me as he finished rolling his cigarette and lit it.

"I was talking about Jonny."

Bozzer slapped his palms down onto his thighs.

"Legs, get ready for hell..." he said, then took a deep drag on the cigarette.

KT2

We'd probably been going for three or four hours and the conversation between us was starting to dry up. It's inevitable when you spend so much time with the same person, but this seemed different somehow. It was *companionable silence* rather than being awkward. We still had to communicate with the necessary instructions for our "buddy" walking system of course, particularly if there was any sort of incline on the slippery stone steps. But these comments were practical observations rather than conversation.

Jonny would occasionally mention the different eco-systems as we passed from rugged, sparse mountain passes, into thick lush forest. There were mini waterfalls surrounded by pink and orange heathers, together with lush tropical vegetation. Often I could sense the change of mini-climate coming, the slightly oxide raining smell was a dead giveaway for cloud forest jungle, while colder damp air was an indication of high, barren mountain passes. During the silences I started to wonder what was going on in Jonny's head. What did he think about this arrangement – us, here? Was he still thinking about Kate Thornly the first?

Me

I suppose our fellow trekkers were curious about our 'unusual' relationship. Perhaps people just assumed we were *together*. At any rate their curiosity meant that we started to become a popular couple to walk with and chat to. Especially after KT2's put down of Mikey, who avoided us like the plague. We found ourselves bonding with the group and I was learning a difficult lesson. I'd never viewed anyone with a disability as 'normal' until this adventure. It's fair to say I was gradually being taken down a peg or two, as only KT2 could.

"Hey you guys, nearly at the top," said a voice behind us. I turned and smiled at a girl of around thirty or so, tall and gangly and red-faced from the climb up Dead Woman's Pass. At over four thousand metres, this was the highest point on the trek. Following her was an equally tall guy in his early twenties. They introduced themselves as Matt and Samantha from Southampton; a brother and sister who were doing part of their travels together before going their separate ways to meet friends.

"I gave you a silent cheer last night, after your brilliant *Highlander* put down," said Samantha.

"Cheers. It was an entertaining evening," said KT2. She turned to smile at them, but gripped my hand tightly as she momentarily lost her balance.

"You okay?"

"Yup, I'm good."

We all walked on for a little while, allowing KT2 to get into a rhythm.

"We were saying how much we admire you Angel... is it scary?" Matt asked.

I glanced over at KT2, wondering how she would answer.

"It can be, but I'm not scared of heights anymore – that's one of the early lessons you learn."

"No reference point, so once your body has made the adjustment, you don't worry?" said Matt.

For some reason I felt he was being a little too intrusive.

"Aye. But the initial adjustment takes a long time..."

"How long?"

Now I was officially getting jealous. But the struggle I was having had more to do with the undefined nature of our relationship, than Matt's advances.

Argh!!

Why was I taunting myself like this? Was this just a petty, selfish feeling of *I don't want you, but no one else is going to have you?*

Or was I still hung up on Kate Thornly the 1st? I couldn't answer my own questions, let alone stop Matt asking his!

"Must have been tough, to come to terms with…"

I'd had enough. I led KT2 over to the side of the path and stopped.

"Water break, we'll catch you guys up."

"I'm happy to wait," said Matt, smiling. Probably in an unthreatening way, but I was way past being able to make such distinctions.

"You're okay, please go on."

"No really, I'm happy to wait, I'm enjoying the conversation…"

I was just about to lose it, but fortunately his sister caught the look of anger in my eye.

"That means a private moment, Matthew. Come on," she said, glancing at me in a *sorry, I know what he can be like* kind of way.

I watched Matt being walked on, his sister hooked on his arm, in much the same way that KT2 and I walked together. He glanced back over his shoulder, prompting me to look away. I shrugged the day pack off and rummaged inside for the bottle of water. I caught the strange smile on KT2's lips, ignored it and took a deep drink.

I placed the bottle into her hand and gently wrapped her fingers around it. A hundred metres or so back down the trail the next trekkers from our group were slowly making their way towards us. I watched KT2 take a long drink, waiting to take the bottle once she'd finished.

"Thanks. It's all getting a bit heated," she said.

Was that a chuckle in her voice? I studied her features, but couldn't tell.

"Are we there yet?"

I grinned at her ability to lighten the potential atmosphere between us. Correction. My mood.

"Probably halfway," I said.

"Then we'd better get going. That's Mikey catching us up and I might have to take a crack at him if he tries to overtake us."

I frowned and glanced back down the path, realising she was right.

"How the bloody hell did you know that?" I said, astounded.

"That, Superman, is for me to know and you to scratch your head over."

I slung the pack over my shoulders and linked my arm through hers. *The bloody woman had some sort of radar!*

I started laughing as we walked on, shaking my head.

"You're a constant surprise KT2."

"That Jonny, is because I have superpowers too."

Nineteen

KT2

It was a relief to snuggle into the dining shelter later that evening for a welcome hot meal. Whilst today hadn't been as physically demanding, we'd been walking for twelve hours and were a pretty weary bunch. But gradually the chatter rose as everyone started eating and energy levels were replenished.

There was an underlying excitement at reaching our goal the next morning. Bob explained we'd be at the Sun Gate at dawn to watch the legendary lost city of Machu Picchu appear through the mist…

"Well, friends, this is it, we are nearly at our journey's end." Bob's voice held everyone's attention.

"We have journeyed together for three days, from kilometre eighty two, through the highest point at forty two hundred meters, which you will remember as Dead Woman's Pass, onwards to Runkurakay at thirty eight hundred meters, then the last big climb to the third pass, Phuyupatamarca. After forty three kilometres underfoot, we have stayed positive and finally rest here at Winay Wayna, the last campsite before the sacred lost city of Machu Picchu. Friends, tomorrow we rise at four am. We have breakfast and will be on our way by four thirty to get to the entrance to Machu Picchu by five thirty. Once we have our tickets we have an hour and a half walk to the Sun Gate, where, through the early morning light, Machu Picchu will reveal herself. Tomorrow will be a very special, unforgettable day. I look forward to completing our journey together."

There was complete silence around the table. I imagine Bob must have glanced around the sixteen faces hanging on his every word and felt a sense of pride. He had something we did not; knowledge and a deep spiritual connection to this very special place. I felt the hairs on the back of my neck stand up. Then there was a jolt in my stomach as I felt a familiar hand gently squeeze my shoulder.

"You did it Angel! A blind girl completing the Inca Trail. Well done," said Jonny, releasing his hand.

"We did it together."

I found myself grinning at the achievement and almost wished we were alone to share this moment. I felt comfortable with this man I couldn't see. A man whose upbringing, job and outlook on life had differed so much to my own at the beginning of our travels. I'd almost forgotten how we first got together, until Bozzer, sitting opposite me, asked *that* question;

"So, how did you guys meet?"

There was a long pause.

"Kind of a dating agency," said Jonny.

I smiled, nodding my head in agreement.

"What's *kind of* a dating agency?" said Bozzer, pushing the point.

Now it was my turn to jump in and head off the connection they were bound to make.

"A charity auction. Up for grabs was a date in London with Superman. I won Jonny."

It was one of those inspired answers that has everyone second-guessing exactly what's meant, including me.

"Superman?"

Shit! Think woman, fast!

"Yup, he had the costume and everything. Of course I had to rely on my friend Maria to describe every curve and bump under the Lycra. Jonny will forgive me for saying this, but he wasn't as fit and muscular back then. In fact he was described to me as being on the chubby side of cute. But for me, any man willing to stand up and make fun of himself, had to be worth talking to."

Me

It was a good recovery, I thought we'd been found out for sure. I held my breath as I glanced around the table, realising that everyone had put their own conversations on hold to listen to ours. I waited for the next question.

"How how much does Superman go for these days?" said Madge.

"There was a lot of interest and I was almost at the point of ducking out at a hundred quid. But then I had an inspired idea. I stood up and said I'd strip for five hundred pounds in order to secure my date with Superman. Several drunken businessmen clubbed together. And that's how it all started."

They were almost taken in, but not quite. It was time for an Oscar-winning closing performance. I took a deep breath, and put on my best poker face.

"But that's not quite the end of the story, is it darling?"

I watched KT2 smile and turn towards my voice, amused that I'd stepped in to up the ante.

"No. You tell them," she said, handing me an imaginary shovel to dig myself an even deeper hole.

"That set a precedent in the auction room. The stakes had gone up in a totally unexpected manner. A group of footballers' wives turned Angel's little ploy on its head. They decided to save her dignity at the expense of mine. So they offered to up the bid to a thousand pounds if Superman would strip down to reveal Clark Kent, in his birthday suit."

I shook my head and dropped it forwards into my hands to hide my grin from the group. Together we'd dreamt up an answer to a simple question far beyond the realms of belief. But somehow we seemed to have pulled it off.

"So did you?" asked Samantha, totally taken in.

I felt KT2 drape her arm over my shoulder.

"We're here aren't we? Hearing the ladies gasp as every inch of Superman was stripped bare, sold me on him. We've been together ever since."

My God, how we howled into our sleeping bags later that evening, until the tears streamed down our faces. We were only trying to avoid the whole *so you're the Kate Thornly* conversation. Instead we'd spun such a ridiculous story, in such a convincing way, that they'd all believed it – how mad is that?!

At last we seemed to have shrugged off the whole eBay-find-me-a-girl-with-the-same-name-as-my-ex-girlfriend thing, and it felt good!

I found myself grinning that we'd left all that behind and because I hadn't thought about work in a month. Granted it had been a pretty intense learning curve taking on KT2. (Perhaps she'd had the tougher job taking on me?) But we were getting through that stage now and I realised I was not only relaxed but actually really enjoying myself, something that hadn't happened for a few years. And this evening had been hilarious. I'd been wiping the tears of laughter away ever since we'd got back to the sanctuary of our own tent. We lay there giggling and talking for hours.

We must have slept eventually because Bob needed a whistle outside our tent to rouse us. It took a few seconds to register before excitement kicked in and I realised where we were and what lay ahead. Machu Picchu was waiting! I sat up, barely registering that KT2 and I had been cuddled up together, making like spoons.

The next couple of hours were a blur; packing up and breakfast were accomplished in near darkness on auto-pilot. All around us torches flickered and danced as everyone hurried to break camp.

After a hasty breakfast we followed behind the excited crowd, hand in hand, the dating agency auction couple on their way to the next adventure.

The last stages of the Inca Trail were fairly flat, but the large stones were slippery underfoot. We slowed down in case we tripped over, so by the time we arrived at the entrance to the Sun Gate, we were bringing up the rear of the group. But we didn't care, we'd made it!

Now though, there was the small matter of eighty of the steepest steps I've ever seen. Waiting for us at the top, looking down anxiously was Bob. He signalled to me – *did we want a hand?* I glanced at KT2, who was waiting patiently for me to lead us up to the Sun Gate.

"Very steep steps Angel. Bob is offering to help…"

"Can we make it on our own? I'd like to try, if you think it's possible," she said.
I glanced up again, then shook my head at Bob, raising my hand to thank him.

"Let's try. Ready?" I said and reached down for her hand.

"One step at a time, no problem," she said, squeezing my fingers.

Bob watched us from the top as we slowly climbed on all fours, feeling our way.

Step by step, we slowly climbed towards the Sun Gate.

KT2

I couldn't feel any steps in front of me. At last we were at the top!

Under Jonny's guiding hand I straightened up to a round of applause and cheering from the rest of our group. Who would have thought a month ago, I'd be standing here, a blind woman at the entrance to the lost city?! I had to tighten my grip on Jonny's hand to steady myself. Perhaps I was giddy from lack of sleep, the altitude, or maybe it was the emotion of the achievement as adrenaline surged through my body. Whatever it was, I felt elated and quite literally on top of the world.

As we walked forwards I didn't have to prompt Jonny to tell me what he saw, I could take my pick of who to listen to; Bob, two or three other guides or any number of excited trekkers. Their enthusiastic voices filled the fresh morning air.

"…the lost city of Machu Picchu, appearing to hover on the top of a mountain, a perfect defensive position to ward off enemies… surrounded by lush greenery… mesmerising symmetrical terraces and exactly proportional buildings, almost as if it's still under construction …"

"Well done KT2," Jonny whispered as he swept me up in a bear hug. Then we walked over to the edge of the Sun Gate where everyone was waiting for a group photo to mark the occasion.

Jonny painted an amazing picture of Machu Picchu through the morning mist. He said on first glance it looked like tightly spaced contours all swirling in the same direction, like you'd see on an ordinance survey map. Then as the cloud patches drifted past, the patterns carved into the mountain top sharpened into precise rows and tiers of stone set out amongst grassy terraced areas. It looked like a miniature medieval village from this distance, surrounded by bushy greenery way down the slopes, deep in the surrounding valleys.

The mysterious lost city was now within an easy walk. There was something about this place, spiritual and unbroken by time. I couldn't stop smiling. Bob was right, it was truly *magical.*

"Do you feel it Jonny? The *strength* of this creation? Shut your eyes. Take a moment to blank out everything else, concentrate, lose yourself in this moment. Do you *feel* it?"

Me

I turned back to face Machu Picchu and closed my eyes, trying to put myself in KT2's shoes to experience what she did. And then, it happened. I felt *something.*

Was it tiredness playing tricks on me? My imagination running wild? Who knows? The sensation climbed from the pit of my stomach, radiating through my limbs. A glow that was real, and for the first time in my life, I felt I was actually right there, living in the moment, soaking up a tremendous energy. I made a conscious effort to try and lock the feeling away.

I prised my eyes open, blinking back the wetness.

"I think you felt it too," she said softly, squeezing my hand. I felt myself nodding. I tried to analyse what had just happened, quickly realising that I couldn't and shouldn't. There would be plenty of time for that some other day. For now I'd just go with it, let my emotions run free. I tried to speak, but couldn't find any words.

"This day may be a turning point for you," said KT2. I squeezed her hand in acknowledgement, and without saying anything more, we made our way from the Sun Gate to follow the path towards the lost city.

Up close, it's the *scale* of Machu Picchu that staggers you. And the construction is so precise, each building or terrace wall perfectly dovetailing into the next; a huge intricate jigsaw puzzle with giant boulder size pieces. No flaws or mistakes. It's completely captivating.

I stood quietly in the centre and watched KT2 trace the outline of the huge stone blocks with her hands, shaking her head at the precision.

137

"Not even the slightest gap. How on earth, with only basic tools, did they engineer this so exactly?"

"The weight alone baffles me. How did they move the stones?" I said.

"A great mystery indeed, Jonathan Cork."

I frowned and turned to look over my shoulder. Stepping out from behind a wall was a rather hot and sweaty British television journalist, complete with cameraman and soundman.

I'm not joking.

Justin's sheepish grin completed the entourage. Simon, the reporter thrust a microphone in my face and started firing daft questions at us, to the bemusement of our fellow trekkers. I turned away, unable to believe my eyes as a sick feeling churned in my stomach.

Twenty

KT2

All I needed to hear was Jonny's words *"...what the hell..."* to know we'd been rumbled. That was when things got really weird and really surreal, really quickly.

"Kate Thornly, are you happy with your eBay purchase? Has Jonathan met up to expectations? What does your *husband* think about you running away with another man?" asked Simon, the slime ball reporter.

Oh shit!

The great shame of that day, other than shattering the magic of Machu Picchu, was how it undermined our bond with the group. It looked as though we'd deliberately set out to deceive our new friends.

Only Bob saw the funny side straightaway. It seems the story of the search for another Kate Thornly had made it all the way to Peru. He probably knew from our application forms for the trek. So that was why Jonny had commented on his mischievous smile whenever they made eye contact.

Bob now came to our aid and shooed away the film crew on the grounds of the site's religious and historical importance. He asked them to please be respectful and to not disturb the spirits. It was a welcome respite, but would only delay the onslaught for a few minutes.

That left us in an awkward predicament with the group. I stood there feeling ashamed that we'd spun such a story and hidden the truth of how we met. As Bob's chuckling subsided, the silence became unbearable. I opened my mouth to speak, but Jonny jumped in first.

Me

"I'm sorry guys. I'd never have thought there would be so much interest in us. For those of you who don't know the eBay story, my ex-girlfriend, Kate Thornly, ran off with a plumber a week before we were due to set off on this trip. The tickets couldn't be changed, so I advertised for a replacement, but this new person also had to be called Kate Thornly, who you all know as Angel. We're not *together* in the traditional sense, nor did we meet at a charity auction. We'd just got fed up with all the eBay attention, so we used a little artistic licence, for which I apologise. We'll take this film crew away and let you enjoy the rest of your time here. We really are very sorry."

I didn't know what else to say. It wasn't fair to screw up their day too.

"You'll meet us for the meal later?" said Bob.

I shrugged, not sure how the rest of the day was going to pan out.

"Please come. We would all like to say goodbye after sharing this journey together. It's bad luck not to come along," he added as he shook my hand and squeezed KT2's shoulder.

There was a general murmur of agreement in the group and as I glanced around, the faces of our travel companions showed mostly warmth and friendship, despite looking a bit bemused.

"Thank you. We'll see you all later," said KT2, as we sheepishly shuffled away, both in a bit of a daze.

This wasn't really happening, was it?

Twenty One

Me

"What are you doing here mate? And who the bloody hell are you?!" I said, turning from Justin to face Simon.

"They've been pestering me since the day you guys left. I held out as long as I could, but their offer is amazing. A hundred grand for your exclusive story. That would set you up, buy you all the travel time you want..."

Simon slid some paperwork across the bar next to my untouched beer. I stared at it for a long moment, then picked it up and flicked through the pages. It had a contract stapled to the back for me to sign.

"Think about it. A hundred grand."

"Fifty," I corrected him.

"Huh?" said Simon.

I turned to face Justin.

"There are two of us in this and I don't mean me and you, mate."

"Okay, *fifty* grand. You could still do a lot with that," said Simon.

"It's not worth the sacrifice."

"What sacrifice?! You don't look too good fella, you're a mess. Can't be much fun, going from one shitty hostel to the next. No hot water to shave, no time to get a haircut..." said Simon.

I started to laugh.

"He's right mate. I nearly didn't recognise you," said Justin.

"That's the whole point of travelling, to become someone else, break away from all that London life bullshit," I said.

"All expenses paid for the rest of your trip and fifty grand in your pocket. But that's just for starters. You'll be a celebrity. Which means advertising endorsements, party invites, more money..." said Simon.

"And all that comes with a hefty price tag," I said, cutting him off in full flow.

"A hundred isn't enough? I've got some leeway on this, so let's talk. What are you looking for?"

I'd had enough of Simon's sales pitch. I shrugged and took a sip from my beer, turning my back on him.

"Kate asked me to give you this. She's worried about you." Justin pushed an envelope towards me. I took it without a word. For the first time since I'd sat down, I started questioning my wisdom in being thousands of miles from home. I turned to face Simon, resisting the temptation to punch his slimy smug face.

"Remind me again of my obligations, if we sign," I said.

KT2

This had to be the weirdest day so far, and not in an adventurous, exciting kind of way. I felt completely deflated. Our magical bubble had been popped, just as we'd started to relax and have a real laugh together. I sat quietly with Jonny in our hotel room as he finished reading the 'contract' out loud.

"So if we agree to be shadowed by the film crew for the next couple of months, we get the rest of the trip paid for *and* fifty thousand each?" I said.

"Yes."

"Is that what you really want? Being followed around, unable to make your own decisions and having to perform for the camera every day? Baring your soul to millions?"

"I didn't manufacture this. Justin thought he was doing me a favour. A bit like Maria stitching you up," he said.

Me

Ouch. I saw the words touch a nerve.

"That's not what I asked. Is this what *you* want?" she said.

"We both need to sign up to this. I don't deny the money would come in handy…"

"For what? It's not going to make a difference to me," she said.

There was a long silence as I thought everything through.

"Maybe there's someone else who might benefit. Your *husband* for example?"

KT2 sat back and folded her arms across her chest.

"That's a cheap shot Jonny. I'd rather you just respect the fact I had a life before that stupid advert!"

"And I'd rather you'd already mentioned something that important! Perhaps when we met for the first time in the hotel lobby?"

I couldn't hide the anger and sarcasm from my voice.

"You could have asked!"

"Why the hell would I? You don't wear a ring!" I shouted back.

I stopped myself as the altitude made me catch my breath. I took several deep breaths, surprised and confused at the intensity of my reaction. Why were my emotions so all over the place? Why did it matter so much to me that KT2 wasn't *available?* I felt my shoulders sag and I slumped down on the edge of the bed.

"What a bloody mess," I said, completely deflated.

"I'm not divorced Jonny, but I haven't been *married* for some time. It's complicated. I don't know where to begin... there are things I have to ask you too, but the timing is..."

"The timing couldn't have been any worse!"

I jumped up from the bed and paced the room. I do that when I'm angry or confused.

Why hadn't she told me she was married?!

I stopped pacing and clenched tufts of hair in my hands.

Was it really such a big deal? This was a business arrangement, nothing more. But was it really that simple?

I turned to face KT2. She looked ashen.

"You should have told me," I said, in a more balanced, controlled voice.

"Why?" We made a deal. No sexual contact, remember. So why should it matter?"

"Because... I thought we were starting to get on, as friends. Starting to trust each other. But now..."

I took a deep breath.

What the hell was going on in my head? Why did all this matter so much?

"It's like we've not been on the same trip, because you've been living a lie..."

"What lie?" she said sharply.

I checked myself, realising that if I wasn't careful I'd really mess things up. How do you ask someone who you're not *with*, why they kept something from you that might make a huge difference to the possibility of something developing between you?

"I shouldn't have found out like this."

"I agree. But you'd never have known if your friend hadn't talked to the media."

"You should have told me!"

"I'm sure you have a past too Jonny. Reasons for keeping some things locked away. If we'd been getting along *that well*, we'd have had *the talk*."

There was a long awkward silence.

"You're not with him anymore?"

"No. Not for a long time."

I studied her, wondering what to make of the revelation and more importantly, the raw nerve it had touched in me. I sat back down on the bed.

"So what happens now?"

"We blame the idiot who wrote the eBay advert," she said.

I had to chuckle as I shook my head.

"Yeah. What a knob."

"Hey, I have a suggestion. It's a bit, um, out there," she said.

"I just shrugged indifferently. In case you were wondering."

"Let's roll back the clock a few hours to before all this blew up in our faces. We forget about Simon, the film crew and the cash and finish the trip the way we want."

I sat there for a while in a detached, *this isn't really happening to me* trance. There was nothing else for it. It was time to bite the bullet.

"One condition," I said.

"Okay," she said, a little hesitantly.

"We have *the talk,* about our pasts."

"We will. But not now. In a month's time. Whatever happens or doesn't happen between us until then, we let the travel gods decide."

Despite my need to resolve the confusion about our *relationship,* keeping my head buried in the sand and enjoying the rest of the trip without any further complications was an attractive proposition.

"Agreed," I said at last.

Watching her smile, I knew what we had to do.

I picked the paperwork up off the bed, watching her grin subside as she heard the pages flutter in my fingers.

"Give me your hand," I said gently.

"I'm not signing anything! We'd never have any fun. Those vultures will probe and try to engineer problems between us to make juicy TV. Do you know how nice it is not to be arguing constantly?"

"Trust me, we're not signing anything."

I lifted her hand and placed her fingertips on Kate's letter.

"This is a letter from my ex-girlfriend."

KT2 pulled her hand back, confused.

"She wants me back," I said, watching KT2 shrink away from me.

I held the letter out and flicked my thumb on a lighter, setting the paper alight.

KT2 wrinkled her nose as the smoke wafted up to the ceiling.

"You're burning it?"

"Yup, unopened. That chapter of my life is closed and there's no going back."

KT2's face lit up.

"My only question now, is will you come with me?"

"I'm in, screw the money!"

Twenty Two

KT2

The rickety old train juddered, rousing me from my thoughts. Since the 'ambush' at Machu Picchu, I was less concerned about hearing Jonny's descriptions of our surroundings, but I was aware enough to know we were in an open plan carriage and were sitting two abreast. I knew Simon was opposite me. I could smell his rank B.O. wafting across the hot, claustrophobic atmosphere.

A couple of hours had passed since we'd left Machu Picchu and we were now bound for Cusco. Last night we'd retired to our hotel room early for a project meeting. It was supposed to be time for us to consider the newspaper and documentary deal. But we were actually working out how we'd make our escape. The brilliant plan was conceived over several drinks at the Inca Trail meal.

Bob had seen to it that the TV crew was banned from the restaurant on the grounds of his religious beliefs. He convinced them his ancestral spirit would be very unhappy if he was captured on film. I have to take my hat off to him, he kept a stern poker face during the confrontation and the film crew scurried away to a nearby restaurant. Bob's grin was apparently as wide as ever as he welcomed us back to the group. Everyone was intrigued to hear our side of the eBay story.

So we told them the story of how we *really* met and some of our adventures so far. Jonny described the embarrassing scene with the customs officers at the start of our trip, which now seemed years ago. Was it really only five weeks since we'd boarded that plane? It wasn't long before someone asked the hundred thousand pound question.

"Are you going to take the money?"
The background laughter and the boisterous conversations trailed off.
I shook my head, but I couldn't *see* Jonny's reaction.

"We may have to do a runner," he said quietly.

"You're mad not to do it, especially if it's all expenses paid," another said.

"I don't think we'd have as much fun with a camera crew in our faces all the time," I pitched in, hoping that Jonny really was of the same opinion.

"Where you gonna go?" someone else asked.

"It's probably best no one else knows, just in case we decide to fly to Las Vegas and get married!" I said, grinning, remembering how my previous reference to New Year in Rio had freaked Jonny out. A gentle tapping of metal on glass caught everyone's attention.

"Friends, congratulations. You have all experienced the magic of Machu Picchu, you have walked many miles with positive steps and now you have memories that will last a lifetime," said Bob. I felt for my beer and lifted it up, relying on the others to chink their drinks against mine. Bob really did have an eloquent way with words. Listening to him was inspiring. He was the sort of person who had a passion for life and the kind of positive outlook that stayed with you long after other memories have faded.

Eventually the rest of the group had to catch the tourist train back to Cusco, which brought the boozy lunch to a premature conclusion. We'd booked to stay on an extra night and visit the hot springs. The plan was to catch the train back the next day. Eight of the group were going to be in Cusco the following evening, so we made tentative arrangements to meet up for a farewell dinner and drink.

"If we don't turn up, it'll be because we've made our escape," I whispered to Madge as we hugged to say goodbye, careful not be overheard by the film crew, who had left their restaurant and followed us to the station.

"Then in the nicest possible way, I hope we don't see you tomorrow. Keep in touch via e-mail and good luck!" she whispered back.

We avoided Simon's interrogation for the rest of the afternoon by saying we needed time to discuss the contract in private. And that's how we found ourselves at the hot springs, sitting up to our necks in hot sulphuric water in one of the dozen or so pools.

"Are they still there?" I asked, sinking back into the hot water, such a luxury in South America.

"Yup, they're sat up at the bar looking down at us. The longer we're here, the more they'll drink and hopefully the less they'll be on the ball in the morning."

I nodded and sank further into the soothing hot water.

"Tell me more about this place, it has a nice relaxed feel to it," I said, my body soaking up the warmth.

"This place is fantastic. We're sitting in the largest pool, about ten feet by twenty. A few yards to our left is the river which flows over a rocky path cut in the rock. In places it's almost a waterfall due to the steep valley sides. There are tropical plants and trees all around us so I can't see the rest of the town from here. It's like we're in our very own hot spring oasis. I could get used to this, it's really quite lovely."

"Uh huh, sounds just gorgeous. You'll have to pinch me, I must be dreaming..."

I heard Jonny chuckle, then felt him shift position, sending ripples of water across the pool. I flinched, waiting for his touch, my heart rate stepped up a notch, but his playful pinch didn't come.

"I think those cheeky buggers have got a camera on us," he said quietly.

"Come on, let's try another pool."

I heard the rush of water cascading off his body as he stood and stepped out.

Damn!

I stood and held out my hand, having to make do with his hand in mine. Before I could get carried away at the thought of our swimming costumed bodies being so close, the cold air made me shiver and I was grateful for the towel he wrapped around my shoulders for the short journey to the next mineral pool.

I sat on the bed in our hotel room as Jonny emptied the entire contents of our rucksacks onto the bed.

"If we do this KT2, we'll only be able to take a small daypack each. Only bring what you really need. Space is at a premium..."

We started on my clothes and belongings first. Jonny would pick up various items, describe them to me, I'd say yes or no and he'd make two piles; stuff that was coming with us and stuff we'd leave behind.

What could have been a potentially stressful exercise was actually pretty light-hearted and fun. Despite having to seriously cut down on our clothes, I felt a buzz of excitement. We were like school kids running off together, only with a touch more life experience under our belts.

Me

I stared at the piles of clothes and wondered how on earth we'd fit them all in.

"We still have too much stuff, we have to be mercenary. KT2, are you with me?"

"Off course, I'm just wondering if we can wear more clothes, you know, to save on space."

I had to laugh. Many women would be in a right strop at having to leave so much stuff behind. I sifted through the first few items from her pile.

"Underwear. How many pairs and which ones?"

"Ten, mix of practical and pretty."

"Angel... think minimalist."

"Okay, four pairs, you choose."

Wow, that was easy. Or was it? I held up her underwear, wondering what to take.

"If it makes it any easier to decide, imagine which you'd like to see me wearing."

Damn! She'd read my mind!

"These are all clean, right? I mean, there's no point taking ..."

She held out her hand. I took a moment to catch on, then handed her knickers over.

"I don't think we're that advanced in our relationship," she said. I watched her hold each pair to her nose.

"Clean. Clean. Clean. Nope. Clean. Hmm, not sure..."

I ducked as she threw the last pair in my general direction, laughing at her wicked grin.

"You choose four from here," she said, passing me the 'clean' pile.

I was a little embarrassed by now, so I quickly selected three fairly practical looking pants, and one black partially see-through pair.

"Which ones did you choose? Are the racy black ones in there?"

"Wait and see!" I said, stuffing them into her day pack.
It took another hour to sift through our remaining stuff and decide what was coming with us and what was staying. KT2 of course was unaware of exactly what I was packing, she had to trust me. Silly girl, because it meant I might get my own back at some point – heh, heh, heh!

KT2
We'd worked out our plan like a military exercise, with code words and everything. There was a stop just before the main Cusco station where we'd jump the train. Jonny would keep an eye on the time and ask me what I fancied for dinner, which would signal a five minute countdown. Then it would be over to me to say I needed to go to the loo. It all worked like a dream.

"Jonny dear, would you mind, I have to visit the facilities..."

"Sure. Please excuse us for a moment," said Jonny.

"You're going together?" said Simon.

"You ever seen a blind girl pick the wrong door on a moving train? It's not pretty," I said quickly, putting the little bastard in his place.

"Jonny, do you have my bag please?"
In preparing for the Inca Trail, we'd brought matching day packs, which fitted the plan perfectly.

"You sure my stuff is in here? I don't think your smelly socks will do the trick," I said.

"Not sure."

"I don't want a repeat of the customs check-in. I was so embarrassed you'd brought our special toys with you…"

"You like Mr Big."

"Not in public I don't. Bring the other pack too."

"Jesus! Come on then woman," said Jonny, the irritation in his voice highly realistic. I heard him rummage over his head for the other pack and I stood, holding my hand out for him. As he led me down the carriage towards the bathroom I felt the train start to slow. Our stop was approaching!

Me

My heart was beating fast as we walked away from Simon, Justin and the camera crew. We ducked around the corner at the end of the carriage, out of sight.

The train was now slowing rapidly.

"One minute to go," I whispered, preparing myself.

From the last couple of stops, we knew the train would wait two or three minutes at the most, less if there weren't many people getting off. I eased the window down as quietly as possible and glanced out. The platform was very basic, just a raised walkway and one dim low energy light.

As the train came to a complete stop I pressed the start button on my stopwatch and waited to see how many people left from our carriage, which was none. I kept glancing anxiously down at my watch, wondering how long we should wait, it was a test of nerves now. I reached out and clasped the door knob.

"Ready?" I said, reaching for her hand.

"Ready!"

I opened the carriage door just as a whistle sounded.

"One thousand... two thousand... three thousand...."

I stepped down and quickly guided KT2 onto the platform then turned and pressed rather than slammed the door shut. I grabbed KT2's hand again and we hugged the side of the train, walking away from its direction of travel until the rear carriage passed us. I finally allowed myself an anxious glance over my shoulder.

"We're clear KT2," I whispered, not sure why, possibly because the platform was eerily quiet.

"Check canopy!" she shouted, completing a parachutist call. KT2 lifted her arms above her head, a huge grin on her face.

We'd made it!

Twenty Three

KT2

It was an exciting but daunting feeling, stepping off the train with only the clothes we were wearing and our small packs. I remember feeling a bit vulnerable because of it – had we done the right thing leaving the bulk of our stuff behind?

As the last carriage rattled away, the cold hard reality began to sink in. The small outlying station of Poroy had sounded interesting and viable when Jonny had read out its name in our planning stage, but now it seemed a bit too quiet.

"Let's get moving. We've probably only got a couple of hours head start," Jonny said, clasping my hand and leading me away from the platform and the distant rumble of the train.

I couldn't tell you much about Poroy. There was little background bustle to speak of, no clamouring taxi drivers desperate for a fare or mass of people transiting through. I guessed it was a local village that just happened to benefit from a train station.

"I hope you've got a plan, because this seems very quiet for our transportation needs..." I said.

"Fortunately I'm not quite as hopeless as you might think. I'd been mulling over the problem of our escape long before we discussed it."

"You did? When?" I said, curious as I heard the rustling of a piece of paper.

"At the restaurant. I had a chat with the only person there who I'd trust not to blab, unwittingly or otherwise. Someone who knows the lie of the land."

"Lovely Bob?"

"Yup. You didn't think I'd throw us into an escape completely blind, did you?"

I had to chuckle, that was Jonny all over, he was such a German, organising everything down to the last nut and bolt.

"Don't worry, from here on it's spontaneity all the way, okay?"

I nodded, grinning. Perhaps a bit of organisation was a good thing.

"We have a few miles walk to get to Bob's village, but I have a sketch map and he's kindly offered to put us up for a couple of days with his family. It seems he's taken quite a shine to you. Not many blind girls walk the Inca Trail, so in Bob's eyes you're a bit of a celebrity."

"Then I can expect celebrity-like treatment from you Jonny. I'd like to start my list of diva demands with a nice hot bath, in ass's milk, nothing less will do. Next, I'd like an Inca throne to take me to Bob's, carried by eight muscular men, naked of course. Hmm, what else?..."

"How would you know if they were naked?"

"Believe me Jonny, I'd check!"

We laughed as we walked, accompanied by intermittent flashes from Jonny's torch. The ground underfoot was rutted and covered in loose stones. I guessed we were way off the beaten track, since there weren't any city smells or pollution. The air was crisp and clean. I'd grown to trust Jonny by now and was happy not to question our route or his map.

We had to be the only couple who would never have an argument over directions or getting lost. It was one of the tough lessons I'd had to learn in the early days of going blind - to hand over a certain amount of control. For some things in my life, I simply *had* to rely on others. It was probably why in other areas, when I could have some input I occasionally came across as being stubborn and bloody-minded.

"What?" he said, reacting to my silence.

"Nothing. Just realising some of my character traits, that's all."

"Obstinate and a pain in the arse?"

"Yeah, you a mind reader?"

"Among my many talents KT2."

"So when am I going to see the rest of them?"

"Whenever I tire of being plain old Clark Kent."

"And turn into Super German?"

I heard him laugh. It was a daft conversation, especially as we were potentially lost.

"Yeah, but I don't see a telephone box around here, so you'll just have to wait."

"How long?"

"Until it's time."

"When will that be?"

"If I told you that, it would spoil the surprise."

Fair enough. I wasn't sure how much I should read into our banter. Perhaps it was just bouncing silly stuff off each other to pass the time; the 'come down' from the adrenaline of having escaped. Or maybe we were both sounding each other out. Perhaps something was developing between us? Who was I kidding, there was definitely *something* going on…

Me

Despite the jovial banter between us, I was concerned that we were miles away from 'civilisation' in the traditional sense. Although I'm not a fan of all those people jammed together, (a la Buenos Aires) there is a certain safety and familiarity there. Not to mention street lighting. Here there was none, and when the moon disappeared behind a cloud it was very, very dark.

I was doing my best to keep things light and cheerful between us. I'd come to realise that honesty was great, but sometimes KT2 was especially reliant on me. So I forced myself to appear confident and relaxed, whatever obstacles or potential dangers lay ahead.

Picking out buildings was particularly difficult, because although there was electricity in places, people here didn't waste it like they did at home. Any illumination from within a house would typically be a dim glow from a single low energy light bulb. I flicked my torch down at Bob's map again and guessed we probably had another mile to go.

Suddenly there was a movement ahead. I felt myself stiffen, my senses more alert. KT2 felt the tension through my hand and gently squeezed it, helping to calm my anxiety. I shone my torch up the path and illuminated two small children sitting by a house constructed out of mud bricks and a corrugated tin roof. As we got nearer the children stood and walked over to us, big toothy grins lighting up their faces.

"Buenos noches amigos," said the taller of the two, a boy of about eight or nine years old. He was holding the hand of a girl, who looked to be about five. She had a shy inquisitive smile on her face.

"Bob said you come with us, yes?" said the boy, as he gently placed his hand in KT2's, while his younger sister offered me her tiny hand.

Off we all went, talking as we walked in a mixture of our travel Spanish and the children's wonderful English. They put us to shame. Bob's kids were charming, as we knew they would be, having just spent four days with their father.

After twenty minutes we found ourselves amongst a mixture of mud brick houses and rough-faced concrete buildings, dotted around a small town square. In the centre was a stone statue. There was music playing from the depths of one of the houses and a rusty old pick-up truck was parked beside a larger building, probably a church or town hall. I could smell wood smoke mixed with faint cooking aromas.

I'd started to unwind as we walked with Bob's children and now I felt my remaining concerns ebb away. There just seemed to be a relaxed *feel* about the village. We were led towards an open door where the most amazing smells drifted out on the night air.

"Is that Elton John?" said KT2.

I listened as we approached the door, grinning as Elton and Kiki Dee belted out *Don't go Breaking my Heart*. They were accompanied by the unmistakable voice of Bob, singing along. The evening had the makings of a bizarre and intriguing mix of cultures.

"Get ready to duck," I said to KT2 as we approached the doorway, much lower than we were used to back home. I had to grin as I remembered who we were running away from by seeking sanctuary in Bob's family home. I realised that given the choice between five star luxury with the price tag of becoming a walking media theme park, and being here, about to have an adventure and enter a simpler life for a few days, we'd definitely made the right choice.

"Duck now," I said to KT2. Bob was standing watching over a large pot of food bubbling away on the wood fuel stove, stirring it enthusiastically. His timing was perfect. As we stepped over the threshold, he spun round to greet us, open armed and singing along to the song's lyrics, waving his spoon baton.

"*...don't go breaking my heart... I couldn't if I tried...!*" Bob sang, enthusiastically.

"*Oh honey, if I get restless...*" sung KT2, nudging me.

"*Baby you're not that kind.*"

"Friends, welcome!... All!"

Bob grinned, using the wooden spoon to count us into the next verse.

"*Don't go breaking my heart... you take the weight off me...*"

"Louder!"

"*Oh honey when you knock on my door, Ooo I gave you my key...*"

And that's how we spent the next few minutes. Bob conducted, all of us sang along. The funny thing was, it should have seemed odd, but it didn't. Bob was so welcoming and carefree we just went with it. I certainly wasn't going to win any karaoke prizes, but KT2 had a pretty good voice and midway through the next verse Bob and I jumped on the Elton lyrics, leaving KT2 to mirror Kiki's. By the end of the song we were all laughing as Bob shook our hands to welcome us to his home.

"Friends, thank you for coming. It's exciting, yes? For me to be hiding runaways, like the French resistance. But where are my little freedom fighters?"

Bob made a show of hunting for his kids, who were hovering by the doorway, no doubt curious as to whom these strange westerners were. He gathered them both up in a bear hug and carried them into the room, setting them down on the bench by a wooden dining table. He chatted and laughed with them for a moment or two in an unusual language. I guessed it was Quechua, the local indigenous dialect. It wasn't Spanish, that much I did know. I looked on and marvelled at how clever this man was, to be fluent in at least three different languages and ably guide a group of mixed nationality tourists on the Inca Trail. Bob put many of my own countrymen to shame, including me.

It seemed rude for me to describe Bob's home aloud to KT2, so I glanced around and made a mental note, to relay to her later. The floor was a mosaic of stone blocks, grey and silver, in a random pattern. Beside the stove was a beautiful hand crafted wooden table for food preparation with knives and cutlery laid out neatly on a shelf under the table top. On the wall above the work surface, pots and pans hung from a precisely spaced row of nails. The walls had some kind of rough-faced plaster that had been painted a cream colour. A sturdy hand-made table and four chairs occupied another corner. There was a partition wall across the back of the room which I guessed must be the bedroom. A single low energy light bulb dangled from the wood beam ceiling. It was a very neat, minimalist, homely house.

My attention was drawn to the open doorway behind us. An attractive woman in her mid-thirties, wearing a mix of local dress and western trekking clothes, was carrying the frame of a small double bed. It was an awkward load that she bumped on the door frame before attempting to set it down along the side wall. I squeezed KT2's hand, our sign that I was going to leave her, then helped Bob's wife to lift the bed frame clear of her shoulder and onto the floor.

"Hola Jonathan and Angel, I am Elizabeth," she said, smiling warmly as she shook my hand. She then approached KT2, a mix of admiration and sympathy in her eyes.
Elizabeth placed her hands on KT2's shoulders and leant forwards to kiss her gently on the cheek.

"Our home is your home."

What a welcome! Here were people who had no cause to help us, but were showing such unconditional kindness. I swallowed hard, a lump in my throat.

"Please sit down, I will be a moment," said Bob, who exchanged a few words with Elizabeth, handed over the spoon and then disappeared out the door.

"Would you like some coca tea?" Elizabeth asked, beckoning her children over and hugging them.

KT2

I know Jonny had been a bit nervous about giving Justin and the TV crew the slip, but within seconds of arriving on Bob's doorstep, it felt like everything would be okay. We weren't fugitives here, we were amongst good people.

I found myself smiling a lot during our stay with Bob, Elizabeth, and their children. Their take on life was full of positive energy, despite not having much materially. But perhaps it was us who needed to understand how little was actually needed?

We sat at their table eating the most delicious stew and listening to Bob's stories of his younger days on the Inca Trail. In those days porters hauled up to fifty kilos on their backs, before the government finally cracked down and regulated the load to half that. Many porters died from over exertion in the early days, one of the cruellest literal examples of survival of the fittest.

Bob told us how as a nineteen year old, he and a group of friends completed the Inca Trail in ten hours. A pretty amazing feat when you consider it's forty three kilometres long, up and down steep stone steps with three high mountain passes and at altitude. *Incredible* is the only word that comes close to describing the fitness and strength of character of this inspiring man. Without any intention of doing so, Bob was gently knocking Jonny and I down a peg or two, whilst filling us with an infectious enthusiasm for the simpler things in life.

I felt as though we were amongst old friends. We heard from Elizabeth how she and Bob were from different villages. They met in his early days working as a cook, an important position on the trail, second only to the guide. Bob had been shopping for provisions and kept going back to the market stall where Elizabeth worked. He charmed her more on each visit until she asked him to show her Machu Picchu, which struck me as one hell of a first date.

With the dinner conversation so relaxed and friendly, it was only a matter of time before we were asked about our *relationship*.

"You won each other?" asked Bob, having picked up some of our story during snippets of conversation over the last few days.

"In a way," Jonny said. He described how we met, the eBay auction and our first meeting at the airport hotel. I chipped in with my take on our unusual *partnership* and realised how entertaining it must have sounded. Bob and Elizabeth were howling with laughter and sheer disbelief as we told our story. I found myself looking back and realising how much amazing stuff we'd already done together. And we were only just approaching the halfway point.

By the time we all stopped chatting and headed to bed, it was the early hours of the morning and my face was aching from laughing so much.

"I suppose it is quite a story, the way we met. Seems like ages ago now though," I said to Jonny just as we started to drift off to sleep.

"And it's only just begun…" he said sleepily.

I waited for him to finish, but his deep breathing signalled that was it. I smiled and felt the stress of the last twenty-four hours slip away as I fell into a deep, happy sleep beside him.

Twenty Four

Me

We spent two wonderful days with Bob, Elizabeth and their children. We helped out on their small holding, taught the village kids English and generally relaxed after the trek. We also read through the Lonely Planet guide, trying to decide where we should head for next.

"Bolivia is beautiful and has even friendlier people," Bob told us, whilst helping us map out a route to keep the TV crew off our tail.

And so after two amazing days it was time for us to move on. We were both getting itchy feet and didn't want to outstay our welcome. I don't know if the family trip into Cusco was planned, or whether it was a special journey just to drop us off, but Bob arranged with one of the other villagers to borrow his pick-up truck and ignoring our protests, we were helped aboard.

This really was living, I decided as we sat in the back of the pick up truck and trundled through remote villages, over rugged mountain passes and skirted around lush green Coca fields.

It had to beat my usual morning commute! As we sat there in the back of the truck, I wondered what we could give Bob and his family as a thank you present. I had already offered money for the fuel but this had been waved aside, accompanied by Bob's standard grin.

"I'm struggling to think what we can leave as a gift," I said to KT2.

"I know, I've been thinking the same thing and kicking myself for leaving most of our stuff behind."
I tried to remember what I'd packed for both of us and mentally examined each item as a potential gift.

"What about your head torch?" said KT2, hitting on a brilliant idea.
And so when we drew to a stop on the outskirts of Cusco, well away from the central square and the tourist area, I'd already rummaged in my day pack and found my neat little LED head

torch. Into the headband I'd tucked enough local currency to cover the fuel into town. As I shook Bob's hand, I parted with our gift, insisting he accept it.

"Always remember. We stay positive and we can get through anything," said Bob as he leaned out of the window of the truck. Bob's kids and Elizabeth waved goodbye as he drove away, leaving us standing on the bustling pavement, as small taxis, trucks and scooters whizzed by in a cloud of two stroke and car exhaust fumes.

I felt excited and nervous that the next stage of our adventure was about to begin.

We had an hour and a half to kill before our bus left, so we decided to stop by an internet café, well away from the centre of town. Being the gentleman I was quickly becoming, I sat beside KT2 and waited for her to log on first so I could read out her messages. This allowed her the time to get on with replying while I checked my own inbox.

"Okay, let's see. The usual junk mail, two from Maria, and a chap called Pete. I glanced across at her. Was it my imagination, or had she gone slightly pale?

"Which do you want first?"

"Um, Maria. The first one, in date order I guess."

I nodded and opened up the message, wondering who Pete was, but that question would have to wait. I scanned through Maria's message before I started reading it aloud. It was a bit odd being privy to only one side of this delayed electronic conversation. I had to try and read between the lines to imagine what KT2 had written to Maria to prompt this reply. It also felt voyeuristic, and underhand, like I was reading a private diary.

"What does she say?" said KT2, reminding me that this was actually her message and I was supposed to be reading it aloud.

"Sorry. Here goes…"

E-Mail From: Maria Stockton
To: Angel
Subject: Wet'n Wild!

How goes it Babe? Or should I call you KT2? Have you been

*brainwashed?! I'm guessing the nickname refers to you being
the second Kate Thornly, but don't forget how unique you are!
Loved the whitewater rafting photo, but as a fashion statement,
the wetsuit isn't working for my people.*

*You're not wrong about the WHOLE WORLD knowing about
Kate Thornly. Everyone is constantly asking how you're getting
on. We are all really proud of you. There has also been quite a
bit of interest in the newspapers because of the eBay advert, but
I've kept my mouth shut and it seems to have fizzled out.
You were pretty elusive in your message as to how well you're
getting on with the city slicker, so I'm going to embarrass you -
is he good in bed? (Sorry Jonny, as I know you'll be reading this
out loud, but I'm sure you'll both be past the first date nerves
and embarrassment by now...)*

*Nothing else to report, or ask, other than have you been wearing
any of the new tee shirts I packed for you?!*

*Write back soon with tales of tall dark handsome strangers and
sordid all-night orgies!
Love ya
Mim*

To my credit, if I may be so bold, I read out Maria's message
word for word. We were indeed getting past that stage where we
were easily embarrassed and I figured our *friendship* could
handle it.

"Do you want some time to reply, or shall I read the next
one?" I asked.

"The next one please, I'll just respond to both. I guess we
don't have that much time..."
I nodded and pulled up the second message from Maria, the tone
of which was very different.

*E-Mail From: Maria Stockton
To: Angel
Subject: Doctor Gadget Warning!*

I guess by now you've completed the Inca Trail. I hope you're not in the pickle I think you might be. You'll know from the title of this message that I've been pestered by you know who. I need to warn you that he's been onto the press trying to find you. If you haven't been ambushed yet, then please try to keep a low profile. I think the press have been twisting Jonny's friend's arm too. (Justin I think his name is. What a dish, in a dippy public schoolboy kind of way...)

The problem is, everyone and I do mean EVERYONE over here is intrigued by the two of you. They want your story. Honestly, it's been bonkers. Dr Gadget came back from holiday and must have been told about you buggering off on your South America adventure. He wants you back Angel. You know how I feel about him. He's been even more of an arse than usual, camping out on my doorstep, going on about how he's changed. I've said nothing, obviously, but it's been in all the papers. It's crazy, like you guys are fugitives or something.

If you get the chance, ring me, but try to get away from those media idiots. It's all blowing up into a frenzy. You've definitely caught the public imagination, I've even had the paparazzi outside the house! I threw a bucket of water over them yesterday, and now they're threatening to prosecute me for assault unless I spill the beans. It's a screwed up world back here Angel!! Hopefully you're well away from this madness!
Love ya
Mim

KT2

"Is that word for word?"

"I'm afraid so, yes."

"Oh."

We sat there in silence.

"Jonny, I'm sorry. This was never meant to happen, I..."

"The doctor is your husband?" he said.

I nodded, ashamed, which I shouldn't have been. That's just life isn't it, getting involved with the wrong person and regretting it?

I heard him take a deep breath. I wondered which way the conversation was heading and prepared myself for the questions that would inevitably follow. Instead I heard him tapping on his keyboard.

"Okay. Well, I'd best check in myself. We can catch up with our backgrounds once we're away from here."

His tone wasn't sarcastic or especially annoyed, so I wasn't sure how to gauge his reaction. Was he upset? If not, how did that make me feel? Did I need him to feel something, *anything* – disappointment maybe? This probably wasn't the time or the place, but I had to know.

"Jonny, I know this is a weird time, but how do you feel about everything?"

"Like I want to escape this place and get on the bus."

"Alone?"

"Sorry?"

"Get on a bus alone - without me?"

"No, of course not. Unless you've other ideas, we're going together. When we're on our own, we'll talk. I'm not ducking out just yet."

I felt him squeeze my shoulder. I wanted to reach out, but the timing wasn't right – the story of my life.

"Okay. Check your messages and let's get out of here," I said, a spark of excitement growing in my stomach.

That was my first secret almost out in the open. The other one I buried deep inside.

"Oh my God."

"What do they say?"

"Don't know, still downloading. Only two hundred and sixty one to go!"

Me

I studied the list for several minutes.

"How are we doing for time?" said KT2 eventually.

I glanced at my watch, mentally counting back from when the bus was due to leave.

"Not enough to read all these. I'm going to whizz down the list and print anything off that looks relevant. There are messages from newspapers and magazines, but also lots of other Kate

Thornlys. Apparently if we get bored, I have offers to replace you. That's nice isn't it!"

I realised the clock was ticking and started printing off anything that looked interesting or was an e-mail address I recognised. I kept glancing at my watch, speeding up my selection process as the minutes ticked away.

There were several message titles that intrigued me, but I didn't have time to stop and read them. In the background I heard the internet café printer whirring away. A message from Justin entitled "The Great Escape" made me chuckle as I hit print and moved on. One from Simon was titled with a not quite as encouraging "You Wanker!"

He'll get over it.

"I'm done. Can you send this for me please," said KT2.

"One second, almost finished."

I ran my eyes down the last page of incoming messages, frowning as I hovered on the last but one. There were many Kate Thornly e-mail addresses that I'd discarded, but this one was distinctive. Not because of the address, but because of the message title.

I've left the Plumber and I want you back, it read, in bold type. I got stuck there for a moment, finding myself torn; one part of me wanted to hit delete, the other was tempted to open the message and read it right there and then.

I glanced over at KT2, wondering.

I hit print, scanned and discarded the last message then shut the computer down. I leant across and clicked on KT2's message to Maria without even glancing at it. Normally my curiosity might have meant I sneaked a curious look, but time wasn't on our side.

"I'll just pay, then we're on our way, " I said as I hurried over to the counter to settle up and collect the wad of printed messages.

KT2

I sat there smiling to myself as I waited for Jonny and thought back over the journey so far. We were hovering on the edge of being celebrities, in the public eye. It made everything all the more exciting. I heard footsteps and stood, offering my hand which Jonny took without a word and we headed for the street.

We were probably being overly cautious, but as we planned the next stage of the trip in Bob's house, we'd agreed to draw out as much cash as we could before leaving Cusco. This meant we wouldn't use our bank or credit cards for as long as possible. Now we had a taste of freedom again, neither of us wanted to let anyone else into our private world. At least not until we had to, which hopefully wouldn't be until we flew home from Rio in six and a half weeks time. By then we'd have had our adventures and they could pester us all they wanted.

Next stop after the cash machine was a supermarket for snacks and water. Then using another of Bob's sketched maps, we walked for twenty minutes to the outskirts of Cusco to pick up the tourist bus that would take us across the border to Bolivia.

"Are you ready for the next stage of the adventure, Angel?" Jonny asked, squeezing my hand as we arrived at the bus station.

"Bring it on!" I said, taking a moment to wonder why he'd just called me *Angel*. It was one of the few times he'd deviated from *KT2*.

For some reason I wondered if Jonny would have survived this trip without wanting to strangle Kate Thornly the 1st.

Very unlikely.

I smiled to myself as I thought back to the first time I'd met him, all London arrogance and blinkered to the ways of the real world. I remember questioning how the hell he was going to manage travelling with someone who was blind.

The answer, as I was finding out, was *easily*.

Twenty Five

KT2

As Jonny described the stunning scenery from yet another bus ride, I wondered if he was growing tired of always having to be my eyes. He'd embraced the job without complaint, which wasn't a compliment I could pay to the last man to stand at my side.

I wasn't looking forward to *the conversation*. I'd been able to bury those memories away, pretend I hadn't been married. I hoped it wouldn't change things between us.

I listened to Jonny's occasional commentary. His tone was much more relaxed these days. He was comfortable with speaking out loud and nowhere near as self-conscious as he'd been at first. There was an underlying excitement in his voice whenever he saw something that surprised or humbled him. When he saw Lake Titicaca for the first time, I knew from the change in his voice that it must have been truly beautiful.

Me

My burning desire to read through the printed e-mails evaporated after the first few miles on the bus. The scenery was spectacular and describing it all to KT2 focused my mind and drew me away from my thoughts of home.

I offered KT2 some water, then took a long drink myself, glancing around the compact tourist coach. It was full of travellers of varying nationalities, no sun-worshipping beach crabs here. These were adventurous types. I found myself grinning as Lake Titicaca, the highest lake in the world, shimmered azure blue and green in the distance. Then a sense of sadness came over me as I watched the water. A tinge of guilt clouded my mood, mixed in with a real sense of how lucky I was. All this was out there, yet until now I'd never ventured out of my bubble-wrapped existence. I stared out of the window and instinctively began describing what I could see.

"The landscape is gradually flattening out, the colours are changing to shades of brown and lighter greens with only patches of dark green trees. The fields have lower lying crops. I've been struggling to sum up the change I've been seeing, but now I think I know. It's like the film set of a western. Barren mostly, but with occasional fields of crops. Beautiful, but not an easy living to be made working the land. It feels less chaotic, more spread out and relaxed. In the distance the lake looks vast. The sun catches it differently as the winding road continually changes our perspective. Sometimes it's dark blue, then light green blending into turquoise or a lighter, Pacific blue. It sparkles, the wind breaking up the surface, as millions of tiny wave crests glint in the sunshine. I'm sorry you can't see the lake, Angel. It's truly beautiful," I said, mesmerised.

"Me too," she said quietly.

"But I still see some of what you do, through your descriptions. You shouldn't feel guilty or sad for that, Jonny," she said, turning towards me.

"We have to make the most of what we have without focusing on the shortfalls. Your lack of prowess in the bedroom department for example."

"Well you're not so hot yourself!" I replied indignantly. She grinned at me and I caught the odd confused look from our fellow travellers. I shrugged in their general direction, enjoying the *something* between us that neither of us wanted to acknowledge, just yet. Instead we left it bubbling away in the background, something to look forward to at an unspecified point in the future.

The bus journey was only four hours, broken roughly in the middle by an amazing ferry crossing over a narrow section of the lake. Everyone disembarked to join a queue, beyond which small wooden passenger boats waited to take us across the water. Not especially unusual in itself, until we saw how the minibuses and cars crossed the water. Our driver lined the empty bus up, then accelerated towards a clapped out barge with a low drop front resting on the slipway. The bus raced towards the barge, over the ramp, then at the last moment, the driver hit the brakes hard. He narrowly avoided squashing the barge skipper standing at the far end next to an outboard engine. The simple brilliance was that the inertia of the bus braking sharply nudged the barge off the slipway, allowing the skipper to spin it around and motor across the water. It was absolutely ingenious! Then I realised we might have a problem. I'd been so pre-occupied watching the bus that by the time I'd finished describing it to KT2, I suddenly became aware how rough the water was around the small passenger ferry. I glanced round the creaking wooden hull wondering if it was seaworthy.

"Jonny, I'm feeling a bit sick. I need a target," she whispered.

"Seriously? This really isn't the time or place..."

"Too late, I'm gonna blow!"

KT2 made to retch, forcing my heart to double its beats per minute in anticipated embarrassment. That's when she turned to me and grinned.

"Just kidding."

I dug her in the ribs, to the amusement of several other passengers as she squealed and tried to wriggle away.

KT2

I was having such a good time on the bus journey, I hadn't even considered whether we'd get any hassle at the border crossing into Bolivia. I'd almost forgotten Simon and his media buddies were even in the same country. So you can imagine my surprise when a car screeched to a halt beside the bus, just as we'd all stepped out to navigate border control. Then I heard Justin's voice.

"Hey, Jonathan. Nice moves on the train."

I froze, cursing. I felt Jonny's grip tighten around my hand. There were snatched conversations behind us, as Simon and TV crew climbed out of the car and started setting up their equipment.

"Hello mate. Which side of the fence are you on?" said Jonny, cautiously.

"Now I know you're both safe, I'm flying home in a couple of days. If it were me, I'd have taken the cash. But I'm a career capitalist with no sense of adventure. Good luck fella, look after her."

Jonny released his grip on my hand for a moment to shake Justin's hand.

"Thanks buddy. Turns out I'm getting a taste for the traveller lifestyle."

Jonny grabbed my hand and led me away.

"Hey, where do you think you're going, *amigo?*"

"Bugger off Simon, this is our trip, not yours," Jonny said, making me grin at his rebellion.

Then he leaned forward and whispered in my ear as we walked away.

"Bare with me Angel. Say nothing, we'll be rid of them once we're over the border."

"But they can follow us into Bolivia..." I whispered back, pretty much resigned to being hassled for the rest of the trip.

"No they can't. Trust me, I'm an analyst."

I felt him squeeze my hand and lead me away from the bus. But Simon wasn't giving up.

"This is the end of the road guys. Talk to me, negotiate yourselves a good deal..."

I felt Jonny pause and turn.

"Simon, piss off!"

Then we were off, fast walking towards the border control.

"We have to sign out of Peru, then walk a few hundred yards to the Bolivian border. Simon and the film crew will catch up with us, but I doubt they'll be able to come with us."

"Why not?" I said.

"Because Angel, fortune favours the brave, lucky and downright cheeky."

Me

I glanced over to see her grinning. I just hoped the Lonely Planet guide was right, otherwise we were screwed.

"Should we run?" said KT2.

I looked back over my shoulder to see Justin wave at me. Between Justin and me, Simon and the camera crew had gathered their gear and were now chasing after us, puffing as they tried to close the gap. I think that's when I realised just how much fitter I'd become. Those regular runs with KT2, frightening and hard though they were in the early days, had really paid off. I chuckled at Simon's red-faced struggle to speed up.

"No, let's just walk and hope my theory about the border crossing holds up," I said.

As we only had our small day packs, we were the first of our coach party to arrive at the Peruvian side of the border crossing. Handing over our thirty day visas and signing out of the country was just a formality. We cleared the office as Simon and the camera crew approached the passport line.

"You can't run anymore mate, give it up..." said Simon, fighting to get the words out between gasps of breath.

"You don't look too good buddy, you need to get fit," I said over my shoulder.

We reached the Bolivian border control and passed through without incident. The guidebook had mentioned the possibility of having to part with a small bribe to gain entry, but not for us.

Whilst we'd been having our documents inspected and passports stamped, the tourist bus had trundled through the border controls and now stood waiting on the Bolivian side. It was tempting to climb aboard, but the devil on my shoulder encouraged me to hold back, have my moment.

"We'll just wait here, to say our goodbyes," I said, watching to see if Simon and the television crew made it across the border. As we waited, the rest of the travellers gradually filtered past us and got on the bus, but still no Simon.

"What's going on?" said KT2.

"Oh, probably just a small matter of their paperwork not being in order."

"But they must have passports to have flown over from the UK..."

"Passports, yes..."

Finally a very red-faced Simon and an angry looking TV crew were escorted out of the Bolivian passport office and ushered back towards the Peruvian side.

"You lucky bastards!" shouted Simon.

I fished a piece of paper out from the protection of my passport, unfolded it and held it up over my head.

"Guess you guys were missing one of these?" I called out, unable to resist a cheeky wink.

Simon stood there, furious. The television crew were also seriously unimpressed and swore profusely at us.

"What's going on?" KT2 asked.

"Our yellow fever inoculation certificates. I seem to remember it was a requirement of the original eBay advert." I heard her giggle.

"Why Jonathan, I seem to recall it was," she said, both of us breaking into laughter as I led her towards the waiting bus. Bolivia here we come!

Twenty Six

Bolivia
Me

This was the life. I forced one sleepy eye open and did a quick sweep of our surroundings, just to make sure I wasn't dreaming. From our vantage point on the hillside at Hotel Cupula, the sandy bay of Copacabana and Lake Titicaca stretched out below us. Fishermen bobbed on small colourful boats, locals drifted along in 1960s pedalos and the line of ramshackle corrugated tin roof fish restaurants on the waterfront were doing a roaring trade.

I glanced across at KT2, asleep in a brightly coloured yellow, red and orange hammock next to me and I smiled. We'd decided to spend a few days here as it was so lovely. The hotel was set half way up a hill on the edge of town. Somewhere across the vast lake was the Peruvian town of Puno. Below and to left of us was the pretty town of Copacabana, with green, white, blue and terracotta walled houses and hotels. But the most captivating view was straight ahead, out over Lake Titicaca. I sighed and sank deeper into the comfy hammock, soaking up the warm sunshine. This was perfect.

Reluctantly, I returned my attention to the e-mails in my hand. The first message made my blood boil.

E-Mail From: Simon Black
To: Jonathan Cork
Subject: You Wanker!

Where the fuck are you?! You ARSEHOLE. Your story is now worth £250k. That's serious cash. Don't be a prick. CONTACT ME!
Simon

I slowly and deliberately tore Simon's e-mail into the tiniest pieces possible.

"Sounds like a bad message," said KT2 as she stretched out in the hammock and yawned.

"Not the best."

"Want to tell me about it?"

"I've forgotten what it said."

"Liar," she said, smiling at me, then lying back, hands behind her head.

"This is a cool place, it smells like the seaside and has a nice feel to it," she said, closing her eyes.

"Wake me when you read something interesting."

The other messages I'd printed had lots of offers for KT2 and I to share our story with the world. There were even enquiries from rival celebrity magazines for a photo shoot. The cash offer would of course go through the roof, they said, if we announced our engagement! Thoughtful of them, eh?

Other Kate Thornlys also offered to step in if things weren't working out between us. I can't believe we were that big a deal; there were still people in the world starving, weren't there? I found myself glancing across at *my* Kate Thornly. She was slumped back in the hammock with her mouth open, snoring lightly.

Would I trade you in, Angel? I asked myself, chuckling and shaking my head. If I'd been asked that question a few weeks ago, particularly after our first meeting, I'd have given a very different answer.

I read on, discarding any irrelevant messages, until I came to the last two.

E-Mail From: Maria Stockton
To: Jonathan Cork
Subject: Please Don't Tell Angel I'm e-mailing you...

Hi Jonathan,
I don't want Angel to think I'm contacting you behind her back and even if you reply to me I'll never acknowledge it. This will be the one and only message I'll ever send you. Whatever you think of me for having a bit of a laugh at both your expenses with the customs thing, (sorry about that, but it was funny, right?) I'm not

a malicious person and I only want the best for my friend. Why do you think I set her up with you to start with?
The thing is, I wouldn't be contacting you now, if it wasn't for the newspaper lot getting involved. All thanks to your so-called friend. As I write this I think they're going to ambush you in Machu Picchu and I wanted to warn you.

They'll probably mention Angel's husband, Pete, because when Simon turned up here with Justin and I told them all to piss off, Simon shouted through the letter box that it would be the first thing they'd say to you.

One thing you need to know: the marriage was dead a long time ago, and the circumstances were not great for Angel. So please, don't think badly of her. They've been apart for over a year and she's so much better off without him.

I don't want you to judge Angel. She's been through a lot but she's still the coolest, most fun person to be around I know, so please give her a chance. If you want the truth from Angel you just have to ask her. I can tell you that from her messages to me so far, she's having an amazing time, so thank you.
Look after her.
Maria

I carefully folded the e-mail and buried it deep in my pocket. I was left holding the last message. I wondered if I should discard it, kidding myself that I had the strength to ignore my curiosity.

E-Mail From: Kate Thornly
To: Jonny Blue Bottle
Subject: I've left the Plumber and I want you back

Dear Jonny,
I hope the title of this message gets your attention. It was never right with Frank and I've realised how good we were together and how much you need me.

I'm sorry for pushing you away, making you take off on the trip on your own. I shouldn't imagine a blind companion is much fun. There, you've done it, drawn blood from a stone and gotten me to apologise. So it's time to sort this mess out, meet up and finish the rest of the trip together. And you'd better hurry up. I can't imagine you'll be able to survive for long without some sort of nut incident, which I'm certain the blind woman can do nothing about. Get back to me while you're still alive and kicking and we'll sort this out.
Your Princess Sparkle

Wow. I had to read back over her message several times to check I hadn't imagined it. She was clever, I'd give her that. And arrogant too, given the tone of her message. But the real question was, had anything in her attitude towards me changed? It's true I'd become reliant on her always being there, complacent even. And in all fairness, sometimes I'd not been terribly easy to get on with. But what affected me the most was that she'd admitted she was wrong. Believe me, that was unheard of.

Bloody hell, what was I thinking?
I shook my head as I caught myself sympathising with her. I instinctively crumpled the page, squeezing it into a tight ball in my clenched fist.

"Now, if I had to guess, I'd say that was a different kind of message to the one that was torn into tiny pieces. Probably no less controversial in content, but one you're going to give a bit more consideration."

"I'm not with you," I said, probably sounding a bit vacant, because that's how I felt.

"Less anger. Am I right? To tear words into pieces would indicate a sort of finality, closure. But scrunching them up, is more of a frustrated reaction, as if there's still unfinished business."

How did she do that? I dropped my eyes to the small paper ball in my hand and frowned.

"I'm right, aren't I?" she said, a cheeky, playful tone to her voice.

I couldn't think of anything to say, so I threw the paper ball at her, which from this range was an easy head shot. I chuckled as

176

the paper missile struck its target and bounced into her hammock. But I'd underestimated her, because she reached out, grabbed my hammock and yanked it hard, spinning me onto the floor.

"Nice pirouette!" she said, laughing at me as she felt around the empty hammock and knew I'd hit the deck.

I lay on the floor propped up on my elbows, laughing with her.

"Serves me right," I said, momentarily contemplating tipping her onto the grass to join me, before stopping myself. She had me fair and square. I'd just have to take it on the chin.

"I've been thinking Jonny, perhaps we ought to think about disguises," said KT2.

"I don't think Superman will blend in that well in Bolivia!" I said, making us both laugh more. I stood up and eased myself back into the hammock, thinking.

"Hair dye and local clothing, that sort of thing?"

"Yeah, why not? Look, you can probably blend in much easier than me, but travelling with a blind girl, must make us pretty conspicuous."

I suddenly felt unsettled at this comment, where was she going with it?

"You want us to go our separate ways? But that would defeat the whole object of running away together…"

"Don't tell me I'm growing on you?"

I had to bite my tongue. The truth was, I couldn't imagine travelling *without* her.

"I've got used to having you around."

She grinned.

"Really? I wasn't actually thinking of dumping you Jonny. That would mean we'd have to get together first and that would be *complicated.* What I mean is, with your beard and longer hair, you're less likely to draw attention to *us*. I'm the one who needs some work, maybe a haircut and a change of hair colour. But we also need to think of ways so that I don't *appear* to be blind."

I took a while thinking this through.

"I guess it's possible. Might be fun too, seeing if we can get away with it."

"See, I knew deep down you'd love the cloak and dagger stuff."

I laughed.

"The name's Bond..." I started to say.

"And if you mention Pussy Galore, I'll flip you straight over onto your back again!"

<u>Twenty Seven</u>

<u>KT2</u>

Never before had planning things out been so much fun. We went shopping that afternoon, scouring the small town of Copacabana for new 'ethnic' clothes, scissors and big sunglasses. But having looked in practically every shop, hair dye was still a problem. The idea was to change my mousy colour to peroxide blonde, and Jonny's fairer hair to jet black. I thought he'd look good as a tall dark, handsome stranger. Great observation, coming from a blind girl! We'd even paid the hotel bill in advance with cash so we could slip out the following morning with our new look. I toyed with my bottle of beer, wondering where we'd get hair dye from.

"The ladies in the market, where we bought our new clobber," said Jonny, after a few minutes silence.

"I'm not with you."

"If they can dye clothes, then maybe hair isn't so different," he said.

"Genius. Let's go," I said, draining the last of my drink. I slipped on my big funky sunglasses as Jonny took my hand and led me out of the bar.

"Are you sure this is a good idea?" I said. My voice was muffled from kneeling down with my head tipped over a bucket of cold water. Old nimble hands carefully rinsed off a foul smelling concoction. I couldn't quite believe we'd managed to explain what we needed.

After fifteen minutes of garbled Spanish exchanges, lots of *si, gracias. Cuanto por favour?* And yet more pointing at clothing by Jonny, (so we could get the colour just right) the woman called for her young daughter to watch the shop. We were then led through to a dark back room where I was now kneeling on the stone floor beside Jonny.

"If she fucks it up, don't tell me." I said.
He sniggered.

"At least you won't be able to see yours. My hair could end up green!" he said.

I felt a towel being rubbed gently through my hair and was ushered to stand. The towel fell away and I stood there wondering what colour my hair was.

"How does it look?"

"Don't know, can't open my eyes yet, they're stinging," I said.

I reached up and ran my fingers through my hair. It *felt* all right. I pulled a few strands round to my eyes and squinted. I heard water being sloshed over Jonny's head, rinsing the dye away.

"This doesn't look very blonde Jonny. If anything it's more…"

"Red," he said.

"Red?"

"Um, yeah. I think I may have confused her…"

I wasn't sure if I was angry or amused. If I was back home in my normal surroundings, I would definitely be upset. But I was a few thousand miles away from home and all that *image* thing.

"Tell me you're blonde and I'll kill you."

"Well, they do say we have more fun," he said, trying to stifle his bewildered amusement.

"Bien, muy bien!" said the lady enthusiastically, pleased with her efforts.

We thanked her profusely of course, it would have been rude to let her see any disappointment. Then we hurried back to the hotel in silence.

"Okay, time for complete honesty."

"But you said if it all goes wrong…"

"Just tell me," I said, guessing from his quietness that he was nervous about my reaction.

"Right. Um, it's not as bad as you might think, I actually like the Toyah Willcox look on you…"

He couldn't hold his laughter any longer, so I dug him in the ribs and tickled hard, locking on even more as he screeched like a girl.

"You bastard!"

"You should see mine…" he said between gasps of air and laughter.

"I don't care!"

I dug my fingertips into his side again, but it was a more half-hearted effort. It ended up with him pulling me into a comforting hug, my head buried in his chest. He must have thought I was sobbing, the way my body was shaking, because he pulled back and started apologising. But I was trying to stop laughing – it was just the sort of crazy situation Maria and I would get into.

"Thank God! I thought you'd be heartbroken."

I shook my head, grinning.

"I used to worship Toyah when I was a teenager, but my mum wouldn't let me dye my hair. I've never been brave enough to do it since. It's hilarious."

"That's not the half of it. I wish you could see mine."

"How blonde is it?"

"Um, Marilyn Monroe could learn a thing or two from me."

"Fantastic! Let me have a look," I said, pulling him close, holding a few strands to my eye.

"Bloody hell! Do the collar and cuffs match?" I said, unable to stop giggling.

Me

We must have been a sight. Both of us stood a couple of inches away from the mirror, examining our strange new looks.

"I still think I need a haircut. A couple of inches shorter would do," KT2 said.

I pulled back from the mirror, watching her clutch her fist around the bottom few inches of her red hair.

"Are you sure? You girls can get a bit protective over things like that, I don't want to balls it up and upset you…"

"Jonny, it's not like I'll know how bad a job you make, is it? And I was joking about the whole wanting to look like Toyah thing. Believe me, red is bad already. Really, really bad. But it can't get any worse, right?"

I'd like to say I made a good job of cutting KT2's hair. It probably wasn't as bad as I thought, but it was *really* short. The problem was, I struggled to cut it evenly. I'd take some off one side, but by the time I'd worked my way round, it was all uneven again. Which meant I cut more off to level things up.

Shit.

"How's it looking Jonny? My head feels lighter, more airflow."

I did the worse thing possible and just went quiet. In that time she ran fingers through her hair, only there wasn't much of it left!

It may have been the effect of our afternoon drinks, or coming down from the energy of our banter and laughter, but she went quiet too, then started to cry. Not hysterical or with any theatrics, she just sat there on the toilet seat and allowed tears to trickle down her cheeks.

Not sure what to do, I just stood there. The thing I realised, as I studied my workmanship, was that compared to her shoulder length mousy hair, the red colouring and short crop opened up her face. It made me realise how bloody attractive she was.

"Say something, Angel."

She shook her head, and wiped her eyes with her the back of her sleeve. I tore off some toilet paper and placed it in her hand.

"It's just a bit of a shock."

I stood there for a few more seconds as she dried her eyes, then did the only thing that seemed appropriate. I knelt down, gathered her in my arms and held her.

KT2

I managed to pull myself together and thought I'd got through my tears. But my composure went out the window when I felt his arms wrap around me.

"Hey, it's not so bad. I actually think being a redhead suits you, and your hair will grow back in no time," he said, holding me into his chest.

His hug was reassuring and safe and I realised I was at a crossroads, that skeleton was trying hard to climb out of the cupboard.

Perhaps it was time.

"It's not just that. It's a reminder, of how things used to be, a few years ago," I said. The words tumbled out, a long kept secret that would no longer stay locked away, deep inside.

It was one of those times where you try to stop yourself, but it feels liberating to fling the wardrobe doors open and boot the rattle man out.

"When you started to go blind?" he said after a pause.

I shook my head, tears welling up, my bottom lip quivering.

"Before that. Going blind actually saved me."

Twenty Eight

Me

I felt KT2 slump forwards in my arms, head in her hands, her body shaking as she silently cried. I sat there in a daze.

What on earth do I do now?

This was sounding like a confession and I wasn't sure I was ready to trade secrets just yet. But when was a good time? I shuddered as I thought back, thinking of my own demons.

"Want to talk about it?" I said, gently lifting her chin with my fingers. Could she see my face? I searched her blank eyes.

"No."

"I think you should. It'll help," I said.

"I can't, it's... too difficult."

She turned away from me, wiped her eyes on her sleeve and sniffed, shuffling away from me.

"I want to reassure you, make you feel safe," I said.

KT2 took a deep, erratic breath, trying to compose herself. I reached out, carefully placing my hand on her shoulders.

"Come on Angel, let me in. I'll understand."

"It's easier like this."

"Independence doesn't mean you shut out your mates. We're running partners. And fugitives," I added, which made her chuckle.

She sniffed and half turned towards me.

"Yeah, outlaws."

She took another deep shaky breath.

"You said going blind *saved* you?" I said, resting my hand back on her shoulder.

She nodded slowly, the motion carrying through to her body. She clasped her hands around her knees and began rocking where she sat. After a long pause she began speaking. Barely able to whisper the words, I had to concentrate hard to make out what she was saying.

"Remember I told you about Katie the Cake?"

"Yes, I remember," I said.

"It didn't stop there. I had an idiot boyfriend, Neil. He destroyed my self-confidence with taunts about my weight. I was a teenager and easily influenced by those waif supermodels. Being the stubborn Scot's girl I am, I made a pact; I would lose the weight once and for all. I saved up and bought a pair of trainers and started running. I ate less, got myself into shape..."

I waited patiently as she struggled to get the words out as more tears fell.

"I hope you dumped him after that."

She shook her head, a sad, vacant expression on her face.

"I tried, but he adored the new me. Wouldn't let me forget how chubby I'd been though. I exercised more and ate less, until I was well past the point of being trim and healthy."

I reached for more toilet roll and waited for her to continue as she dabbed her eyes and blew her streaming nose.

"I fought my weight issues for years. Seeing myself in a mirror made me feel worse. *Anorexia* is a horrible, debilitating, vicious disease. I was in hospital, painfully thin. At the lowest point of the illness, I looked in the mirror and hated what I saw. Hated what I'd done to myself. So I cut off my hair. My beautiful long hair that should have helped me to look attractive had failed me. I'd failed. Feeling how short my hair is now is a reminder of somewhere I never want to be again. Back then, I lost all perspective and at times, even the will to live. But then, the cruellest of miracles. I started to lose my sight, aggravated by the anorexia. I woke up one day and there were no more mirrors. None that I could see my reflection in."

KT2 shook uncontrollably as she let go and sobbed her heart out. I pulled her towards me and held her as she cried and cried and cried.

We sat there for a long time as she slowly calmed down.

"Was that when you met your husband?" I said, as delicately as I could, holding my breath as I waited for her to answer.

"No, I met Pete a year before. He helped me. I think he saw me as his personal crusade. Being a doctor, it probably went with the territory."

I waited for her to continue, but she was lost in her thoughts.

"So what happened?" I asked.

"I started to go blind. But my weight was becoming less of an issue, so I wasn't a challenge to him anymore. Not seeing made things so much clearer and I realised how stupid I'd been. I started to get better. I ate hearty meals and started running again, for fun, not to lose weight. I began to live."

KT2 let out a big sigh and sank forwards, resting her elbows on her thighs. I sat back against the wall, my head spinning.

Bloody Hell.

KT2

I felt completely exhausted. Where was Maria when I needed a friendly, understanding hug?

The silence hung there for a long, long time. Finally I heard movement. His feet shuffled on the floor, I heard his footsteps leave the bathroom. I can't say I blamed him. It was one hell of a let's *get to know each other* conversation.

Me

I simply wasn't equipped to deal with this. I paced back and forth across the bedroom, at a complete loss.

What to do?

How do you treat someone with *anorexia?* It's one of the last taboos, trying to starve yourself to death, it just doesn't sit right. I stopped pacing and stood there with my hands on my head, staring out of the window at Lake Titicaca, the inky water glistening in the moonlight.

But if she was a bit *unstable,* where did that leave me? Wherever it was, I had to stop running away from difficult emotions. It was time to man up, or wimp out.

KT2

I heard his soft footsteps pad back into the bathroom, felt him sink down onto the floor beside me.

"I wasn't expecting you to come back..."

"Neither was I."

I sat there wondering what to say. But there wasn't anything left to say about me, it was all out there. Only time would tell how he'd react and he was here now, so it was a start.

"What about you?" I said quietly.

"Me?"

"Uh huh. That's my skeleton well and truly kicked out of the closet. And if you don't have any, then make something up, it will make me feel less of a nutter."

Me

I sat there without saying anything for a few minutes.

Baggage, piled high on the bathroom floor, was all I could think about.

She turned to face me, a prompt; *your turn.*

I took a deep breath.

It wasn't that I was shutting her out, I just wasn't sure if... Oh what the hell.

"I went through a tough time, after mum died and Kate Thornly the 1st dumped me. It's insignificant compared to your *issues...*"

"Is it?"

Something about her tone of voice made me wonder if she knew, had already guessed. I lifted my eyes from the floor to see her still looking at me. I wondered how much of my features she could make out. I watched as she attempted to smile, a contrast to her red puffy eyes. She reached into her pocket and pulled out the screwed up e-mail from Kate Thornly the 1st.

I felt my heart rate jump up a notch as she opened up the crumpled paper.

"If I wasn't blind, I'd have been tempted to read this. I guess you might want it back."

She held the piece of paper. I took it from her hand and stared at the crumpled text.

"Do you love her?"

"I thought I did."

"And now?"

I hesitated, flicking my eyes over the text.

"Now is different. But it seems wrong to moved on so quickly. Especially considering... "

I thought back for a moment or two, wondering if I should leave things there, or carry on, get everything out into the open. The problem was, I wasn't completely sure in my own mind what I'd *intended* that night.

"I won't judge you," she said softly.

I took a deep unsteady breath.

"I'm not totally sure what happened. I don't want to label myself with something like that…"

She just smiled her sad smile and waited for me to continue.

"When Kate Thornly the 1st cheated on me, it was such a *betrayal*. Everything was planned out, for after the trip I mean. We'd come back and get married, move away from the city, then probably have kids. I was going to set up in business as a gardener, do some fancy landscape design stuff and enjoy being outside and away from a stuffy office. I was desperate to escape from the London treadmill and I saw all that dissolve when we split up. I hit a real low."

I paused, wondering how much more to say.

"What was her reason?"

"She was fed up always having to nursemaid me."

"Was it that difficult a job?"

"Maybe. I probably took her for granted, got complacent."

"It happens."

"Yes it does. I went a bit off the rails, drinking to excess. I ended up at a party, already pretty drunk. My friends humoured me because of the break-up. They didn't stop me drinking, they thought it was part of the healing process. So I drank more. I have memory blanks, but I remember some pretty dark thoughts flashing through my head."

"What sort of dark thoughts?"

I slumped back, resting my head against the wall.

"I'm not entirely sure. I had no one to watch over me anymore, tell me not to eat certain foods. I was angry and hurt that she'd cheated on me. I should have gone home, slept it off, but I stood in the corner brooding, drinking even more. None of my friends asked how I was holding up. *Didn't they care?* I remember thinking that my life was worthless. I gave myself a hard time for being so reliant on Kate, but now she wasn't around anymore, I wanted to punish her."

Now I was struggling to speak. A lump started to swell in my throat, tears welled in my eyes. I fought the emotions back. I knew I needed to finish telling my story. I turned to face her.

"I ate something I shouldn't have."

"Deliberately?"

"Possibly. Yes."

Tears ran down my cheeks. I stifled a tremble in my bottom lip. I felt her squeeze my shoulder again and we sat there quietly until I'd composed myself.

"I woke up the next morning in hospital and felt so stupid and ashamed."

"Do you still feel low now?" she said.

I realised immediately what she was thinking.

"No. I haven't since that day. Realising I'd tried to top myself brought me back to reality. Don't worry, I'm not a suicidal nutcase."

Angel felt her way over to me and slipped her arm over my shoulder.

"Not yet. But give it another few weeks with me..."

I laughed, shook my head.

"And you thought you were the bonkers one," I said.

Twenty Nine

KT2

We eventually went to bed, with little more said. I lay awake for some time after, wondering how mad he thought I was. I also thought about his story and wondered how I felt about him now.

Where on earth did we go from here?

It seemed like only a matter of minutes since we'd closed our eyes, when the alarm went off. I'd had some strange dreams and was a bit disorientated as I woke. I instinctively touched my hair, shocked again to find it so short. Then, I thought back and cringed as I recalled my *confession*.

A shudder ran up my spine and I felt sick. Before the uneasy feelings got a hold, I ran my hands over my body, reassuring myself that I could feel healthy curves. Thankfully those dark days of skin and bone were no more. I could hear Jonny breathing close by and was comforted by knowing I wasn't alone, that he had a story too. To be honest, I'd half expected to find myself alone in bed. Perhaps he had the same pleasant surprise to find I was still here too.

"Don't worry, shorter hair suits you," Jonny said in a sleepy voice.

"Been awake long?"

"Mmm... mulling things over, quite a night. For both of us I mean," he said, yawning and rubbing his eyes.

"Yeah. That's all my skeletons made homeless."

"Mine too."

We lay in silence. I'd been here once before, at that awkward but necessary stage where the past comes out and the other person makes their excuses and leaves.

"How are you this morning?" he asked in a tentative voice.

"Better. And you?"

"A bit too early to tell. You ready to hit the road?"

Jonny packed for us (which didn't take long) while I freshened up. I was starting to get used to the feeling of air around my scalp, but I still felt a bit sad each time I ran fingers through what was left of my hair. But in a way it just added to the excitement of the next stage of our adventure.

We were ready to go in less than twenty minutes, sneaking out of the hotel room as quietly as we could in our new Bolivian clothing; a white embroidered blouse and a mustard-coloured alpaca wool smock for me and a blue and white stripy shirt for Jonny with a cream and brown alpaca fleece.

We walked downhill through the sleeping town, the cobbled stone backstreets and uneven pavement gradually giving way to rough tarmac and then compacted mud and gravel. We passed a rubbish tip because for a while I could smell rotting vegetation and household waste. After that we must have hit open country, I could *sense* the space around us.

Jonny had sketched the route of a day hike through Bolivian villages to Isla Del Sol, the 'Island of the Sun,' from a hotel guidebook. This really was off the beaten track and despite some uncertainty about how we felt following last night's revelations, I found myself grinning as we trudged through muddy puddles away from Copacabana.

"I feel like a proper traveller Jonny," I said, squeezing his hand.

He was quiet for a while as we walked, withdrawn.

"Can I ask you something?" he said, his serious tone of voice putting me on edge.

"Sure."

"I was wondering if you mind me calling you KT2?"

We walked on for a bit as I thought about my answer. I had the feeling it was a slightly loaded question.

"Honestly?"

"Always."

"Okay. Yeah, I do a bit. It feels like I'm in *her* shadow, a second-rate travel companion."

"I wondered about that. I have to say I'm not that keen on being called Jonny. *She* used to call me that. It always sounded a bit patronising, a put-down."

I nodded.

"I prefer Angel, if that's cool with you," I said, pleased with the way the conversation was heading. It was like a tentative fresh start. We'd both aired our dirty laundry and now it was time to try and move on.

"Completely cool," he said, his voice lifting, no longer so cautious.

"What about you?"

"Anything but Jonny, if you don't mind."

I thought for a moment, then grinned.

"What about your initials, 'JC'?

"Fantastic, The Angel Gabriel and Jesus Christ!"

We both chuckled.

And so it came to pass, we both had new nicknames…

JC (aka Me)

The drizzle eased off during the morning and we gradually began stripping off waterproof and fleece layers as the sun warmed the air and we left the town behind us.

The real beauty of the route was that it followed the coast, giving us spectacular views out across the lake. It was a liberating feeling, walking away from the town along a route seldom used by westerners.

"Breathe in that fresh air Angel, isn't it fantastic?"

"But surely you're missing the London smog, the pollution of your people?" Angel said, unable to hide the amusement in her voice.

"Ah yes, my people. I think it's time they made do without me for a while. After this trip I mean."

We walked on, enjoying the morning, without any traffic noise.

"You been thinking about the future JC?"

"A bit. I can't go back to that way of life. Not now. The scary thing is, I don't know where the time has gone. I wish I'd done this years ago."

"Guess we always regret the things we don't do more than the things we do."

"Definitely. What about you?"

"You know what, I'm taking one day at a time. I wasn't even supposed to be here a couple of months ago. Life shouldn't always be planned out in detail, it takes the surprise and spontaneity away."

I found myself nodding. It was a subtle observation about my organising ways.

"I do tend to do that, don't I. My job was very structured, safe. I'd like to try and be a bit more like you. Let things happen without trying to always control the outcome…"

"Ah, but I often have no structure to my life, so maybe we can learn from each other."

"Maybe we can."

We walked on for another hour or so, then stopped by the side of the track to look out over patchwork fields. In the distance I could see local families working the land, with the sparkling backdrop of the lake beyond. We'd picked up a few bits of food the night before and I unpacked the cheese, cold meat and bread rolls. We ate this simple breakfast miles from any recognisable civilisation. This was an uncomplicated existence, almost like time had rolled back a hundred years.

"Thank you…" Angel said between mouthfuls of food. I glanced across at her smiling face. Aside from her cute short red hair, she looked more relaxed, happier than I could remember.

"…For bringing me here, to this amazing place. And for not selling us out. You're a good man."

"That works both ways. You've opened my eyes Angel, helped me see a way out, but also a way *in,* to enjoying life more."

"I hope you're not going to try and convert me JC. Each to their own, but I'm a bit sketchy on the whole religion thing." I grinned.

"Perhaps we could make up our own religion."

"The church of the peroxide blonde analyst and the blind fiery redhead? Not very catchy is it," she said.

We walked on through several villages, past families cultivating their fields. Waving and calling out greetings in Spanish, we received gold-capped grins in return. We were passed by occasional villagers on bicycles or on foot and once by a farmer escorting his noisy sheep and reluctant pig, both of whom had rope 'leads' around the leg and didn't seem to like each other very much!

After fifteen kilometres walking we were greeted by a Bolivian man perched against a building. He was holding a Spanish copy of the Lonely Planet Guide to Bolivia. He asked if we were going to Isla Del Sol in a mixture of Spanish and English and offered to take us in his boat for ninety Bolivianos, around nine pounds.

"What do you think?" I asked Angel.

"How much more walking does it say until we reach the normal tourist boat across?"

"Maybe five kilometres."

"A longer boat ride from here sounds more adventurous..."

"And spontaneous," I added, chuckling at myself. I had to admire this man's resourcefulness – he'd probably spotted us coming a way off or, maybe someone had warned him potential trade was on its way.

Angel (aka KT2)
The boat trip was hilarious!
I heard the voice of Javier, our excited boatman as we followed him through his small holding, which JC described as a tiny 'farmhouse' surrounded by fields on one side and a shallow reed-filled lake on the other. Chickens, a pig and goat roamed free in the yard. Our guide reappeared with a fuel container, while his wife nodded and smiled at us as she hurried past. JC explained how we were following the couple through the waist high reeds along a rickety wooden walkway. It led us towards a colourful wooden boat with 'Tourismo' lettering and ancient outboard engine, tied up in the reeds.

"But that's not the best bit, Angel. He's sent his wife to row out to the motor boat in a battered rowing boat. I can see her furiously bailing water out - we could be waiting here a while!"

Eventually, safely on board JC and I sat up front as we nudged out through the reeds and into open water. I felt the breeze on my cheeks as we picked up speed and grinned when occasional droplets of spray splashed across my face. This was the life. And then the boat spluttered to a halt! I heard a couple of tugs on the pull cord and it fired up for about thirty seconds, then died again. This carried on another nineteen times – I counted! In the end Javier gave up trying to fault find and rowed us to the island, another back breaking thirty minutes. I felt for the man, he was really having to earn his fare, but the sudden quiet was wonderful. I could hear water lapping at the side of the boat and the oily two stroke engine smell had disappeared, it was heaven. JC later told me that as our speed dropped without the engine, water started seeping in through joints in the wood planks. No wonder he'd gone a bit quiet, I thought he was just enjoying the silence!

JC

Later that afternoon we arrived on *Isla Del Sol*, where the Incas believed the sun had been born. I thanked Javier and gave him a hundred Boliviano note, waving aside his offer of change. We also left him with the remains of the food and water from our breakfast for the long journey home. I watched his small muscular silhouette row the boat away from the shore as the sun crept towards the horizon over the glistening water and felt my enthusiasm soar. What an amazing experience!

The thousand steps to the top of the island were steep, but all in a day's work to Machu Picchu veterans like us.

We passed through neat terracing, segregated into shades of yellow, green and turquoise and saw a beautifully tended herb garden. Its small paths connected neat sections of shrubs, with much care and nurturing in evidence.

I remember marvelling at my fitness as we climbed the steps. I'd never have made such short work of them without Angel's regular runs. I no longer had my office tummy and didn't run out of puff after a flight of stairs. It amused me to think of all the fad diets people try and mostly fail at, when all they had to do was come travelling!

We reached the top after forty-five minutes to see a gorgeous view opening up. The back of the island looked out over an endless horizon of flat calm water, sheltered from the wind. Smaller islands dotted the water, peppered with clusters of village shacks. We found a room for the night with a rickety bed, bare floorboards and a balcony that looked out over the lake. It was basic, chilly and perfect.

We dumped our bags, put a few layers back on as the sun began dropping below the horizon and headed for the local 'cafe' which was a handful of log tables and tree stump stools that looked out over the lake. The view was spectacular, like looking out over an endless volcanic crater, filled with water, the rugged far shore just visible through the lingering low cloud.

I described the shifting colours of the setting sun against this magical backdrop and we drank cold beer as the world stopped for an hour.

All too often in life I thought, we're rarely aware of a turning point until it's passed us by. Then we look back and think, oh yeah, *that's* when things really changed. From the moment we'd left the hotel room to dye our hair, we'd triggered a change of direction and I was fortunate enough to realise it was happening. Right now.

I shut my eyes to enjoy the sensation, knowing that when it passed, things would never be quite the same again.

Angel

I could still *feel* JC there, despite his companionable silence. My instinct told me not to say anything, let him enjoy the moment on his own. So I sipped my beer and allowed my mind to wander too.

So much had happened over the past few years and I found myself enjoying some time to reflect without criticising myself. And who would have thought I'd end up here? I shook my head, amazed to be sipping cold Bolivian beer with JC, two miles up in the clouds, far away from home, but without feeling lonely.

As I sat there thinking about my feelings towards him, I became aware of voices approaching. The different accents suggested three Irish guys and two girls, one English. I couldn't place the other accent.

"I say good luck to them. They must have been offered a big pile of cash, but they still chose to take off on their own," said the English voice.

"Nah, they're an urban myth. They don't really exist. There'll be some kind of advertising spin on it."

"Don't be daft. I saw the advert on eBay. A friend of a friend applied."

The voices were getting closer. They passed to our right and parked themselves at a nearby table.

"Jesus, what a beautiful view."

"Which is exactly the reason it's an urban myth – what's to see for someone who's blind?" said a male voice, very close to us.

I froze, kicking myself for daring to believe we'd escaped.

"We'll be fine, just trust me and try to appear normal," whispered JC.

"Try to be normal yourself, man from Krypton!" I whispered back, the humour helping to calm me down. I slipped on the dark glasses and took another swig from my beer as we listened to the conversation developing at the adjacent table.

"I don't believe they managed to escape the press. I mean, if the girl really is blind, how could they possibly manage it? They'd stick out like a sore thumb."

There seemed general agreement to this observation and I allowed myself a secret smile – turns out JC and I were more resourceful than we were being given credit for.

"How do you think their sex life is? Do you reckon she knows he's a fat gawky analyst?"

"Nah, she's probably gagging for it!"

Uh oh. I sensed JC stiffen, anger clenching his muscles. I placed a calming hand on his arm, nuzzled my head into his cheek, to appear as any other loved-up couple.

"They're young and naive. Let's not blow our cover," I whispered in his ear, squeezing his arm.

"Do you think she could tell if he got a mate round to have a go too?"

"I don't reckon so, not if he took her from behind..."

"Size boys! A woman can tell!" said a girl's voice, joining in the male bravado.

The group laughed, and I felt my skin start to crawl. My fingers tightened around the bottle of beer. A red mist of anger descending...

"I fancy getting some food babe, you ready?" said JC in a fairly even voice. But I could tell he was still angry and trying to suppress it.

"Sure," was all I could manage as there was another burst of laughter from the nearby table. The sexual comments were getting even more graphic, making my blood boil. I felt JC grasp my hand, leading me away.

"Nice and steady Angel, it's a bit uneven underfoot. You're doing a great job, they've not even noticed we've gone," he whispered and squeezed my hand, but I was angry and didn't acknowledge his support.

JC

I'm not an aggressive bloke by any stretch of the imagination. Neither am I particularly keen on confrontation, although when I have to, I'll dig my heels in with the best of them. But hearing those travellers talk about us like that, insulting Angel, was humiliating. It was all I could do to clench my teeth and lead us away. I reasoned that they weren't insulting us deliberately. It was only because we were so well disguised that they were completely oblivious to our real identities. But it didn't make it any easier to walk away from. To be honest, the strength of feeling they'd stirred up had surprised and scared me. Perhaps this was all part of the travelling, exaggerating my usually measured *control* of my emotions…

We sat in silence in the simple restaurant, unable to make conversation. We were both still way too angry and also conscious that they could walk in at any moment; there weren't that many places to eat on the island. It wasn't until we got back to the hotel room and sat out on the balcony, that we were able to say anything about what had happened.

"I was ready to launch into them, it wouldn't have been pretty," Angel said.

"I know. Believe me I was annoyed too. But they were young, just laughing with us and at our brilliant escape."
Angel turned to me, her face like thunder, mimicking a gruff Irish accent.

"I bet she's better in bed for being blind, she tries harder…"

"I know, I'm sorry…"

"Sorry for what? Not beating the crap out of them? I'd have respected you more. I shouldn't have to listen to that."

"No. I know. But sometimes being spontaneous can be reckless. Don't worry, I've something in mind for them…"

"Yeah? Well it's too late, the moment's gone."

I watched her stand and feel her way around the wall for the door to the bedroom, open it, then slam it shut. I cringed.

Damn.

She was right of course. But although reacting on the spot might have sent Angel a message about my feelings for her, it would also have sent us right back to square one with the press. We'd lose not only our anonymity, but also the chance to experience the rest of our trip as ordinary travellers. I slumped forwards in the chair, dropping my head into my hands. *Who was I kidding, how could we ever be ordinary?*

The only saving grace I had, the ace up my sleeve, was that I saw the Irish arrive earlier that afternoon and knew they were staying a few doors away. I only noticed because all five of them had piled into one room and I'd wondered about the sleeping arrangements. Now as payback I came up with a plan for early the next morning. I spent a few moments setting the alarm on my watch and allowed myself a mischievous smile. Tomorrow I'd take sweet revenge.

I might be late defending Angel's honour, but defend it I most certainly would…

Thirty

Angel

I felt a bit bad about my outburst, but damn it, was he completely gutless?! I waited until he went to the bathroom, then crept into bed and pretended to be asleep when he came in.

I should probably have apologised and tried to talk things out, but I was still simmering and he did the right thing by saying nothing. The trouble was, his silence irritated me even more, especially as I'd gotten used to hearing his voice.

I was vaguely aware of the alarm going off and remember thinking it seemed really early. It was quiet for a few minutes after JC turned it off, so I thought he'd gone back to sleep. But just as I was drifting off, he slipped out of bed and started fumbling around, presumably getting dressed.

"What's up?" I mumbled.

"Secret mission. I'll be back in zero three minutes."

And before I could say anything else, he was gone. I felt a bit lost and guilty and wondered if he'd buggered off and left me after my outburst last night. For someone who was extremely independent at home, out here I was almost totally reliant on JC. I started to get a bit worried, then pinned my hope on the thought that he wouldn't abandon me. He'd be back. And at that moment, he was!

"Brrr, cold out there Angel."

"Where've you been?"

"Why, did you think I wasn't coming back?" he said, a cheeky, upbeat tone to his voice.

"No, I knew you couldn't survive without my sparkling personality."

I was vaguely aware of a small light beside me. Then several beeps followed, which meant he was setting his alarm for a more respectable time.

"What have you been up to?"

"Something most unchristian, Angel. I fear the Big Man would not be amused. On second thoughts, he might have a little chuckle."

JC giggled, wriggled around a bit to get comfortable, and then went quiet.

"I think I may have been a bit hard on you last night. If I was, I'm sorry," I said.

"You weren't, no apology needed. See you in a couple of hours," he said, his breathing gradually getting deeper. I lay there for a while wondering what on earth he'd been up to, but eventually drifted off, glad to have his warm body back in close proximity.

The second alarm brought brightness to the room and warmth from the sun, encouraging us out of bed to see what the new day would bring. I was desperate to ask what he'd been up to earlier, but he said nothing. So I busied myself by ducking under the ice cold shower, screeching, soaping up, and then rinsing off with more shouts. It was bloody freezing!

Conversation between us was friendly and without an atmosphere, but I knew something was amusing him. He had that playful way about him. But I wasn't going to ask, even though it was driving me mad.

JC packed up our stuff and we were ready. I heard the door open and smelt the cool fresh air as he led me out into the sunshine.

"Okay, I can't stand it anymore. What have you been..."

"Shhh. Grab a seat here on the balcony. Imagine the beautiful sparkling water of Lake Titicaca stretching out far below with its rugged islands and endless horizon and just listen. All will be revealed in the fullness of time..."

"You stole a book on poetry didn't you? What has got into you..."

"Have patience, Angel."

We sat back in the chairs, lapping up the sunshine. It was all very pleasant, but I was getting fidgety. I was hungry and desperate to know why we were waiting here. Then I heard something. It sounded like metal rattling.

"Do you hear that?" he said, a snigger in his voice.

I listened, there it was again, only louder this time, more aggressive. There was a muffled voice and a door banged in its frame.

"That's our cue Angel, breakfast time. Don't say a word until we sit down again, okay?"

I felt JC slip his hand in mine and off we went. The noise got louder, someone was hammering on a door from inside a room. Several Irish voices shouted out in anger and frustration. JC led me down some steps into a warm room where he guided me into a chair.

"Did you hear that Angel? That was the sound of sweet revenge. The locks on the rooms here are a bit unusual. If I say to you hasp and padlock on the outside, do you know what I mean?"

I nodded, still confused.

"One of the items I took from your big rucksack, was a padlock. Maria must have packed it thinking it might come in handy. Well, I found the perfect use for it. I've locked the Irish in their room. I even left some cash rolled up in the hasp for the hotel owner's trouble in removing it!"

JC started sniggering again. It took me a moment to catch on, then I giggled, but quickly stopped when JC pressed his finger to my lips. It quietened me down, but also felt kind of erotic. It was difficult not to laugh over breakfast, so JC settled up and we left, scurrying away like two mischievous school kids.

"Are we a safe distance away yet?" I asked.

"Yup. Ready?"

We both exploded into fits of laughter, which continued all the way down the thousand steps to the tourist ferry back to Copacabana.

JC

That little prank set us up for the day. The Irish didn't make the 9:30am ferry with us, but I set any guilty pangs aside by reasoning that they'd asked for it. Perhaps in future they'd be a bit more respectful.

"Feck! Some fecking feck has fecking locked us in! The feckers!" Angel whispered in my ear over and over again, pulling me close to her so I felt her hot breath on my cheek. Funny as it was, her mouth nuzzling up to whisper in a fake Irish accent was starting to push my buttons.

I'd almost forgotten that we had to start being vigilant again as the boat chugged into Copacabana. The hour and a half journey from Isla Del Sol had flown by.

"Back in character Angel, sunglasses on. I'll squeeze your hand once for a step up, twice for down and I'll pull your hand left or right to turn. Okay?" I said, reminding both of us of the silent code we'd been practising.

"Oh yeah, back to reality," she said, squeezing my hand as we followed other passengers off the boat.

We had an hour or so to kill before the tourist bus to the capital, La Paz. I was tempted to head for an internet café, but I decided not to risk it. We could do all that in La Paz, where we'd easily lose ourselves.

As we walked up from the port I glanced around the street to see stalls of handmade crafts and jewellery. I slowed down, prompting Angel to glance up at me.

"It's okay, I just think we need some decoration," I said, leading her to the nearest stall.

"Decoration?"

"Yup, we might as well look the part. I'd like to buy you something for being such a good travel companion. What sort of jewellery do you like?"

She beamed and we browsed a few stalls, making a pretty good job of projecting the image that we were a couple of normal travellers. Angel would wave her hand vaguely over an area of the display and I would select a necklace or earrings I thought she'd like.

After three-quarters of an hour we'd kitted her out with some dangly silver feather earrings, a shell bracelet and a colourful beaded necklace. Angel looked amazing and blended in even better as a traveller 'type'.

"What about you JC?"

"I don't normally wear anything at home, apart from a nice watch. It's not really *me*." I said.

"But this is the *new you*. Go on, live dangerously. Don't worry, I'm not going to suggest a ring… that can wait until Rio," she added, a mischievous lilt to her voice. I had to smile at that. So with me trying to describe my preference from several necklaces, we eventually made a decision. It was pretty comical because Angel kept agonising over the different choices, as though she had a firm opinion. Difficult when you can't actually see anything!

Once we'd bought our stuff, Angel-style, we strolled up to the bus stop. It was actually just a side street where the small coaches pulled up next to a handful of competing travel agents' shop fronts.

As we rounded the corner and slowed down to pick out the right bus, I froze. Standing on the opposite side of the road was Simon, with one of the camera crew. I turned away from him and carried on walking. Fortunately we'd ditched our daypacks by now, opting instead for local-style shoulder bags to help us blend in even more. At the time I'd questioned the logic of leaving the more practical and comfortable rucksacks with the lady in the shop, but I was glad we had.

Angel

It's amazing what a difference a bit of cheap jewellery can make. I walked up the hill towards the bus stop grinning. I felt like a million dollars and all for only a few quid. I told JC he'd have Maria worried for her job as shopping monitor. I can't remember the last time I went shopping with a bloke and actually had fun, especially since I lost my sight.

My good mood was kicked into touch as we rounded the corner to jump on our bus and I felt three rapid squeezes. This meant we were in danger of being spotted.

JC left me by a wall, allowing me to sink down against it and sit on my bag, hopefully making me look less conspicuous.

"Hi, Ingles?" said a voice that sounded suspiciously like Simon.

Bollocks!

"Feck off! Don't be insulting me now. I'm Irish!" I replied, tilting my head up in his general direction.

"Sorry. I'm looking for a mate. I lost track of him back in Peru...." said Simon.

"You got a photograph fella?" I said, holding up my hand, raising the other to make out I needed to block my eyes from the sun.

"Sure."

I felt the glossy paper in my hand and rotated it several times.

"Ugly fecker, even upside down. Nah, sorry fella, good luck with that though," I said, in my best Irish accent, offering the picture back to him.

"Okay, cheers," said Simon.

I heard his footsteps start to walk away, then they stopped.

"What about a blind girl? Mousy hair, early thirties, pretty, in a girl next door sort of way."

"Can't say I have, but fair play to her. Can't be easy finding your way out here," I said, wondering how long we had before the bus left.

"God knows what he sees in her, but they say love is blind."

"So they do. You have a good day now," I said and looked down at my bracelet, toying with it, signalling that our conversation was over.

Now bugger off! I murmured under my breath.

It was several long minutes before I heard JC beside me.

"Ready my Irish Angel? Five quick steps and we're on the bus. I've left it to the last possible moment."

I nodded, relieved to feel his hands slip into mine as he pulled me up. I counted five steps, felt JC's hand jerk up, the signal to lift my foot and I climbed onto the bus behind him. There was a pause as JC handed our tickets over, then we made our way down the coach to a vacant pair of seats. I heard the engine rumble into life and I started to relax.

"Turn to face me, Simon's walking back this way!" he said urgently, making my heart beat faster at the possibility of getting caught. I turned away from the window and felt JC's beard bristle against my cheek. He was very close to me. I started to say "you'd better kiss me then..." but I didn't get to finish because he pulled me close and pressed his lips against mine. I was oblivious to the bus engine revving up as we pulled away from the curb. We were on our way – in all directions!

With the build-up over the last few days, weeks even, it was inevitable that this wasn't going to stay a staged kiss for long. I reached up and stroked his cheek with my fingers, pulling his lips more firmly onto mine. My excitement soared as we slowly kissed, parting only as the bus gathered speed.

"Now tell me, was Simon really there or did you pull a fast one?"

JC

I smiled at her question but didn't answer. I was buzzing inside as I studied her face, it was such a turn on to be this close to her. I reached up and gently pushed up her sunglasses. I wanted to look into her eyes, *see* her.

I stroked her cheek as I studied every inch of her face, conscious of her unsteady breathing and slightly parted lips. I tried to read her eyes, but they were clouded and gave little away.

I found myself hesitating.

"Am I taking advantage of you Angel?"

"Jesus! What a stupid fecking question!"

Angel tipped her head and leaned in, our lips only just touching again when the bus hit a pothole and knocked our heads together. A cheer erupted from the other passengers, either at us, or the bus driver. I didn't know and I didn't care. We laughed as we rubbed our foreheads, the intimacy of the moment gone.

Thirty One

Angel

By the time we arrived in La Paz it was mid afternoon and we were both starving. The breakfast on *Isla Del Sol* seemed days ago. After finding *The Republica*, a quiet courtyard hotel, we dumped our stuff and headed out. Jonny had described La Paz as a sprawling ramshackle capital city spread out across a valley, with US style wide roads and wild spaghetti overhead power cables. Big boxy and colourful 1960s Detroit minibusses lumbered past, always full. Unlike Buenos Aires, La Paz felt more relaxed, despite still being busy, hectic and loud. Yet Jonny didn't get irritable or flustered, he seemed to be embracing the city.

Perhaps he was adjusting to travelling and was a bit more chilled out now. Whatever the reason, we took advantage of his willingness to explore and drew some US Dollars from an ATM, then we walked a half hour loop to check out what was nearby. There were some unusual sights that Jonny pointed out. Many of the street sellers had had telephones with temporary cables strung out to their stalls, a variation on a British Telecom payphone. Some sort of celebration was in progress in the central island in the middle of the main road – lots of school kids around fifteen years old danced, played instruments and partied in a fountain, splashing water everywhere. We ended up at a Chinese restaurant on the tail end of its afternoon shift and just managed to get in before they closed. We'd not spoken much since the kiss, there didn't seem any point. But now there was a definite sexual tension between us and small talk wasn't going to help.

JC

Okay, I admit it. Simon was nowhere to be seen when we got on the bus, I pulled a fast one!

I can't explain why. I just had the urge to step out of the *old* me for a moment, be a bit cheeky. Perhaps her mischievous enthusiasm was rubbing off. I'd taken the bull by the horns and blagged it and had been pleasantly surprised by the results. That was until the bloody bus hit that pothole!

The trouble was, knowing how much I wanted Angel now, reminded me of how badly I'd viewed her blindness in the early days. I'd had a dismissive attitude towards her back then. The old me was not a particularly nice person and I found myself hanging my head in shame.

Perhaps I was finally starting to find out who *I was* (as the cliché goes) and who I wanted to become. It was time to start breaking free.

Happier with this view of myself, I lifted my head and looked across the table at Angel. She was right, KT2 wasn't the right name for her at all. I took a deep breath to steady my nerves and prepared to start out with my new self.

"I suppose this is a bit like a first date," I said.
With all the butterflies in my stomach, it certainly felt like it.

"Maybe, but I don't remember being asked. I might be washing my hair later."
I saw a smile twitch across her lips.

"Don't worry, it won't take long, there's not much left!"
Her smile widened.

"Is that supposed to encourage me to say yes?"

"Whoa, easy. I haven't even asked yet."
She pulled a face.

"So where are you taking me? For this date that you've yet to ask for, to which I haven't agreed."

"Yet."

"So ask me."

"Angel, would you like to meet me for a drink sometime… perhaps this afternoon?"

"Sorry, I'm growing my hair."
We both laughed. I counted out some cash and paid the waiter, who was hovering, keen to usher us out the door.

"I need a drink. Fancy coming along?" she said.

"Are you asking *me* out?"

"Yeah, girl power. And knowing your misplaced sense of duty, and the fact that I can't go on my own, you're bound to agree. So I'm taking that as a yes. Shall we go?"
I nodded, chuckling.

"Yes," I said, still grinning as I held her hand tightly and led her out of the restaurant.

Angel

Despite having spent the last six weeks or so living in each other's pockets, twenty-four hours a day, seven days a week, I found myself tingling with nerves and excitement, just like I would on a 'proper' first date.

JC got the drinks in and we sat nursing them for a few minutes, neither of us saying very much. It was almost as if the rules between us had changed, and we didn't know how to play the game now.

One of my biggest problems when meeting someone new is lack of eye contact. How is the other person reacting to me – what's their *body language* saying? Do I get butterflies in the pit of my stomach? Does my heart rate increase? It was one of the hardest adjustments, having to rely on tone of voice, or touch to let me know how things were going. So I often find myself being more extrovert to try and get a reaction, so I can decide if I like someone. I also need to get a feel for whether they like me, so I don't make a fool of myself and play up to someone who isn't interested. Maybe that's why I seem a bit loud and outrageous sometimes; I know it's scared men off in the past.

"You okay Angel? You're a bit quiet."

"Actually I'm struggling a bit."

"Oh. With me? We can go back to the hotel if you like…"

"I don't want to, unless you do?"

"No, I'm good."

We sat there for a few awkward moments, then I heard him chuckle.

"Look at us, acting like two shy teenagers. I sometimes wonder what you're thinking, but it's difficult to tell. I wanted to ask how hard it is for you, not seeing someone's face, gauging what sort of mood they're in. Is that what you're struggling with?"

I nodded, surprised at his perception and started to feel a bit tearful.

"It's difficult. Whatever you think of me - tough outer shell, loud and obnoxious at times, I'm a softie inside. Us sitting opposite each other like a business meeting, makes it hard to get a sense of how we're getting along."

JC said nothing for a moment, but then I heard him get up and I felt him slide into the booth beside me.

"I've been sitting there thinking the same thing Angel, trying to put myself in your position. It can't be easy."

I felt my body tingle as he brushed my hand.

"Just try shutting your eyes, then you'll know."

"I've been doing exactly that from the moment we sat down," he said, resting his hand beside mine, so close I could feel the soft hairs on the side of his wrist.

"You're joking."

"I've had my eyes shut trying to understand some of what you have to deal with every day."

I've heard a lot of cheesy chat up lines over the years, but actually all someone had to do was sit next to me and say they'd been trying to understand how I felt by shutting their eyes.

"You don't know the half of it," I said quietly, reaching out with my little finger, touching his hand, stroking his skin, enjoying the nervous excitement in the pit of my stomach.

JC
I know we'd been holding hands every day for the last six weeks, but this was no longer out of necessity. Now I wanted to.

I felt my skin tingle as she caressed my hand and we talked about the adventures we'd had so far and laughed, filling in some of the gaps for each other with our own take on the different situations and people we'd met.

Time just flew.

I don't think we had more than three or four drinks all evening, and by the time we left I hardly felt the effect of the alcohol at all. I did have a few stomach pains though and remember wondering why I wasn't feeling quite right. Earlier in the evening I'd put the unsettled feeling down to nerves, but this was different, now the cramps were getting uncomfortable. I tried to forget about them as we wondered back to the hotel, hand in hand.

210

Another cramp hit me just as we were nearing the main entrance and I had to stop to catch my breath. I doubled up, feeling bloated, concern hovering at the back of my mind.

"What's up?" said Angel, as I groaned. I took a minute to steady myself, then straightened and hobbled into the reception.

"Stomach pains, not good. Sure it will pass in a minute..."

"This isn't setting the scene for a tactical retreat is it?"
I tried to laugh, wanted to, but was feeling decidedly groggy. I collected the key and hurried us along to the room.

"I guess not!" said Angel, excitement and amusement in her voice.
I only just made it back to the room. I unlocked the door, led Angel inside and made a dash for the toilet. I didn't even have time to apologise.

"ARRRRAAAAHHHH!!!"
I have never been so ill in all my life! I knelt with my head in the toilet bowl for ages, throwing up constantly.

I felt completely drained, sprawled out on my hands and knees, clutching the side of the bowl, my arms scarcely able to hold myself up, all strength sapped from my body. It was a horrible state to be in.

"This is probably one of the more extreme reactions I've had to a first date..." Angel said outside the open bathroom door.
I could barely respond as another wave of retching overcame me. But it didn't stop there. Having gotten rid of everything, including my stomach lining, the other end started. This went on every hour. Each time I tried to sip some water and get some fluids down me, it came straight out again.

"Sorry Angel, it's not pleasant in there," I said, slumping down on the edge of the bed.

"I'd say you have food poisoning JC."

"Oh bloody hell, excuse me..."
I ran back into the toilet and let rip again, unable to believe I was so ill. I was gutted that it had happened today of all days. By the time I made it out again I was seriously drained. I felt as though I'd lost two or three stone, yet still the stomach cramps continued.

"We need to get some water down you, is there any bottled stuff left?" she said, shuffling along the bed to drape her arm over my sagging shoulders. *God I felt rough.*

"Only a few mouthfuls, forgot to get any more."

"Okay. I'll ring reception. Now JC, if you'd wanted to let me down gently, you just had to say."

I attempted to smile, not that she could see it of course, it was more to encourage my own state of mind. Angel hugged me gently, then shuffled back towards the head of the bed and felt for the phone.

"Hola Senora, es posible un poco de aqua por favor? Si. My boyfriend, very ill. Si. Muchas gracias**."**

It wasn't long before one of the girls from reception appeared at the door, bless her. I took the bottles of water and mumbled a thank you. She glanced over in Angel's direction, smiling. I think she may have noticed her lack of eye contact, so there was a good chance she'd realise Angel was blind. To be honest, the way I felt right now, there was nothing I could do to try and cover things up. It was over to the receptionist's integrity as to whether she let on to anyone else we were staying here.

"Sorry Angel. This is a bugger," I said as I sat down next to her, nursing the water bottle, trying to force small mouthfuls down my raw throat.

"You sure know how to show a girl a good time," she said, putting her arm around me as I slumped forwards, elbows on knees, waiting to see how long it would take the water to go through me.

"Timing was never my strong point."

"Shame, because you were about to find out if the old saying is true."

I frowned, lifting my head to turn towards her.

"What saying?"

"That there are two *sure things* in life; death and a nurse."

I chuckled, shaking my head. Then I leapt up and staggered to the toilet again.

"I offer myself to you as an Inca sacrifice and you run away, bloody typical!" she shouted at the door, but her humour was lost on me as I purged my system again.

And again.

Angel

It wasn't quite the end to the evening I'd been hoping for!

Poor JC, if he wasn't so ill it would be funny. I tried to lighten his suffering with some good old nurse humour, but he wasn't having any of it. In a strange way, I felt a sense of comfort in his being ill. It seemed to boost my confidence, because I could now put my training to some use and look after him for a change. I doubt he'd appreciate my upbeat take on the situation though, boy was he suffering.

He was up regularly during the night, returning after every visit to the loo a little weaker and more despondent. Fortunately I'd insisted we brought the medical kit with us from the main packs, which contained some rehydration sachets. They didn't seem to help though, because an hour or so after he'd mixed it up and drunk a few mouthfuls, out it came again.

It goes without saying that neither of us got much sleep that night. But at least he wasn't being sick anymore. JC returned from his latest visit to the bathroom groaning.

"How long do you think it'll go on for?"

"The rest periods are getting longer, so I think your system is on the mend. But you'll probably be like this for another twelve hours or so. Keep drinking the water, try and force it down, even if you don't want to. Is the liquid getting clearer?"

"Um, yeah, a bit."

"Okay, good. Your body is flushing it out. It's just a case of keeping going. Stay in bed today, drink as much fluid as you can manage and I'll look in on you this evening."

It took him a few moments to register what I'd just said.

"You're leaving me?"

"Of course. I have a new city to explore," I said indignantly, wishing I could see his face.

"Gotcha!" I said, reaching out to tickle him gently.

"You cow! And I'd be careful tickling me at the moment unless you want an accident in the bed. My bum is a loaded weapon, the safety catch is off and it's pointing in your direction!"

We laughed, exhausted from the lack of sleep, but at least he could see a funny side to all this.

213

"What are we going to do about food? For you I mean," he said. I was touched that he was concerned about me.

"You know what, in a completely level headed, non-dieting kind of way, I think I'll survive for a few hours. Maybe when you're up and about, we'll go out for a slap up meal. If you're lucky I might let you have some bread and soup."

"Great, more liquid!"

JC

I guess it was pay back time, being ill and having Angel to look after me. She helped keep my spirits up. This trip was turning out to be a real partnership. Who would have thought that when we'd started out? Not me, that's for sure.

Just as Angel had predicted, the visits to the toilet became less frequent and by late afternoon it was nearly three hours since I'd last gone. I still had stomach cramps, but Angel was sure they were now hunger pangs. It certainly felt like I'd lost a whole lot of weight.

I had a shower and by seven o'clock that evening I felt I was ready to brave the outside world without needing the comfort of a toilet less than ten yards away. I dressed and shook my head at having to use an extra notch on my belt.

This time I studied the Lonely Planet for a restaurant recommendation and we ended up at a little place called *100% Natural*. The food was excellent, but Angel was right, bread and soup was all I could manage. She on the other hand ate for Scotland. I watched her stuff her face, feeling slightly envious, hoping I'd be well enough to eat properly again soon.

Having had some food, my first in thirty-six hours, I suddenly felt exhausted.

"I'm going to have to go to bed Angel, I'm shattered," I said, fighting to keep my eyes open.

"I'm not surprised. You body has been through hell. Now it's had some energy, it wants to shut down everything non-essential so it can start repairing the damage."

We picked up some more bottled water on the way and stopped by reception to collect the key. Was it my imagination, or did the lady behind the desk give us a strange look? No matter, I was too tired to register it as a problem and escorted Angel back to the room.

I suggested she go to the bathroom first, just in case… and that was the last thing I remember until the morning.

Angel
I smiled at JC's light snoring, which guided me into bed. I wasn't surprised he'd crashed out, that was a really nasty bout of food poisoning and he was lucky to have got through the worst of it so quickly. I slipped into bed next to him and lay awake for a few minutes, fighting my own tiredness to think about the build-up over the last few weeks.

I wondered where we went from here, how strong the feelings really were and how they might change if our pasts came back to haunt us?

I suppose we'd need to be *together* first, I reasoned, my last thought as I too drifted off into a deep sleep.

Thirty Two

JC

I slept in late the next morning, dangerously close to checking out time. I woke with a pounding headache and realised I needed to keep drinking as much water as I could. But the good news was I hadn't needed to get up in the night and although I still had a dull ache in my stomach, I put this down to hunger and soreness rather than the food poisoning. Angel was already up and dressed, listening to her headphones.

"Morning Nurse. Top of the morning to you," I said, propping myself up in bed.

"Wow, you look so much better!" she said in an overly loud voice.

I chuckled and climbed out of bed to find a bottle of water.

"How you feeling, man of steel?"

I drained the water as I wondered around to her side of the bed and gently pulled the earphones out of her ears.

"Not so loud Angel, feels like a sledgehammer battering the inside of my head."

"Oh, sorry. Water is what you need, lots and lots."

I grinned at the empty plastic bottle in my hand, which of course she couldn't see and bopped her on the head with it.

"Ah, I see you're ahead of me. What's the plan today, you feeling up to a wander around?" she said.

"I reckon that's a good idea. Fresh air, maybe check out an internet café…"

"Hang on, are you standing there naked?"

"I am."

"All dangly jangly? I'm not sure that's appropriate after not even half a first date. You should be mindful of your manners Superman."

I laughed, which made my stomach twinge, prompting me to head off to the bathroom.

"If you were a lady you wouldn't be asking those sorts of questions."

"Like you were a gentleman and didn't look that first night?" she said, her voice muffled through the bathroom door.
I opened my mouth to answer then thought better of it.

I smiled at the receptionist as she looked up from the desk and I passed her our key.

"Gracias. Senor Cork, follow me please?" she said, with a sheepish look. I frowned, leading Angel into the small dining room, where the receptionist shut the door behind us. I'd not noticed before, but she held a newspaper in her hand.

"Please, excuse. You are eBay couple, no? Kate Thornly, yes?"
I felt Angel squeeze my hand as I watched the receptionist open the Bolivian newspaper and spread it out on the nearest table.

"Be careful amigos."
The receptionist traced her finger over the newspaper headlines and the first few lines of the story underneath. I could see a grainy photograph of me on a boozy night out and Angel's infamous shower picture.

"Twenty thousand Bolivianos. Blind girl taken by English um, how you say, thief, no, er…"

"Con artist. Trickster. Bad man," said Angel, in a playful tone.

"Bad man, yes. Report you, this telephone number."
It seemed we now had a price on our heads!

"Simon's off my Christmas card list," said Angel.
I shook my head, bemused. The world had gone mad.

"But I see you. You no bad man. Look after Kate, smile much. Bolivian people good people, but poor. This much money. You understand?"
I nodded.

"Passports. Don't give Kate Thornly to hotels. That how I know. I not know you blind Kate. I am sorry."

Shit! How bloody stupid can you get? We'd thought about the credit card, paying only in cash and had disguised ourselves, but had forgotten about our passports. It was so obvious we'd both completely overlooked it.

"Thank you Senora. Muchos gracias," I said, holding eye contact with this lovely kind lady. Angel offered her open arms and hugged her.

I paid the outstanding amount for our room in cash together with a sizeable tip and left Angel in reception while I took the key and packed up our room. It was a shame to be moving on so soon, particularly as I wasn't feeling great, but it didn't look like we had much choice.

Angel

"I wish I could remember which bank we robbed, Butch," I said as we stepped out of the hotel into the street.

"They all merge into one when you've hit as many as we have, Sundance."

We both laughed.

"Fugitives again. You're a bad influence JC."

The only plan we had now was to find an internet café to check in with friends back home, and pick up the latest news on the search for us. Then we'd decide where to go next. Preferably somewhere well off the beaten track.

JC led us to *Oliver's Travels,* a bar and restaurant serving the best English breakfast in Bolivia, where we quietly discussed our next destination.

"What about the jungle?" he suggested, reading me snippets from the Lonely Planet guide on Bolivia.

"We could fly there in an hour. Ordinarily that would be better than the bus, but they would definitely have to check our passports.

"How long by road?"

"Fifteen to eighteen hours, depending on the weather," he said.

Not an especially appealing option, but if it meant escaping capture for another couple of weeks, then it was worth considering.

"Why the hell not, let's bus it to the jungle and meet some of your ancestors!" I said, making JC splutter, mid-mouthful.

JC

We had a new system for our visit to the internet café. I rented a terminal and Angel perched behind me on a stool, leaning over my shoulder, staring into space in the general direction of the screen while I went through both our e-mail accounts. Our theory was that to a casual observer we were just like any other travelling couple on a tight budget. Not that it was expensive, this was Bolivia after all.

I logged into Angel's account first, wondering what would be waiting for us in cyberspace. I scanned down the list of messages and printed off anything that looked interesting. If nothing else it would help to pass the time during our bus journey to the jungle. There were a couple of messages from Maria in Angel's inbox and one from Pete. I hesitated, wondering if I should delete that one, then stopped. It was a matter of trust.

"Do you want all of them printed off, including ex-husbands?" I said, deciding to play the game fair and square.

"Might as well get the whole picture on what's happening back home," she said, squeezing my shoulder. I nodded and tabbed down through the list, printing off relevant messages, then closed down Angel's account. I logged onto my e-mail and watched as sixty messages appeared.

"I've never been so popular."

"Especially with that new hairdo!"

"You're not wrong. Old friends creeping out of the woodwork, work colleagues, the press of course…"

"Any other Kate Thornlys?" she whispered, her voice sending shivers down my spine, despite my still delicate state.

"Let's see… yup, one or two. And Kate Thornly the 1st. It seems the plumber might not be doing it for her anymore."

"No longer able to clear her U bend?" said Angel, making me laugh out loud.

"Lovely turn of phrase."

"You know me."

I turned back to the screen, printed off messages from Justin and one or two others that seemed interesting, then shut the system down. I wanted to get out of there as soon as possible.

Thirty Three

JC

The bus journey was a bugger! Cheap as chips for the distance, but we were jammed into the back of a small minibus. Our knees were tight against the seats in front as we bounced on the back axle over every pothole and rut. Clearly we were sitting in the seats that no local wanted.

At least there were no passport checks, but it didn't get away from the fact that it was bloody uncomfortable. We didn't even get a chance to read the e-mails, firstly because I'd stuffed them in my pack, which was under a tarpaulin on the roof, and secondly because even if I'd had them on me, I'd feel sick reading them in this hot, cramped roller coaster.

"I'm sure the SAS use these very stress positions as part of their escape and evasion training," I said, making no attempt to disguise the grump in my voice.

"No, I think we're missing the thumb screws," said Angel. Another reason for my less than impressed state of mind, was that this environment wasn't exactly conducive to re-establishing a romantic air between us. I hoped we'd get it back, but this really wasn't the time or place to lean across and start whispering sweet nothings in her ear!

I tried my best to describe what I could see, but soon gave up shouting over the road noise and hot air blasting in from the open window. I vaguely remember reading that part of the journey to the jungle town of Rurrenabaque was along a stretch of the infamous 'world's most dangerous road' – they weren't joking. The loose grit track looked barely wide enough for one vehicle, let alone two being driven at speed. I peered over the edge of one mountain pass as we inched past a cattle truck. We had maybe three inches of road on my side before we'd plummet five hundred feet to the dense jungle below. Car and truck wrecks littered the side of the road every few miles. Out here there were no crash barriers, no street lights and no speed limits. I was quite glad Angel hadn't pestered me for a detailed description of our surroundings – perhaps she's picked up on the tension in my voice and had decided she was better off not knowing!

There were stops every few hours to stretch our legs, visit the toilet or grab a bite to eat from the small village stores. The trouble was, having taken ten minutes to get the blood moving, the thought of having to squeeze ourselves into the bus again wasn't pleasant.

Sixteen uncomfortable, hungry and miserable hours later, we finally arrived in Rurrenabaque. It was one of those times when the first hotel with a room would do. We crashed out under a whirring fan that just about kept the stifling heat and humidity at bay, long enough for us to drift into a fitful sleep. Something told me the journey here was an ominous omen for our time in the jungle...

Angel

According to JC, we'd lucked out with *The Oriental Hotel*. There was a central outdoor courtyard with half a dozen hammocks strung up under shelter. Our room was big, had a really comfortable bed, proper deep pillows and a bathroom bigger than many a previous hotel room. The journey here should have prepared me for the stifling heat of the jungle, but stepping off the bus it still hit me. We'd thought we'd be more comfortable here at sea level, but the humidity is sky high. It's sticky and uncomfortably hot all of the time. Wearing shorts and tee-shirts instead of fighting off the cold was a novelty that soon wore off!

The *smell* of the jungle heat is weird, it exaggerates everything – rancid trash smells, two stroke motorbike fumes and B.O. And the whole place resonates with a high pitched squawk from untold bugs that made my skin shudder, despite the heat. But the worst sound was the scream of incoming mosquitoes, buzzing around my face, freaking me out – little bastards!

Despite my normal enthusiasm and energy, I struggled from the very start in the jungle. It was such an alien environment, riddled with hazards. I felt my confidence dip as I realised I had to be so much more careful than normal. It also meant I wasn't as relaxed around JC. I'd have to rely on him even more and we wouldn't be on the reasonably level ground that we had been.

An invisible force field seemed to descend between us and I felt powerless to do anything to dissolve it. But this was only the start. We'd planned to spend a few days up river away from the town at a jungle village lodge with even more heat, insects and hardcore hiking.

For the first time since starting out on the trip, I felt a sense of gloom.

JC

Jesus it was hot! Like being in a furnace, sauna and steam room all at the same time. It didn't take me long to realise that even once we'd managed to recover from the bus ride here, neither of us was going to cope that well. And we hadn't even got to the jungle lodge yet!

We got up the first morning after a poor night's sleep. Both of us had been restless in the heat and were unable to settle because of the noisy whirling of the ancient overhead fan. We sat at a table outside one of the few shack-type buildings open for breakfast and fended off the bugs. We were both jaded and not in the best of moods. Usually when one of us was a bit low or quiet, the other would be upbeat and would be able to lift the others spirits. But here we were both struggling.

I wasn't in the right frame of mind to read the e-mails, so I left that delight for another time. Instead, I ran through a mental list of things we had to do, including confirming our booking with the jungle lodge.

"You're quiet this morning JC," Angel said, an edge to her voice that I hadn't heard before.

I looked over at her, seeing her agitation as she swatted buzzing insects away from her face. Normally I might have felt sorry for her; not being able to see the mozzies but hearing their high pitched 'Stuka' scream can't have been very pleasant. But I didn't allow her any latitude.

"Yeah, making a list of things to do. Starting with…"

"You and your bloody lists."

Ouch.

"Sometimes they're necessary to get things done."

My tone could have been reeled in a notch or two, but unfortunately I was also tired and irritable. Blind or not, if looks could kill I'd be well and truly six feet under. We sat there in stony silence for the rest of breakfast.

"Come on, let's go and pay for the jungle lodge. We've come all this way, we might as well experience the whole travel thing. Good, bad or bloody awful.

"That was a barbed comment."

I sighed and stood there for a moment looking down at her. I wondered what else was going on, but doubted I'd get a straight answer.

"I know it's bloody hot and there are lots of insects, but let's just try and make the best of it. We're here now."

I offered my hand, leaning down to slip it into hers. She reluctantly accepted and stood, sighing for effect.

Rurrenabaque is built on a grid layout, with wide straight mud roads and mostly single storey terraced buildings in bright colours; cream, turquoise, yellow and green. It's a fledgling tourist resort located beside a wide fast flowing muddy brown river. All around the edge of the town is dense jungle – bush trees right up to the water and lush green ferns. There weren't many cars here, the odd jeep or Nissan Patrol dodged two stroke motorbikes that were usually driven flat out – their screechy engines and smoky exhausts hanging in the thick air. There were loads of hardcore travellers milling around and one or two European residents who looked like they'd come to visit in the seventies and never left. One made a living selling banana cake from a flatbed trike, another ran jungle tours.

I checked the directions in the Lonely Planet and took a left past an elegant modern building which was the town's only bank.

"Nearly there, Angel," I said, squeezing her hand, but she barely responded. It looked like I'd have to jolly things along for the both of us.

The lady in the *San Miguel del Bala* office was very enthusiastic about our four day trip and passionate about the villagers. Apparently this was a community-based project that had evolved five years ago after the government declared much of the village's hunting ground a national park. This meant they had to look for other ways to sustain themselves and future generations, so the growing tourist trade was an obvious opportunity. I was really impressed with the whole set up and asked lots of questions that Danni, the Dutch volunteer seemed to revel in.

"Would you like to see some photographs? I'll just be a moment," said Danni, as she disappeared into the back of her office.

"I bet she's early thirties, blond and has big tits," Angel hissed.

"That's actually not a bad description."
I'd not seen Angel in a bad mood before, and it wasn't pretty. Her face was angry, all humour and energy had drained away.

"Perhaps you should carry on with her instead. She'll be less of a burden and is obviously better eye candy."
I bit my tongue as Danni reappeared holding a large photo album and with a big smile on her face.

"Here we are. This is the education and meeting shelter…"
Despite her dark mood, I felt I'd been a bit short with Angel and had probably contributed to her state of mind. As I sat there looking through Danni's photos, I thought about whether we should mention that Angel was blind. I reasoned that it would be difficult to hide it, and now we were here, there was less chance of anyone being aware of who we were. But above all else, if I didn't do my usual descriptions of what I could see, Angel would miss out on the whole experience of the rainforest.

"Excuse me Danni, but I just need to describe these lovely photographs to my friend, her eyesight isn't brilliant and we lost her glasses on the journey," I said, smiling at Danni as I squeezed Angel's knee.

If only I'd been a mind reader and known that that was totally the wrong thing to say!
Fortunately Danni was oblivious.

"Of course. My goodness, I'm sorry to hear that. Okay, the first picture here shows the community hall and the villagers during the grand opening ceremony…"
Danni went on to carefully explain all the photos, which can't have been easy for her without feedback from Angel. I felt I had to be overly enthusiastic to make up for her silence. Half an hour later I paid, thanked Danni and escorted Angel away.

Once away from Danni, Angel shrugged off my hand and insisted on dawdling along at a snail's pace. Finally, I couldn't take any more. I grabbed her shoulder, stopping her in the street.

"What's the matter?"

"I'm fine."

"No, you're not. Come on Angel, we've been through too much together to fall out now..."

"So we've fallen out have we? That's news to me!"
I stared at her, shaking my head.

"Tell you what, you just go on your merry way and I'll book you a flight out of here in the morning. I'll ring Simon and tell him to expect you. He'll get you home with a few quid in your pocket. Is that what you want?"

"So you're going to abandon me. Great guy you turned out to be."

"Oh for Christ's sake! I know we're both tired, but what the hell has got into you?"

"Me?! I thought we'd agreed to maintain the illusion I could see, so we didn't attract attention to ourselves. But all that went out the window in front of saint fucking Danni!"
I dropped my arm from her shoulder.

"I told her you can't see very well, because I'm guessing that of all the places we've been, this is probably the most threatening, the most hostile but also the most beautiful. So I decided here, of all places, you need me to be your eyes. Which incidentally, I'm more than happy to do. Unless you want to continue being a bitch, in which case you're on the next plane out of here while I head in the opposite direction. What's it going to be?!"

Angel

I know I'd behaved like a brat, but we were both tired and these things are never completely one-sided. I took a calming breath. Deep down, I really didn't want to screw this up, but I had a nasty feeling it was already too late.

"This is a difficult environment for me and I don't want you to leave me. I've just got stuff on my mind."
I felt him put his hand back on my shoulder and heard him sigh.

"What sort of stuff? Let's find a bar and talk it out."

I shook my head.

"It's a girl thing. I could do with finding a pharmacy. Have you noticed one anywhere?"

"Oh. Are you feeling okay?" he said, concern creeping into his voice.

"I'm not ill, just the usual monthly visitor," I said, a bit sheepishly.

"Right. Okay, no problem," he said, slipping his hand into mine.

We walked on for a few minutes in silence. Bless JC. After making a couple of attempts to ask directions for a *Farmacia,* it seemed there was one a few streets away. No great problem you might think, but I'm afraid I was being slightly economical with the truth.

It wasn't my period that was the issue. It was the *lack* of one.

Thirty Four

Angel

"Here we are Angel, *Farmacia*. It's also a general store, is that okay?"

I nodded, wondering if he might have seen through me and was starting to guess because of my quietness. He led me into the shop. My nerves were starting to kick in now.

"Do you have any preference?" he said, pulling me out of my trance-like state.

"What do you mean?"

"Tampons or towels? Believe it or not, you have a choice."

Great. As if I wasn't embarrassed enough. I was tempted to tell him to choose, but my normal sense of mischief had abandoned me. I wasn't in the mood.

"Towels would be great. Thanks."

I'd been racking my brains about how to hide my next purchase from him. I waited until he'd paid and he'd handed me a plastic bag.

"Um, JC, this is also a general store, right?"

"Yup, bit of an Aladdin's cave…"

"That's great. Would you mind waiting outside the shop for a moment? There's something else I need."

He was quiet for a moment, God knows what else he thought I wanted.

"Okay," he said, hesitantly and left me on my own.

Without a phrase book I was a bit stuck, but I had to have a go.

"Senor, es posible… bebe?" I said, making a round tummy gesture with my hand. I didn't understand the reply he rattled off, but then I heard a softer, female voice answer and I sensed a girl at my side, perhaps his daughter. I pointed to my eyes, waved my hand to indicate I couldn't see. Over the next few minutes various baby products were placed in my hands, packaging that varied from nappies to feeding bottles. I shook my head to them all. Thanking them both I felt my way out of the shop, helped by the girl who was chattering away to me in Spanish. I felt the bright sunlight outside and waited for JC to appear at my side.

"Okay? All sorted?" he said, amused but also intrigued. I put on my best smile and nodded.

"Uh huh. I need a drink," I said, wanting some thinking time.

I wasn't myself that evening, but I hoped he'd just put that down to hormones, the heat and adjusting to the jungle environment. Fortunately the bar was fairly lively with loud music, so we'd have struggled to have a conversation anyway.

Over the course of the evening I decided the only person I could ask for help was Danni. There'd be an opportunity in the morning to ask her. At least then I'd *know*.

Honesty and full disclosure, I'd decided, weren't an option.

JC
Of course that explained everything – women's problems!
I started to feel better about being here after the visit to the pharmacy, despite Angel acting a bit oddly. Perhaps she just wanted a big bar of chocolate and was worried I'd tease her. Whatever. At least there was a rational explanation for her throwing a wobbly.

She was pretty withdrawn that evening, but I guessed it was stomach cramps and generally feeling a bit low. So we just had a quiet evening and got an early night. In a strange way, Angel's monthly thing also meant it took a bit of pressure off us getting together. The jungle wasn't the best place for that anyway, it was hot and claustrophobic, so our moods were bound to be affected.

I rested my head on the pillow, quite content. We'd have an amazing experience in the jungle and see some fantastic things. There was also a good chance that our feelings would be re-awakened once we left and we might still get it together. Man logic - simple!

Angel
My night's sleep was awful. I was worried but the worst bit was that although I might have a chance to set the wheels in motion tomorrow, I'd still have to wait several days before I knew for

certain. Counting back, I already had a pretty good idea I was pregnant. And it frightened the life out of me.

We stood outside The Oriental Hotel at seven the next morning waiting for Danni to come and get us. JC had woken in a positive mood and was going out of his way to be nice to me, which made my deception harder. What was he going to think of me?

JC
Angel still wasn't herself, so I decided to fill some time and try to describe our surroundings.

"We're standing in what looks like an old town square. There's a bandstand with delicate balustrades and a cobbled road around the perimeter. I can see the river drifting past and there are seven long and thin flat bottomed wood boats tied up along the bank. Some have modern outboard engines, others have old car engines and long propeller shafts bolted to the back. Most have plastic sheeting sunshade roofs and chairs beneath, two wide. It looks like there's a neighbouring village across the water, I can see wood smoke drifting up from random bamboo houses. On our side of the river there's a Mississippi-style houseboat with two wooden storeys and ornate handrails. Beyond it, the river widens out, a big swirling mass of water running with a fast stream. It's very beautiful."

Angel
I nodded, but hadn't taken in any of JC's description. When Danni arrived, I immediately grabbed my opportunity.

"Can I have a minute please Danni? Sorry JC, women's stuff." I said, squeezing his hand as we parted.

"Of course," he said, unconcerned.

I walked several paces away, sensing Danni at my side. I kept my voice low and relayed the speech I'd mulled over in bed last night.

"Will you help me please Danni? I need a pregnancy test, but I don't want my boyfriend to know. He'd get too excited and I need to be sure. I have some money, would it be possible please?"

My voice was unsteady, just for me to say that word, *pregnancy*, here of all places, freaked me out.

"Of course!"

Danni hugged me.

"When you get back from the lodge... or sooner, because I visit on the third day. Would that be okay?"

"Yes, thank you so much. But it needs to be kept a secret."

"No problem. I know how men get. I'm so excited for you!"

Danni hugged me again, a lovely gesture, but it just made me feel even worse. Not just because of the predicament I was quite likely to find myself in three days from now, but because I was deceiving JC.

"All sorted?"

"Yup, we're good," I said, attempting my best smile, saved from further interrogation by Danni's enthusiasm.

"The boat is this way, your jungle adventure begins!"

JC

The boat ride was amazing! It was one of the fifty feet long wooden boats that had been tied up by the hotel. It was only just wide enough for two people to sit side by side, with a big modern outboard on the back. It skimmed over the muddy brown water, speeding upstream at a rate of knots. The breeze was lovely, cooling and refreshing, but it didn't seem to lift Angel's mood. She was still quiet and withdrawn. It concerned me for a while, but with my own spirits soaring, I decided to try and cheer her up and go back to my normal running commentary.

"I could do with some quiet time JC... to enjoy the sensation of the ride," she said, turning away from me.

"Are you okay Angel? I know it's not the best timing for you, but we're in a place few people will ever go to..."

I studied her indifferent reaction but gave up trying to push her further, she was probably best left. But I wondered why I hadn't noticed such a change in her last month.

Perhaps it's just the heat and humidity here.

I turned my attention outside of the boat to the lush green rainforest zipping by.

After about an hour, the boatman skilfully slued us across the river and beached the nose of the boat onto the muddy river bank. We were helped ashore by the lodge manager, a lean muscular man in his forties called Monty. I pointed to my eyes with two fingers, then waved my hand - *Angel can't see.* He nodded his understanding.

We were then given a tour of the lodge set-up. There was a large bamboo octagonal meeting and teaching area. It was open sided, but clad in thin mosquito netting, with three hammocks strung up in a corner. Next came the separate kitchen building come dining room which was for around thirty guests. We headed up several sets of steep wooden steps and passed along an interconnecting walkway and mud paths to reach the six individual guest cabins, that looked out through the trees at the river below.

"This is a lovely bamboo and wood hut Angel. It's raised off the ground by short stilts, with a stone walled shower, plank floor and two single beds with mosquito nets. Simple, but beautifully clean and functional," I said as I sat on the bed furthest from the door.

"Be a bit strange, not sharing a double bed with you. I might get lonely," I said, trying to jolly along the conversation, but failing miserably.

"I won't. Be nice to have enough room to sleep for a change," she said, a sour edge to her voice.
I stood and touched her lightly on the arm.

"Come and sit down Angel, you're not yourself and I want to know why."

"I'm *fine*. It's this place. It's so fucking hot and full of nasty bugs!"
I gritted my teeth and struggled to stay calm.

"Have a drink of water. There's a cold shower if you want to cool down before the nature trail. Hey, we might see wild monkeys."
Reluctantly she came and sat down, but seemed agitated. She fidgeted, rubbing her arms, unable to sit still. This wasn't the Angel I'd got to know and had started to develop feelings for.

"Please don't be nice to me, it doesn't help."

231

What on earth do you say to a comment like that? I gave up, walked outside and sat down on the porch decking, dangling my legs off the side.

This had all the hallmarks of a doomed friendship, and despite all the positive vibes over the last few weeks, I was really starting to think this whole trip had been a terrible mistake.

Angel

I sat on the bed feeling awful. My predicament was worrying enough, but I was also upset because of the atmosphere between us. I was screwing things up, but had no way of making everything right. For the first time on this trip, I felt really alone. If I could've pressed a magic button and whisked myself back home I would have. I was dreading the rest of the trip now and was quickly coming to the realisation that I couldn't continue. The only way I could salvage any long-term respect from JC was to leave him.

My emotions overcame me and I felt my eyes fill with tears. How the hell had I fucked up this badly? I started to cry, feeling completely alone in the world.

I didn't hear the door open, or the footsteps across the floor. I had my head in my hands and was rocking back and forth trying to comfort myself as I felt his arms wrap around me, pulling me into a close hug. I completely let go and sobbed my heart out, my shoulders juddering uncontrollably as I buried my head in his chest.

He held me there for ages, rocking with me, saying nothing, just gently stroking my hair. His embrace felt so safe, but it somehow made me feel worse. My stupid mistake had already sealed our fate and I was convinced he was going to hate me.

"It's okay Angel. Shhh…"
But of course it wasn't.

Thirty Five

Angel

Eventually I calmed down and regained some of my composure. Before any awkward questions began, there was a knock at the door and Monty called out a happy greeting.

"Amigos, are you ready to meet the animals?"

"Can we have just a minute please?" JC replied.

"No problem, I'll be by the steps."

I eased back from JC, rubbing my wet eyes.

"I'll get you a towel," he said, leaving me on the bed feeling alone. Then he sat down beside me again and carefully dabbed a hand towel against my face, soaking up the tears.

"Later, after dinner we'll talk this out."

I started to shake my head to protest.

"I've gotten to know you well enough to care about you Angel. There's something else going on here and you're going to tell me what that is so I can help you. I'm not taking no for an answer. You *will* get it off your chest and you *will* feel better. Don't forget, I know where you live!"

That made me chuckle a bit.

"Okay?"

I nodded, reluctantly.

It wasn't a conversation I was looking forward to, but I'd made my bed. Now I had to lie in it…

JC

God knows what was going on, I'd never seen Angel that upset before. True, we'd only known each other for a very short time, but it was an intense experience and I reckoned it was probably worth at least a year of 'ordinary' dating.

By the time we joined Monty at the steps, Angel had calmed down. Her dark glasses helped to hide the redness of her eyes. But she was still withdrawn, not her usual enthusiastic self at all. I was worried about her, but also for myself as well. I didn't want to lose her, or what had seemed to be building between us.

233

As we walked and listened to Monty explaining what the different animal and insect sounds were, I was deep in thought, wondering what could have upset her so much.

Angel

The worst thing about the day for me, other than carrying the burden of my secret, was how *nice* JC was being to me. He was extra attentive and made conversation for both of us to jolly the day along. He was trying so hard to look out for me, but it was just making me retreat further and further into my guilty self. I wanted to blurt it out, tell him, but I couldn't. It wasn't something I wanted broadcast to our hosts either, it was going to be painful enough.

It was almost a blessing that the trail was such a challenge for me. The narrow twisting jungle path was slippery underfoot and scattered with tree roots and other obstacles to get over or around. It was also so very, very hot.
And then the rain started. Bullet size droplets pelted down relentlessly on us – they don't call it the rainforest for nothing! Despite the dense jungle we didn't have much shelter and within seconds were saturated. I began slipping on the muddy path, tripping over tree routes and tangled plants with tentacle-like grips, nearly pulling JC to the floor with me many times. Added to this were the animal noises – some bloody tree frog calling his mate, far off screeching monkeys, branches crashing as they swung across the treetops and screaming insects flapping their wings around my head – they sounded as big as rats. *Challenging* jungle conditions didn't even come close...

I fell over again and again, flustered by the threatening sounds and slippery path, but JC was always there to pull me back up. How ironic that he was coming into his own now when I *really* needed him, just as I was about to burst his bubble…

JC

I guess walking *blind* on level ground is difficult enough, but now I really felt for Angel. She was having to navigate the jungle path without being able to see any of the hazards ahead. I took my hat off to her for gritting her teeth and hanging in there, especially in the stifling heat and pummelling rain. We did at least have plenty of water, but by the time we got back to the camp for lunch we were both drenched in sweat and rain, exhausted from the intensity of the walk.

It was a strange sensation, having to tread water emotionally. Lunch came and went, a fantastic local meat and rice dish, served in the marginally cooler dining hut, where we had the luxury of a gentle breeze blowing off the river. We made polite conversation with Monty as we ate, who appeared clued up enough not to push questions about the two of us. He must have sensed things weren't great between Angel and I. A look we exchanged during the meal seemed to suggest he understood. He must have seen countless couples struggle with the oppressive heat and physical demands of the jungle.

We had some free time before setting off on a different afternoon trail, so we crashed out in the communal area hammocks for half an hour. Somehow I doubted we'd have enough time for our discussion before the walk, which was to be 'the medicine trail' as Monty called it. We were joined by one of the village elders, who, with Monty interpreting, showed us natural plant remedies for every kind of ailment the villagers were likely to suffer in their lifetimes; *nature's problems all had solutions, it was just a case of knowing where to look.*

I'd been willing the evening meal to arrive all day, so as soon as we'd finished eating dinner (which was in virtual silence) we made our excuses and headed off to our guest accommodation. My heart rate was up. I was anxious about what might be said, but was determined not to sleep until everything that needed to come out into the open had been well and truly aired.

I frowned as I approached the front door, noticing that I'd left the light on. This was easily done as there was no electricity between ten in the morning to six at night. I unlocked the front door and led Angel in, only to be confronted with a mass of buzzing insects – some of which were as big as flying hamsters! They were using the light like a punch bag, constantly bashing into it, mesmerized.

"Shit!"

I heard Angel scream as she frantically swatted bugs away from her face, her arms flailing, getting extremely upset and agitated – on the verge of totally freaking out. I grabbed her hand and quickly led her into the main room, sat her down on her bed and threw the mosquito net over her. I switched the overhead light off and opened the door, waving my arms trying the encourage the bugs out, but with little success. After a while I gave up, realising that I was deliberately delaying things. I didn't really want to have *the talk* either, but it had to be done.

I ducked down and used my torch to find my way back, illuminating several pairs of eyes, some as big as coat buttons, hovering in mid air. I sat down on my own single bed opposite Angel's and pulled the mosquito net down over my head. I sat there for a moment, letting my eyes adjust to the darkness, wondering if I should have plonked myself down on her bed, but that might have felt like I'd invaded her space.

So I sat on my bed waiting patiently, quite a feat after practically tearing my hair out all day wondering what had upset her so much.

Thirty Six

Angel

The insects screeching and buzzing around inside the hut didn't help, but it was the torturous silence between us that really upset me. I don't know why, maybe because we'd shared a bed for most of the last eight weeks. But when he led me to my bed, then left me, it really hurt. Didn't he care at all?

I reached out to touch the mosquito net, knowing it was essential, but it felt like an emotional force field had dropped between us.

Perhaps that was no bad thing.

"Here we are," he said softly from across the room.

"Yup."

Silence.

Where on earth should I start?

A distant rumble built into a muted crack of thunder and rain started pattering against the thatched roof, bringing with it a decomposing vegetation kind of smell.

"You seem to have gone through a dramatic change in outlook Angel. What's triggered it? Was it something I did?"

I sat there thinking.

"Not exactly, no."

I wiped tears away from my face, fighting the urge to ask him for a hug.

"The thing is… oh crap."

I said a silent prayer and with a shaky voice I began.

"It's like this, JC. I'm late."

Wait for that penny to drop…

There was a long pause.

"Late. As in your period?"

There you go.

"Um, yeah."

What the hell must you think of me?

"Was I any good?"

I almost laughed, covering it up with a cough. If this wasn't such a hopeless situation, I'd have laughed my head off.

"How late?" he said, before I had a chance to explain.

"Maybe six or seven weeks."

"Oh. I see."

"The first month we were here I didn't even register what the date was and what should normally be happening. I suppose I got caught up in the excitement of our travels, the fun we were having. During the bus journey I had all that time to think about how happy I am travelling with you. Then it hit me and I started counting back…"

JC

Stunned didn't even come close.

My heart was racing and my throat bone dry. I struggled to get any words out, but I had to ask.

"This is going to sound awful, but did you sneak off with someone else while we were travelling?

"No, of course not. Even if I'd wanted to, when would I have had the opportunity? It happened before I even met you."

I didn't really want to hear the details, but I couldn't stop myself.

"What happened? Aside from the obvious."

I watched her silhouette behind the mosquito netting. The rain was growing in intensity on the roof, accompanied by distant thunder booming closer overhead.

"He wasn't some random bloke. Look, the downside to being blind, despite my apparent outgoing personality, is that my confidence can dip. It takes a lot of getting used to, not being able to *see* yourself look desirable, *feel* attractive. I suppose that's how Pete was able to work his old charm on me."

"Pete your husband?"

"Soon to be ex-husband. That's the reason he came round, to sign the divorce papers… I suppose I was at a low ebb and he's a real charmer…"

I heard her sigh. There was movement behind the netting, perhaps she was rubbing her eyes.

"We shared a bottle of wine, ended up laughing a lot of painful stuff off. He was full of himself, going on about a research study in Australia looking into hereditary eye defects.

He said that in a few years people like me could have most of their vision restored. I don't know how accurate or honest he was being, it may just have been a line. Even so, there was still a familiarity between us, we'd shared time. Perhaps that's how we ended up in bed together."

"For old times' sake?" I said, regretting saying it as soon as the words left my mouth.

"Does it really matter? I made a mistake."

"Do you know for sure?"

"Danni is bringing me a pregnancy test kit."

That explained the *Farmacia* and her private chat with Danni before we got on the boat. I'd thought little of it at the time, but it was all making sense now.

"Does Pete know?"

"No, how could he? I've only just realised myself that something was amiss."

She laughed a hollow laugh.

"Something amiss. That sounds pretty flippant," she said, scolding herself.

We sat quietly for a while, listening to the rain pound the straw roof from the sanctuary of our separate beds. Then an unpleasant possibility occurred to me.

"Do you have any memory gaps from that evening? Did you wake up in the morning with a fuzzy head?" I said.

She hesitated before replying.

"I can't remember my conversation with Pete word for word, but no major memory gaps. Why?"

I took a deep breath, took my time deciding how best to respond, acutely aware of the delicacy of my question.

"Is there any chance something was slipped into your wine and…"

"No. Pete's a smooth talker, a loveable rogue perhaps, but he's not capable of that."

"Are you sure? You were vulnerable Angel. It would have been easy for him."

There was a long pause.

"It was consensual. I made a mistake. I'm sorry."

I sat there in silence, trying to get my head round everything. I wanted to say to her *why are you sorry? This happened before*

239

we'd even met, and you didn't know you might be pregnant. But I was unable to say a word.

Angel

The thunder that had been distant when we'd started our conversation, was now getting really loud, a cascading drum roll that exploded overhead. Mother Nature was unleashing her anger on me for screwing up so badly.
JC's silence was the real killer though. Couldn't he think of anything to say?

There was a bright flash that must have been lightening as more thunder exploded close by. The noise was a convenient cover as all my pent-up anxiety and stress came pouring out again.

I leant forwards, hugging my knees, crying again.

Thirty Seven

JC

What's actually changed between the two of us? She made a mistake, but it was before your time. Okay, it has massive consequences, but does it change how you feel? No. Yes, and no. Bloody hell! I'm so glad we didn't end up in bed together. Are you really? No. Bollocks! So the question is, what are you going to do about it? Nothing I say will make any difference. You sure about that? No. So there's only one thing for it...

I could have gone on wrestling with myself for the rest of the night, taking my normal analytical, measured approach, or I could just follow my instinct. I took a deep breath and made my decision.

I rolled out of my bed, lifted the mosquito net surrounding Angel and climbed in, making her jump as I pulled her close and held her. I felt a dampness on my tee-shirt as her tears soaked in. I hugged her tightly, calming her shuddering body, overcome with emotion myself as I felt the tears spill from my eyes.

Above all else, whatever happened from here on, we'd been through too much together for me to let Angel suffer alone. We sat there like that for a long, long time. The storm became increasingly loud and violent overhead, until eventually it started to blow through.

"What am I going to do?" said Angel between sobs, her voice muffled on my chest.

"Not you Angel, *us*. We're going to wait until Wednesday when Danni comes. Then, we'll know. And when we do... we'll cross that bridge when we get to it."
I closed my eyes and held her even tighter, a feeling unlike any other washing over me.

Angel
I don't know what time it was when JC finally left my bed to try

241

and get some sleep in his own, but it must have been the early hours.

Little more had been said since he came to comfort me. It was a waiting game now until Danni arrived. How would either of us truly know how we'd feel until after the test result?

The waiting was agonising, but we just had to put a brave face on it and tread water for a couple of days. Despite this, or because of it, the jungle seemed a little easier to cope with. JC was as attentive as ever, but it seemed a relief to him that the unknown was now out in the open. And there seemed to be a closeness between us, despite all our developing feelings being put on hold.

JC

I suppose it was to keep occupied, stop myself going crazy, that made me rummage in my pack for the e-mails I'd printed off in La Paz. We'd had dinner and were killing time before going to sleep, which we both desperately needed after the previous night's thunderstorms. I sat on my bed under the mosquito net and started reading the messages by the light of my torch.

There was another message from Simon, more rational this time, pleading with me to get in contact. The deal he was negotiating would set us up for life. He couldn't understand why we were being so dismissive over so much money. I smirked as I discarded the page.

There were several other e-mails from newspaper and media reporters, which I read with amusement, then also cast aside. The last handful of messages I spent a little more time over.

E-Mail From: Maria Stockton
To: Angel Eyes
Subject: Butch Analyst and the Sundance Sexpot Ride Again!

Hi Guys,
Whether or not you're a couple yet, (in the carnal, romp between the sheets sense...) I'm writing to you as one. You are after all fugitives, being hunted like wild animals, pursued by the world's

press and still managing to stay one step ahead of them... (by the way, did you like the title of this e-mail?!)

No let-up back here, I'm still being hassled most days to dish the dirt on you. I can only vouch for Angel of course, but I tell them there aren't enough hours in the day to tell all the stories. Then I put the phone down or slam the door in their faces. Make sure you don't get caught, I'm quite enjoying all the attention!

I'm not even going to speculate where you might be now, the computer could be bugged, but I hope you're still having an amazing time. One thing's for sure, it can't compare to the routine and boredom of life here! That said, the supermarket has become rather fun, paparazzi-bashing with my trolley - I kid you not. Last week I was pursued round the freezer section by a young lad, firing questions at me. I swung my trolley round and caught him squarely in the balls. It brought tears to his eyes. I did at least do the decent thing and offer him a packet of frozen chips to calm the swelling down. Funny, he didn't seem interested in asking any more questions after that!

We're taking bets at work on how long you'll last without getting caught, I reckon you'll make it to the end. I've got a tenner on you both, don't let me down!

Gotta run now, my paparazzi need me! Take care of yourselves and keep up the good work. Angel, you'll be amazed when you get back to see how many people you've inspired; if you can travel all that way being blind and avoid capture, just think what everyone else can achieve if they put their minds to it. I'm serious, you're becoming a modern day heroine, so keep going and show them all!
Maria x

I had to smile. Maria had a way with words and was a true friend to Angel. I put Maria's message on the bed away from the pile to be binned and held the last two e-mails in my hand. One was from Kate Thornly the 1st and the other from Pete, Angel's soon to be ex-husband. In the confusion since her bombshell, I couldn't quite remember if they were still married or not.

I sighed, wondering if it actually mattered. I dropped my eyes back to the e-mails.

E-Mail From: Princess Sparkle
To: Jonny Blue Bottle
Subject: I Messed Up, I'm SORRY!!!

Dear Jonny,
If the first apology was unusual, this second one is unheard of. I'm sorry Jonny. I just felt we'd drifted apart. It was flattering, the attention I got from Frank, but with hindsight I should have taken it with a pinch of salt and stayed faithful. I'm sorry I didn't, and I really regret it. I know I messed up. Will you forgive me?

I've had reporters hounding me. It's horrible. They shout nasty probing questions through the letterbox, ring me all the time and go through the bins looking for juicy gossip. It's embarrassing and if I'm honest, humiliating, especially as it rubs in how much I messed up...

I couldn't read anymore and took great pleasure in slowly and clinically tearing the page into the tiniest pieces possible.

Bugger off Kate Thornly the 1ˢᵗ. You made your decision. You only get one chance, and you blew it.

That felt much better. I had a thought and glanced over at Angel, wondering if she could hear me reducing the message to confetti, but she appeared to be listening to her MP3 player. I hoped the music was taking her mind off her predicament. Correction, *our* predicament. I was left with the last e-mail, the one from Pete. I wondered if I should read it. Normally I wouldn't even consider prying, but I'd have to read it aloud to Angel anyway and I'd already set a precedent reading Maria's message.

I held up the paper and began to read.

E-Mail From: Dr Pete

To: Angel
Subject: How about a Rematch?

We've made a breakthrough, discovered a new genetic treatment for your condition! We've had remarkable results in younger patients, improving their vision enormously. Get in contact. I know people who can fast track you through the waiting lists. Imagine being able to see again! Call me.
Peter
PS. Fantastic evening, I didn't think you'd be up for it. When you're done with the analyst chap (who doesn't look much fun) maybe we can hook up from time to time?

Christ! What the hell should I make of that? I scanned through the message again, knowing I'd have to read it to Angel. If Pete wasn't exaggerating and she had a chance to regain her sight, that would be amazing. My mind started running away with itself. If she had a child on the way, the chance for her to *see* her baby would be fantastic, the stuff dreams are made of. But what about Pete? Did she belong with him? There didn't seem to be much warmth in his message, it was pretty aloof and clinical.

I shut my eyes, trying to clear my head and be objective about a friend. I needed to set aside my own deeper feelings for a moment. How the hell was I going to get my head round all this?

Angel
I'd been lying back thinking when I heard JC tearing paper, which I guessed was one of the e-mails. The music had taken my mind off things for a while, but I'd switched it off to have some clear thinking space. I lay there wondering if I should ask him who the message was from, but I decided against it. With everything else going on, it would probably only complicate things further. So I said nothing and trusted that if it was important, at some point he'd tell me.

JC turned in for the night and so did I. Tomorrow was very likely going to be life changing. I removed the earphones and shut my eyes, drifting in and out of sleep until morning, when I woke to one of the scariest days of my life.

Thirty Eight

JC

It was the day of the pregnancy test and now the tension really set in. We washed and dressed quickly, walking in silence down the long walkway to the dining hut. I couldn't remember whether Danni would be there in the morning, afternoon or evening. I should have asked Angel, but my mind was racing and I couldn't concentrate on anything.

As we descended the last step, I saw Danni chatting to Monty.

"Hi guys, how are you?" she said.

I felt Angel's grip tighten and my heart went out to her. If I was nervous, how must she be feeling?

"Jonathan, can I ask you to give Monty a hand with the boat, we have some supplies for the village to unload. Don't worry, I'll look after Angel," said Danni, as she took Angel's hand and led her away.

I watched them leave and felt a sense of helplessness. I wanted to be there with Angel to support her, whatever the result.

Angel

I sat on the edge of a hammock as Danni crouched on the wood floor in front of me, rummaging in her bag.

"As you might imagine, Rurrenabaque has a limited stock of these products and I had no luck finding anything locally. But fortunately I had a friend arriving from La Paz, so I sent him off on an errand, after convincing him it wasn't for me! Men are so funny. Here we are," she said, as she placed a packet in my hand.

I sat there cradling the answer to the question that had been on my mind constantly for the last few days. My throat was bone dry, my heart racing.

"There'll be some time after breakfast, before we go off in the boat to see the Macaws nesting, if you want to try then? You must be desperate to know..."

I found myself nodding, lost in a trance. Danni placed a hand gently on my arm.

"We'll have some breakfast first. These things shouldn't be faced on an empty stomach," she said, placing her hand in mine to lead the way.

JC

I helped Monty with a couple of trips between the boat and the dining hut, my heart racing. It was just a decoy of course, Monty didn't really need my help.

I joined Danni and Angel at the breakfast table, not wanting to eat, but I forced half the normal amount down. I'd probably need all the energy I could get for later. Nerves were burning through my reserves at quite a rate. Fortunately Danni did all the talking, chatting away happily, until at last it was time for us to collect our stuff from the cabin for the day's trek. She gave me a big encouraging grin as we left the table, but I struggled to be as enthusiastic.

Angel

This was a totally new experience for me, sitting there on the toilet. Waiting. I couldn't get my head round the fact that I wouldn't be the first to know. Any ordinary girl would at least have a few moments to register the result before an anxious boyfriend or excited husband started pestering. I realised it was pointless waiting on my own, because even held close up to my eye, I couldn't make out the result.

"How long do I have?" I called out.

"Another thirty seconds. Here, come and sit down."

We sat on the edge of my bed and waited. When it was finally time, I held the tester up for JC to read. He sat there for a long time in silence.

"What does it say? Is it positive?"

"I don't know how to say this Angel… but I don't know."

"What?"

"I can't be sure."

AAAARRRRHHHH!!!

JC

We got our stuff and legged it down the steps, nearly slipping over several times as we rushed to find Danni, who was sitting with Monty on the meeting room decking. She looked up as we ran over, her face lighting up. Her happy expression dropped, confused as we hurriedly tried to explain. Angel thrust the tester under her nose. Danni took the plastic tube and examined it closely, then showed it to Monty, who nodded, his expression giving nothing away.

"What does it say?" we both said, almost in unison.

Thirty Nine

JC

"It's positive, you're pregnant. Congratulations! I'm so excited for you!"

Danni threw her arms around Angel and hugged her tightly.

Oh bloody hell!

"Are you sure?" Angel said, in a quiet voice.

"Yes. Definitely. Do you want to sit down? This is a big thing for you both, yes?"

Danni guided Angel to a seat on the decking, just in time because I could see her starting to shake. She dropped her head over her knees, shock kicking in. She wasn't the only one. Danni hugged me too, then Monty shook my hand and clapped me on the back, grinning at me. The adrenaline of the last few minutes started to ebb away, leaving me wobbly on my feet. I sat down next to Angel, resting back against the mosquito netting and closed my eyes.

Where on earth did that leave *us*?

Angel

Fuck.

Pete you fucking bastard!

But I was also elated too. I was going to be a mum!

I felt JC slump down next to me. He must have been shell-shocked. The problem was, it was bound to stifle anything that had been building between us and I still *wanted* him. Jesus, my head was spinning.

"It must be a shock, finding out the first time," said Danni, uncertainty in her voice as to how I was taking the news. I managed to nod.

"This is good news, or... unexpected?" said Danni.

That was a good question. I opened my mouth to answer, but JC beat me to it.

"Both," he said.

The perfect answer! I could have kissed him, if I hadn't been feeling so sick. I felt his hand rubbing my back, which was reassuring. I wondered how long that would last before reality set in and he ran a mile. Because if I'd been in his shoes, that's exactly what I would have done.

JC

I found myself starting to laugh. Inappropriate it might have been, but it helped to diffuse my emotions – how my life had changed. At least it wasn't boring!

"We're going to make quite a story Angel, you and me." Angel sat up straight, her breathing still unsteady. She turned towards me and broke into a grin, her cheeks glistening with tear tracks.

"Aye. You should have put a government health warning on eBay!"

She started laughing with me. I glanced up at Danni, who was looking confused.

"It's a long story…" I said, laughing some more. It just seemed like the only thing to do to keep my sanity.

Angel

I'd been sitting toying with my drink for a while, something at the back of my mind nagging away at me. I lifted the glass to my lips, tasted the alcohol, and then hesitated, realising what it was. How stupid, I shouldn't drink! I pushed the glass away and sunk my head onto my hands.

"Sorry Angel, I wasn't thinking," said JC over the bar music.

"This is going to take some getting used to," I mumbled.

"Yeah. I'd better drink that for you."

I heard him pull my drink towards him, there was a pause, then a clunk as he placed the empty glass back on the table.

"I'm gonna grab the waiter. Soft drink for you?"

I nodded, completely spaced out. We'd got back to Rurrenabaque that morning. I'd tried to finish the last day and night at the lodge, but couldn't face it. We'd got the boat back with Danni, checked back into The Oriental Hotel, then found the nearest watering hole, ironically called the Mosquito Bar – wonderful!

I heard JC's stool squeak as it was dragged towards me and felt his arm drape across my shoulder.

"Cheer up chicken, it'll be okay," he said.

"You figure?"

JC

I pulled Angel close to me, but there was a reluctance about her. It wasn't hostility, more a sadness and unwillingness to open up. And let's face it, this wasn't the ideal place to cheer her up. We were in the middle of the Bolivian jungle in a bamboo-built travellers bar with thumping dance music and every cocktail you could imagine for only a pound a go. It was also bloody hot and raining, again.

"Put her down, you don't know where she's been," said a vaguely familiar voice. I turned and looked up at Bozzer, standing there dripping wet, wearing a wacky Hawaiian shirt, surf shorts and flip flops.

"Bloody hell! Small world," I said and stood to shake his hand.

"The world of the traveller is never that small mate, similar psyche and all that."

"Now where did you learn such a complicated new word?" said Madge, joining Bozzer as she dragged two stools from a vacant table.

"Fancy some company?" she said, more of a statement than question.

Madge reached over and hugged Angel then kissed me on the cheek.

"So, what we all drinking?" said Bozzer.

"Beer and a coke, thanks mate," I said.

He nodded and hailed a waiter.

"I'd ask you where the film crew are, but your escape has been splashed all over the news. You're quite a team," said Madge.

"Yeah, cult heroes. Nice hairdos by the way. Suit you both," Bozzer chipped in.

"Sorry about the way it was left at Machu Picchu. We had no idea they'd be waiting for us," said Angel.

Her voice sounded reasonably together, but I knew she was making a big effort to engage in the conversation. Madge reached out and squeezed Angel's arm, a concerned look in her eye. I guess some people are intuitive, they know when things aren't right. Bozzer of course was oblivious.

"It was a bit of a shocker, but a few of us met up in Cusco the next evening, had a good laugh about it. Especially when we heard you'd done a bunk. How'd you manage it?"

I explained about the train, Bob and our journey from Peru to here, with Angel pitching in occasionally. We spent some time talking about Bob, his generosity and the classic sing along to *Don't go breaking my heart*, which had them in stitches.

The beers kept flowing and Bozzer and I got more and more drunk. I guess the evening was a much needed pressure relief. It had been quite an emotional roller coaster these last few days. They noticed Angel was sticking to soft drinks, but I fobbed them off by saying she'd had a heavy session the night before. Bozzer shrugged and chinked his glass against mine.

"More for me and you then, Jon boy!"
Madge eased back on the booze part way into the evening though. I think she was keeping an eye on Angel.

"Excuse me boys, nature calls. How you fixed Angel, I'm off to the ladies if you need a ride…" said Madge.
Angel nodded and stood, allowing Madge to hook her arm under hers and lead her away. I looked after them, thinking Angel could probably do with a girlie chat.

"Got yourself a cracker there mate. She seems a bit quiet though, heavy one on the sauce, eh?"
I nodded, then drained the last of my beer. I picked up the cocktail menu on the table. Bozzer grinned.

"I'm liking your style mate. What'll it be?"

Angel
I started crying almost as soon as I pushed the cubicle door shut. I didn't know if they were happy or sad tears. It was just a way to get my head around stuff. How could I be here, in the Bolivian jungle with a man I met a matter of weeks ago, (and one I've started to care about a great deal) pregnant with someone else's child?

There was a soft knocking on the door.

"Want to tell me about it?"

I reached out and flipped the door catch, allowing Madge to ease the door open. One look at me and she knew. I heard the door shut and Madge crouched down in front of me, stroking my hair.

"How late are you pickle?" she said, in a soft, gentle voice. Which of course set me off again. She hugged me and I buried my head into her shoulder.

"It's such a fucking mess," I managed to say, before my breathing became erratic and I couldn't speak anymore. I sat there with Madge holding me and cried and cried.

JC

It must have been an hour later that I wondered where Angel had got to. I was pretty plastered by then, but I wasn't overly concerned. As Madge had led her away to the ladies she'd winked at me. She must have guessed that Angel could use some female company.

"So where you heading next?" said Bozzer.

"Probably try and fly out tomorrow or the day after. The jungle has been a struggle for us."

Bozzer nodded, squinting at me through his cigarette smoke and the alcoholic haze.

"I can see in your eyes you need out. I understand that, pretty hardcore travelling here, eh. But there's a flaw in your plan, aside from your passports flagging you up on the radar…"

"We're past caring mate, we both want to leave. We're not going out on the local bus, it nearly killed us getting here. If Simon and his film crew catch up with us at La Paz airport, so be it," I said, cutting in.

"Nah, you're missing the point amigo. It's been raining solid for the past week. They don't call it the rainforest for nothing. Me and Madge have been trying to fly out for the last three days. We're gonna swing by the Amazonas office in the morning, but if nothing comes in, then nothing's going out. We've got to be in Argentina to meet my brother in a few days, so if there's no plane tomorrow, we're gonna ask around, see if anyone else wants to split the rental of a jeep to La Paz. Should be twelve to fifteen hours rather than eighteen on the bus. A seven seat jeep with four passengers and a local driver who knows the roads should be much more comfortable."

I drained the last of my cocktail and sat back, glancing over my shoulder at the rain lashing down beyond the mosquito screens. I weighed up the chances of a flight leaving in the morning, then as any good analyst would, I factored in the grass runway (which would be waterlogged) and the waiting list of delayed passengers all trying to fly out ahead of us.

"Count us in mate," I said, as we raised our glasses to seal the deal.

Angel

I told Madge everything. By the end of our mammoth chat I felt much more composed and together. Somewhere at the back of my mind, a decision about my future was being forged. I hugged Madge for the hundredth time and thanked her, then stood, ready to face the world again.

Back at the table it was apparent that the boys had been going through the cocktail menu, which I guessed was JC's coping mechanism. It reminded me of the one question of Madge's I'd not been able to answer, because I honestly didn't know.

How did I feel about JC and how did he feel about me?

Forty

Angel

I was no closer to answering that question the next day when I found myself sitting in a jeep preparing to set off on our marathon drive back to La Paz. As I waited for everyone, I thought back to my conversation with Madge. On her advice, I tried to talk to JC that night, but all he was good for was collapsing in bed and snoring all night. I didn't blame him for getting blind drunk. Had I been able to, I would have done the same.

The following morning was wiped out until lunchtime while he slept off his hangover and was then grumpy for the rest of the day. So not the best timing for an in-depth discussion about our feelings for each other, or whether we could get ourselves back on track to almost getting together. But despite everything that had happened, and his mood, he had been as attentive and thoughtful as I'd gotten used to. It was a surreal combination.

Our plan was to get back to La Paz, spend a day or two getting over the journey and then make our way overland to Paraguay, ending up at the Iguazu Waterfalls on the Brazilian border with Argentina. I guess somewhere along the way we'd each work out how we felt about the other and this crazy *situation* I found myself in.

I felt the jeep engine rumble into life. The door to my right opened and Madge shuffled in beside me, while JC spread out on the bench seat in front of us. I guessed Bozzer was riding shotgun with the driver.

"Got us some water and snacks," said JC, squeezing my shoulder as we pulled away, leaving Rurrenabaque and the jungle behind.

JC

It had taken me a whole day to recover from my hangover, those cocktails were lethal! We'd met Bozzer and Madge that afternoon at the only swimming pool in town, and had swum between downpours for something to do. The girls sheltered in the bar, deep in conversation, which was good for Angel. She must have missed female company, being stuck with me all the time.

To be honest, I'd not given myself that much time to think about the two of us. The problem was, I think Angel thought I felt sorry for her and if we ended up together then that would be the reason. But in truth I'm not sure how I felt, now there were *three of us.*

I glanced around the empty streets as we trundled out of town. It was early, and we had a long journey ahead, but I felt much more comfortable this time around, despite our previous vow to fly out. Bozzer had been right, no planes left the previous day and although it wasn't raining at the moment, the lady in the Amazonas office thought it would take two or three days to clear the backlog of stranded travellers.

My eyes rested on Angel and for the thousandth time I wished we could have the intimacy of eye contact, so that we could really know how we felt about each other. I found myself smiling as I recalled how she ended up with red hair, and how different she looked. *But no less lovely.*

I turned back to face out of the side window, but saw Madge looking at me - caught in the act. I smiled sheepishly and she winked at me. Was that a green light? Or was the wink just to encourage me not to do a runner now Angel was up the duff?

Looking out of the window, through the rain, I was quite relieved Angel couldn't see the state of the road, I'd forgotten how perilous the bus journey had been. The 'road', no more than a gravel track clinging to the side of spectacular jungle-clad mountains was notorious. Sheer drops without any crash barriers plunged away at almost every hairpin. Wreckage far below was worryingly frequent, perhaps I was more aware of our mortality now Angel was *with child...*

I flinched as a pick-up truck loomed from behind a blind corner. We crawled past at walking pace, wing mirror to wing mirror. My nerves were not handling this journey particularly well...

Angel

Although quicker than the bus, it was still a long journey. We stopped a couple of times for food and loo breaks, but not for long. Our driver, Pedro, sounded like a young lad of maybe nineteen or twenty and he spoke pretty good English.

Conversation inside the jeep had died off an hour or so ago, as we'd exhausted all discussion about how we'd met our 'other halves' and where we were in life. Tiredness now took over and we sat in companionable silence.

I asked JC what time it was and worked out we'd been on the road for just under nine hours, which meant we were well over half way. We were making good time according to the driver, who had his foot down all the way. Although driving fast and slightly erratically at times, I was assured that he was doing a good job of avoiding the traffic coming the other way. I had someone else to consider now. It's a strange feeling when your sometimes reckless outlook on life is pulled up sharp.

I smiled to myself, instinctively rubbing my belly, worry and excitement creeping into my thoughts. Suddenly I felt the jeep swerve and jolt violently to the left, it bounced up, slamming back down on the gravel road, before sweeping hard right, careering out of control...

JC

Jesus Christ!! We hit the verge then swerved to avoid an oncoming minibus. My face spun forwards as the packed bus filled the jeep's windscreen. I barely had time to yell "HOLD ON!!!" before we smashed into the front quarter. Then we spun backwards into the steep verge, trees breaking as we rolled onto our side, part of the roof caving in, crashing to a stop.

"Bloody hell, everyone all right?!" I shouted, my eyes darting around the inside of the jeep. Because I'd been stretched out across the bench seat I was fortunate to have landed on my feet when we'd tipped over. Adrenaline surged through my system, I had a few scratches but I was okay.

Angel!!

"Guys! Are you okay? Talk to me!" I shouted, climbing over my seat, finding Angel's limp body pinning Madge to the side of the jeep.

"I'm alright mate, driver don't look good, but I can see his chest moving. What about Madge?!" Bozzer shouted, scrabbling to release himself under the weight of the driver, who was slumped awkwardly across him.

"Madge! Talk to me!"

It was one of those moments of clarity where you slow yourself down and force yourself to think logically, desperately trying to set panic aside. Bozzer was talking, which meant for now he was okay.

"Bozzer, can you kick the windscreen out? If you can, get out and get the door above us open!"

"Madge!"

"Mate, get a grip! Your best chance of getting her out is to get yourself free first."

I looked at him, shaking his head, his breathing all over the place. I realised shock was kicking in, sapping his energy. I turned back to the girls, weighing up the best way of getting to them, then shouted over my shoulder at Bozzer.

"Bozzer! Kick that bloody windscreen out! Get angry, hate it! Come on you worthless criminal descendant!"

BANG! BANG!

That did it, he was good and mad now. I climbed over the seat and took a look at the girls. Although I could smell petrol, there was no immediate danger, I prayed the rain would wash it away. I carefully ran my hands over each body, checking vital signs, feeling for damage. Were they still breathing? Broken bones? Bleeding?

Up front Bozzer was yelling all sorts of obscenities as he kicked the shit out of the glass, but it was working, he was nearly free. I stared down at Angel, my heart pounding, feeling myself start to lock up, shock hitting me hard.

"You trying to touch me up JC? Bit forward for a first date," Angel mumbled, her eyelids flickering open as she came round.

"Jesus, don't do that to me! Where does it hurt, can you move? Be careful of Madge…"

As far as I could tell she had no major injuries. There were cuts and grazes, but it was the baby I was most worried about, a reaction that surprised me. There was another crash up front and with a euphoric yell, Bozzer kicked the windscreen clear and scrabbled out onto the road.

"Must have cracked my head…" said Angel.
Together we untangled her from Madge, who was out cold. I heard Bozzer climbing over the jeep and saw his wild eyes appear at the side window above us. He crouched over the door and tried to heave it open.

"Fucking door's jammed mate!" he shouted.

"Okay. Hang on a moment, let's check Madge out first…"

"I'll find a rock, smash the glass from the outside," said Bozzer, glancing around, his face red with blood that was washing down his face with the pounding rain. He looked like something out of a horror film. By this time Angel had managed to turn and support herself and was slowly examining Madge by touch.

"She can't be moved JC, not yet. She's got some damage here, I can feel blood. I need time to examine her. And if we take her outside she'll freeze in this rain."

"Okay, we'll clear the boot and get you some room to work," I said, completely deferring to her knowledge. It didn't even enter my head that I had to look out for her, her blindness was no longer an issue.
I heard Bozzer climb back onto the jeep and saw his rain and blood soaked wild-eyed face appear at the window above. He didn't even shout out a warning, he was completely focused.
WHACK!

"Shut your eyes Angel!" I yelled as Bozzer smashed the rock down again, raining fragments of glass into the jeep. Then Bozzer's feet dropped in through the open window.

"Madge!"
Bozzer was all but elbowing me out of the way, but I grabbed him before he could move her.

"Mate, pass that luggage from the boot forwards to me, I'll throw it through the window…"

"No! She's coming out the window, we've gotta get her out…"

Bozzer tried to get to Madge again, so I increased my grip on him.

"Bozzer, listen to me. Think! We're not on a cliff edge here, there is no immediate danger, but if we move her too soon we could do more damage. I know you don't want her in a wheelchair so <u>listen</u> to me. Pass me the luggage, kick that back screen out so we can move her quickly and easily when we need to, but let Angel do her job – she's a nurse, okay!"

Bozzer struggled to get free.

"She's fucking blind!"

That was it. My own adrenaline pushed me over the edge. I clenched my fingers around his windpipe and squeezed hard, pulling his face close to mine.

"Listen you colonial fuckwit, THINK! Do <u>you</u> have any medical training? NO! We have a trained nurse here, she can tell us what to do. Give Madge a chance. Do your job and clear that luggage. NOW!"

I stared into his eyes, waiting until I saw the small nod of acknowledgement. I eased my grip and pushed him towards the boot.

"Let's go! Chuck the bags back to me, we need to work together."

Bozzer climbed over into the boot and started heaving bags to me, which I tossed out the open window above. If nothing else, distracting Bozzer allowed Angel the time to finish examining Madge unhindered. We cleared the last bag and Bozzer set to work kicking the rear windscreen out. I eased myself down to Angel.

"How's she doing?"

"She's damaged her pelvis, there's bleeding from the side of her head and she has some sort of neck injury. Her airway was blocked, but she's breathing on her own now. If we're careful and we all support her we can lay her out. I need lots of clothing to make a bed."

"Right. How you doing?"

"A few bumps, but okay. Poor Madge took the brunt of it."

"Okay."

I climbed over into the boot to help Bozzer.

"Ready? Together mate."

We kicked the last of the glass out and I dragged Bozzer out onto the muddy road, rain lashing down, instantly soaking me.

"Mate, go through our bags, grab any clothing, make a bed for Madge. You heard Angel, she's breathing on her own, she has a fighting chance. Okay?"

"Yeah, no problem, mate, I'm sorry I lost it back there…"

"That's okay. Go!"

I ran back to the front of the jeep, pausing to glance back down the road where the minibus lay on its side. I could see movement, people were starting to climb out and in the distance headlights were approaching through the rain. I turned away and climbed through the open windscreen. Pedro was slumped down in the footwell, blood seeping from his face.

"How's the driver?" said Angel, calm yet assertive.

"Not good, blood everywhere…"

"It always looks worse than it is. Find the source, get some pressure on it, and try not to move him in the process."

"Okay," I said, glancing back, pleased to see Bozzer's legs running back and forth to the jeep as he lay out clothing in the boot. I looked back at the driver and shouted out to Bozzer.

"Mate, I need a tee shirt or something!"

I didn't hear a reply, but in less than ten seconds Bozzer appeared, handing me two tee shirts, then disappeared again. I began mopping up the blood on the driver, searching for the source. He had a nasty gash from behind his ear to his forehead, but he was breathing. I folded along the length of the tee shirt and tied it around his forehead, tight enough to put pressure on the wound. I checked his body for other injuries. His arm seemed a bit banged up, but thankfully I found nothing else.

"Ready when you are JC," said Angel.

Leaving Pedro for a moment, I dashed back to the boot, where Bozzer had finished laying out a bed of our clothing. Under Angel's instructions, Bozzer and I positioned ourselves so we could hold Madge's head and pelvis as we carefully eased her back into the boot and lay her out on her side on the bed of clothing. Angel checked her over as I tied clothing together to form a neck brace.

"Bozzer, she's stable, breathing on her own, just unconscious. Stay here, support her neck. If she comes round don't let her move. We need to check Pedro again. Was there another vehicle involved?" said Angel.

"Yes. Hundred yards back down the road," I said.

"Okay. We need to help them too," said Angel. I helped her to climb out into the rain, which seemed to be easing a bit.

"You're doing a fantastic job Angel," I said, squeezing her hand as I guided her fingers onto Pedro's limp body.

"You too."

I watched her check Pedro over, in awe of her skill. In a bizarre split second flashback, I wondered if the chance to regain some of her sight was really possible and not Pete's *I want you back* bullshit.

"His arm's broken, the one he's lying on. Can you lift him while I hold his head? Let's straighten his arm in a splint and then check out the minibus. Ready?"

We worked together, lifting and turning the driver who fortunately wasn't too heavy. It was awkward to get the leverage in such a cramped space.

"We need a splint. A branch, something like that. And a strap from one of our rucksacks."

I heard Angel call to Bozzer to check in with him too. I had a quick scout around outside, found what I needed and returned to the jeep. I helped Angel patch up Pedro, then we left the jeep. Angel gave Bozzer strict instructions not to let anyone move Madge.

"Thanks. Sorry I insulted you…" Bozzer called out as we left the jeep.

Angel and I ran hand in hand as fast as our bruised bones would allow towards the crumpled minibus.

Angel

They say it's like riding a bike, you never forget your medical training. Only this time I didn't have my own visual assessment, I had to rely on JC's observations and answers to my questions. We worked together at the minibus, assisting and instructing the local helpers with my medical knowledge, helped by JC's hand signals and our pigeon Spanish.

I've no idea how long we worked for, stabilising, bandaging, trying to help these poor victims, but it must have been several hours. We kept running back to the jeep every twenty minutes or so, checking in on Madge and the driver. By the time help finally arrived, we were completely exhausted. But of course this being Bolivia, help didn't come in the form of half a dozen fire engines, ambulances and police. It was all very basic.

Apparently car and truck wrecks littered the side of the road between La Paz and Rurrenabaque, good job I couldn't see any of that on the journey into the jungle, or we'd have been flying out, no matter how long we'd had to wait.

From what we could gather, the minibus that would normally seat eleven, had fifteen adults and three children crammed into it. The driver had been playing cards on the dashboard with his brother. There'd been an argument, causing the driver to veer across the road and smash into us. Pedro had done an amazing job to avoid a full head-on collision. The driver of the minibus had taken the brunt of the impact and was dead when we got to him; the injuries described to me by JC were horrific. A mother and her eight year old daughter sitting immediately behind the driver had terrible injuries. Even with the help of other passengers we couldn't get them both out of the wreckage in time and the mother died at the scene. The young girl fared better, being shielded from the worst of the crash by her mum; she had a deep cut to her thigh, a broken leg and some injuries to her face. But being smaller, she was pulled out in time for JC to get pressure on the wounds to stop her bleeding to death.

I have no idea how the word got through to the 'emergency services' about the crash, but as they started to arrive, JC pulled me away from the minibus and we trudged wearily through the mud back to the jeep. I crawled into the boot and checked Madge's vital signs. She'd been awake for a while now, but luckily Bozzer had done his job and stopped her from moving. I'd been able to ask her where it hurt and established that she had a fractured pelvis and serious whiplash. We'd all been extremely lucky. The jeep's solid construction had saved our lives. Pedro had a broken arm, concussion and a head wound. He'd come round whilst we were at the minibus and had climbed out of the jeep to come and help us. He was amazing, acting as an interpreter to those less seriously injured and flagging down other traffic to come and help pull people out of the mangled wreckage.

JC

As help arrived, we handed over the casualties with Angel running through the injuries and Pedro translating. Once we'd sorted out all of the minibus people, we met back at the jeep to help with Madge. Under instruction from Angel, we carefully lifted her out of the jeep, holding her flat. Once she was safely clear, fifteen or so Bolivians heaved the jeep upright. I remember standing there in disbelief as they rolled it back on four wheels and it was started up.

"Good for many more miles, yes?" said Pedro.
My jaw dropped in disbelief. We watched as the jeep was cleared of glass, loaded up with our sopping wet gear, and driven round to face towards La Paz. We carefully returned Madge to the back with Bozzer by her side and the rest of us climbed in. Pedro sat up front next to me whilst I drove. Angel kept vigil beside Madge all the way to La Paz. It was a long journey as we were doing no more than twenty miles an hour on Angel's strict instructions.

Once on the road, shock really hit home. I think privately Angel was very worried about Madge, but she didn't want to let on to Bozzer. It had been enough of a job for her to persuade him that a slower speed was essential. The potholes in the road were bone-jarring and hitting them would speed up any internal bleeding. I don't know how long we drove for, but by the time we pulled up at the hospital in La Paz my head was pounding with exhaustion, my mouth was parched and I felt weak.

It may have been my imagination, but Angel seemed to be checking Madge over a lot more frequently. There was an urgency in her manner, concern in her body language.

"How's she doing?" said Bozzer.
Angel didn't reply. I helped her out of the way as two doctors and a nurse arrived.

We all stood back as we watched the doctors go to work on Madge. I told Angel what I could see and she fired questions at Pedro and the medical team, an edge to her voice. I heard a word that I recognised, only because it was accompanied by a senior looking doctor rubbing his index finger and thumb together as he spoke. I saw the look on Bozzer's face and shuddered as it was translated and repeated.

"Insurance."

Bozzer said nothing. He looked completely spaced out as Pedro explained the doctors needed to see a copy of their travel insurance. Running a hospital in Bolivia is an expensive business.

"I'm not sure they're giving her the best medical treatment," Angel said to me as we were shown into a corridor.

"It's not going to improve when I can't produce any insurance documents," said Bozzer, stopping us all in our tracks.

"It ran out three weeks ago and it was too expensive to extend. We thought we'd take a chance…" Bozzer said, starting to get upset.

Oh shit.

"You're going to have to wing it for as long as you can, she needs urgent treatment," said Angel.

My mind was racing. The senior doctor appeared, getting quite insistent with Bozzer, who was holding his palms out in an *I don't have any* gesture.

"What happens if you have no insurance?" asked Angel.

"No US dollars, no medical," said Pedro.

"How much?" said Angel, beating us all to the inevitable question. Pedro shrugged.

"I have a credit card. There's probably a couple of thousand left on it, I could get it extended…" I said, but Bozzer sank down onto a chair, shaking his head.

"They want cash or the insurance documents," said Bozzer, his hands placed over his face, muffling his voice.

"What about our insurance? Madge could become Kate Thornly for a bit…"

Bozzer shook his head.

"They took her passport, they know who she is. Fucking nightmare," said Bozzer. I found myself looking round the waiting room again, my eyes resting on the young girl who'd lost her mother in the wreckage of the minibus. She was lying on a rusting trolley huddled up in a blood stained blanket. She didn't have any doctors fussing over her, attending to her injuries. She'd just been left. I looked away from her, back to Bozzer and then Angel.

"Can I talk to you?" I said, leading Angel away. "Have we had a good run, you and me? On our own I mean."
I watched her frown, trying to figure out what I was getting at, too exhausted to read between the lines.

"On our own? I don't understand."
I realised I didn't have time for the exploratory *how do we really feel about each other* conversation, the clock was ticking.
It was time for a leap of faith.

"Angel, I have had the most amazing time. I want to finish this trip with you. We've done well to stay away from all the hype that has surrounded us because of that bloody eBay advert. It was a blessing because it got us together, but it's also been a curse. Maybe we can use our 'celebrity status' to help Madge and the rest of the victims from the crash. It'll mean we'll have to give up our anonymity. They'll be media attention focussed on us. More than anything I want to be with you, but we can help Madge and these people with just one phone call."

"What about the baby? It's not yours and yet you'd be willing to…"

"Yes. Completely. I care about you Angel. You've shown me so much, made me *see* everything so differently…"
I didn't have to say any more, I was babbling, fatigue making me struggle with my words. Angel was nodding, tears trickling down her face. She held her arms out, I pulled her close, our mouths searching for each other and we kissed tenderly.

"We're strong enough to cope. Make that call," she said.
I nodded, kissed her again, then lifted my head just enough to call out.

"Bozzer. You got a mobile phone?" I said, hoping I could still remember Justin's number.

Forty One

Angel

Things happened very quickly after JC's phone call to Justin, who contacted Simon. It's amazing how money can move mountains. Apparently there had been a number of false sightings of us, locals desperate to claim the reward money, which meant Simon and the camera crew had been hanging around La Paz checking the airport and bus station.

The agreement JC struck was simple; unlimited medical treatment for Madge and the Bolivians on board the minibus, together with compensation for their injuries. We were to be checked over at the hospital, before being flown to the Iguazu Falls for three days rest and recuperation in a decent hotel without being pestered by anyone. In exchange, we would sit down for a series of exclusive interviews before finishing the last two weeks of our travels into Brazil with the camera crew in tow. We'd spend Christmas on a beach in Paraty, New Year in Rio, then fly home. Exclusive rights to our story finished the moment we got on the plane home.

During the negotiations, Simon told us we'd have to surrender our passports to him the moment we cleared customs in Brazil. He needed some guarantee that we wouldn't try escaping again!

"We should take up a new career as criminals, I think we'd be quite good," I joked with JC as we waited to be checked over.

"Yeah, by all accounts you weren't much good as an analyst," said Simon. From the tension in his voice, he wasn't very happy.

"Funny you should mention that, because I've moved on from that old life," said JC, barely hiding the hostility in his voice. I smiled to myself, remembering our first meeting in the hotel lobby. How bizarre to end up here, under these circumstances. It was definitely a story to tell the grandchildren. That thought killed my good mood as I instinctively felt my stomach, hoping that everything was okay. I felt JC's hand cover mine and gently squeeze it reassuringly.

"It'll be okay. I'll look after *all* of us," he whispered, making me tingle.

JC

Simon had arrived at the hospital with his entourage within an hour of my phone call to Justin. My meeting with Simon had been frosty and it wasn't showing any signs of thawing out. So long as he kept his end of the bargain and didn't try any 'buddy routine', that was fine by me.

Madge had been in with an American doctor for a while now and I was wondering how it was going. I looked up as Bozzer walked over. He looked shattered, much like the rest of us. He sat down heavily beside me.

"She's pretty banged up, but she's gonna be okay. The doc wants to fly her to a private hospital in Argentina. He's making the arrangements. Thank you, both of you. You saved her life, and mine, her dad would have murdered me."

We shook hands and Bozzer leaned in to kiss Angel on the cheek, then disappeared outside for a smoke.

"Hope your lot brought their chequebooks," I said to Simon, as I watched the tall middle-aged doctor walk over, a friendly smile on his face as he offered his hand.

"Good evening sir, ma'am. I'm Doctor Pacer. I'm extremely privileged to meet you both. Jonathan Cork and *the* Kate Thornly I presume?" he said in an American accent. I grinned and shook his hand.

"The very same," said Angel.

"After we're done, would you be kind enough to let me have your autographs? My street cred will go through the roof and my kids will clean their rooms for a week if I come home with proof I've met you both. Please follow me and we'll check you over."

We followed the good natured doctor into a treatment room, with me leading Angel by the hand as always. The doctor shut the door behind us and smiled reassuringly.

"Now, before we start, are there any medical conditions I should know about?"

Forty Two

Angel

I took a long deep breath and settled back into my seat as the plane accelerated down the runway. I stretched my legs out, exhausted, but so glad to be leaving Bolivia behind. It was a shame to think like that, because up until the jungle we'd had a great time and met some fantastic people. But it was time to move on.

This was going to be a long flight, despite the relatively short distance to the Iguazu Waterfalls, as we had to go via Buenos Aires. The media lot were paying, so there was little to do but rest my eyes and sleep. Thankfully Simon was a few rows back. I didn't fancy being anywhere near him and I doubted JC did either.

I must have drifted off, because the next thing I remember hearing was JC thanking a stewardess.

"Did you sleep too?" I asked, my head fuzzy but without the throbbing headache I'd had when we took off.

"Yup, Zonko. Needed to though, do you know how many hours we'd been up for?"

"No, but you being the analyst, I bet you've got a pie chart and graph to demonstrate it…"
I yelped as his dug me in the side, making me laugh and cringe as he touched a bruise.

"Got you some orange juice," he said, guiding my hand onto a plastic glass.

"Cheers. To surviving this long without killing each other…" I said, raising my glass.

"To the three of us," he said, tapping the plastic against mine. Oh yes, *the three of us.* I sipped the sweet juice and let that thought settle. So it wasn't a dream, I really was pregnant.

The doctor had been surprised, but delighted for us. It was still very early days of course, but he'd run all the checks he could at this stage and confirmed I was definitely still pregnant and congratulated us. We were both still a bit stunned by everything that had happened, but mostly we were just so knackered, nothing would make much sense until we'd had some sleep.

"We probably need to have a chat about that at some stage," I said, preparing an escape route for him, wondering how he really felt now we were out of the jungle.

"I'm not going anywhere for the next few hours and this is probably as much privacy as we're going to get for the rest of the trip."

"Okay. It's lovely that you're willing to give us a go, particularly given the *circumstances,* but I'm wondering if it's not just a bit of bravado, or misplaced sense of duty. We've spent a lot of time together and it's natural that we've grown fond of one another but perhaps that's all it is…"

"Look, we both know there've been a couple of occasions when something *was* going to happen, but didn't quite because of other factors. I've felt it, and I think you have too."
I had to hand it to him, it was a brave move baring his soul.

"But how do we know it's not just the romance of travelling, a result of spending so much time together? Do you *really* know how you feel? Things have changed now, massively. I have someone else to consider, it's muddied my thoughts. I don't know how I feel about us because it isn't just you and me."
There was silence for a while as he thought this through.

"I'm going to go out on a limb and say I think you feel the same way about me as I do about you. I guess you need some reassurance, but I know how I feel about you and I'll prove it right now."
My heart was starting to race. I was excited at his honesty and the emotion in his voice, but I was also intrigued as to what he was going to do. My mischievous side wanted to call his bluff.

"How?"
Another silence. Was he contemplating backing out, or gathering the courage to continue?

"By making a complete tit of myself. I'm going to prove how much I love you."
I caught my breath, did he just say *how much I love you?* I found myself grinning, which must have spurred him on.

"Excuse me for a moment."

He stood and shuffled out of his seat, into the aisle. I felt for his arm as he left.

"Are you going to get us thrown off the plane?"

"Don't worry, if we're jettisoned mid-flight, I'll fly us home."

Huh?

I felt him kiss the top of my head, then he was gone.

Forty Three

JC

There comes a time in a man's life when you have to face your fears, no matter what the consequences. I knew after the crash that I couldn't imagine being without Angel and having broken out of my comfort zone by coming on the trip in the first place, I never wanted to look back with regret. I was determined that if she ended up being the one that got away, it wouldn't be through lack of trying on my part.

I walked away from her, past all those strangers' heads, my heart racing, ignoring the little voice inside that screamed *what the hell are you doing?* I locked the toilet cubicle door behind me and started taking off my clothes as fast as I could. I was afraid that the longer I took, the less chance there was of going through with my plan. I laughed as the layers came off. This was going to be a very interesting few minutes...

Angel

I sat there grinning and for a while there was just the usual dull background hum of the jet engines and murmuring of quiet conversations. But then, something started. A ripple of gasps, some chuckling, then a burst of applause resonated from the front of the plane. The laughter and cheering grew louder and I found myself going red – the bastard was making *me* blush, and that never happens! How on earth had he done it? I felt JC plonk himself down in the seat next to me, with passengers still laughing and cheering.

"What have you done?"

"Who me? Oh, just stripped off a few layers, it felt a bit warm in here."

I gasped, and reached out to touch him...

"Senor. Please, this is not appropriate clothing," said a voice that must have belonged to an air stewardess.

I frowned as I touched JC's arm, which wasn't bare, it was clad in some kind of thin stretchy material.

"Senora, I'm worried about this plane crashing. We're flying awfully close to Krypton," said JC.

"You didn't..." I said as I felt up his arm, across his chest, tracing the outline of a large 'S.'
I burst out laughing.

"Afraid so. I've been wearing this bloody thing since the jeep ride out of the jungle. It was meant to cheer you up when we stopped for a break. I didn't figure we'd crash - I've been wearing it ever since."

"You brought it with us from Machu Picchu, when we legged it from Simon?" I said, struggling to get the words out.

"Yup. Thought it might come in handy! Thing is, it's not the only one of Maria's gifts I brought with us."
My laughter died away as I racked my brains. What else had Maria stitched us up with? A cold shudder shot up my spine as I recalled the items.

"You haven't?"
I felt something cold slip around my wrist, heard a ratchet click and the cold metal bracelet touched my skin.

"Senor!" the stewardess said, but now there was a giggle in her voice.

"Even Superman can't escape Kryptonite handcuffs. It looks like the man of steel quite likes you, Angel. The only problem is, the Clark Kent side of me can be such a clot. I managed to drop the key down the toilet!"
Oh my God, I've never laughed like that before. JC was even more crazy than me!

JC
It's fair to say we caused quite a stir when we landed at Buenos Aires for our connecting flight. Airport security was definitely interesting! Simon followed red-faced behind us, perhaps the television crew was giving him grief for all the attention we were getting. We were supposed to be under wraps until they could interview us properly.

Our flight was delayed whilst the airport staff found someone with a set of bolt croppers. It turned out to be a fireman based on the edge of the runway. We were driven there by a security guard who was chuckling to himself all the way.

"I should have worn one of Maria's tee shirts, can't have you getting all the attention!" Angel said, cuddled up next to me in the back of the car. Once freed of the handcuffs we were escorted back to the terminal building and I was made to change out of the Superman costume. I reappeared from the gents' toilets feeling no less of a superhero; I'd won Angel back, that was all that mattered.

Angel had been right, all those adventures ago when we'd first met. Life is so much easier and so much more fun if you can laugh at yourself.

We were still giggling and making superhero jokes all the way to the Iguaza Falls, an hour's flight from Buenos Aires. Perhaps being a *someone* wasn't so bad after all. The best bit for me was seeing how many people on the plane (and at the airport) had smiled and laughed at Superman handcuffed to a Scottish Lois Lane with bright red hair. For a short time we'd made a difference and would become the talking point of their day.

Angel
Despite being a dickhead, Simon was as good as his word and the hotel was very grand compared to the cramped places we usually stayed at. It had a cool fresh smell and an airy feel that even I could appreciate.

The place had an outdoor swimming pool, gym and internet access, but by the time we arrived we'd been on the go for almost two days, so the facilities were wasted on us that night. We were tired, hungry and in desperate need of a wash and a fresh set of clothes.

We just about managed to shower but didn't make dinner as all our spare clothes were soaking wet from the crash. So we collapsed into bed, cuddled up and slept for twelve hours solid.

I woke in the morning to an empty space next to me which was still warm, so I knew JC couldn't have gone far. I heard him finishing off a conversation on the telephone, then felt the mattress shift as he climbed back into bed.

"I've told Simon to find us some new clothes," he said, lying back down beside me, his warm body just inches from mine.

"Shame, I was getting used to seeing you without any…"

He laughed and turned towards me.

"Me too."

"I thought you were a gentleman and didn't look."

He sniggered and I felt his hand brush my hair off my cheek, making my skin tingle.

This had been a long time coming…

I shuffled onto my side, reached out and touched his arm, running my fingers down towards his elbow, my whole body was waking up, quivering in anticipation. As the gap closed between us, I felt the heat from his body. He ran his hand through my hair, trickling his fingertips down my neck, onto my shoulder, travelling across my collarbone down towards my breasts. They tingled, firming up as I became more aroused. I reached up behind his head and pulled his lips to mine. We kissed urgently, passionately, the bristles of his beard tickling my chin.

Christ I wanted him!

Our bodies locked together, pulling each other tight, tongues connecting, gently probing. I ran my palm down his back, clenching his bottom cheeks in my fingers, his taut muscles exciting me even more as he responded. His hand slipped between us, over my hip, past my rib cage until he cupped my breast. He toyed with my erect nipple, sending pulses of ecstasy through my body. I broke away from his lips for a second to gasp at the sensation as he gently squeezed, making me wriggle and cry out with pleasure. I reached round his stomach, finding him already hard.

"I've wanted you for so long…" he moaned as I slipped my hand around him, gently squeezing and rubbing up and down. We kissed deeply, tongues searching, hungry for each other. I felt him start working his hand down from my pert breasts towards…

KNOCK, KNOCK!!

"Senor," a voice called from outside the door.

For fuck's sake!!

275

"NO! You've gotta be joking!" JC shouted , breathless, whacking the bed in frustration as I rolled over and doubled up, panting from the excitement.
Of all the lousy bloody timing!

JC
Bollocks!
I scrambled around for a towel and yanked the door open, cowering behind it to shield my obvious bulge from the porter's wide eyes.

"Senor. Breakfast finishes in ten minutes," he said, handing me a shopping bag of clothes.

"Gracias," I managed, then pushed the door back for a moment as I hunted around for some loose change, oblivious to the fact that we were in Brazil now and that the Portuguese language and currency were the order of the day. I shot a look at Angel as I fished the money out of my trouser pocket. She'd pulled the sheets up under her chin, her face flushed.

I poured a handful of coins into the porter's hand then shut the door, leaning back on it, breathing hard. I started to laugh as I suddenly felt wobbly and in desperate need of food. I made my way to the bed and shuffled up alongside Angel, laughing at her shaking her head.

"Shitty bloody timing!" she said.

"I know, story of our lives! One of these days we'll get it together. Tell you what, I'm starving. Do you fancy breakfast, a day at the Waterfalls then a nice meal and an early night?"
She nodded, a wicked smile on her lips as she stood and felt her way around the bed towards the bathroom.

"This time you can look, keep it in mind for later..."
I felt myself shudder as she disappeared into the bathroom, my eyes lingering on her naked body. She was one sexy woman. I didn't know if I could wait until this evening...

__Forty Four__

__JC__

As bad timing as it was, the interruption was probably a blessing. I didn't appreciate how hungry I was until I stood staring at the breakfast buffet. I realised we'd not eaten anything substantial for two days.

I handed Angel a plate and loaded it up with eggs, sausages and cheeses and we devoured a hearty meal, each filling our plates twice more before we were done.

"That was delicious. Thank you."

"What for? I didn't cook it," I said, sitting back with a full tummy.

"You made this happen, with one phone call."

"Don't thank me yet, there'll be a fallout from all this..."
I watched her shrug her shoulders and for a moment my eyes saw past her cotton tee shirt, mentally undressing her.

"Madge and Bozzer will be in Argentina by now. She'll be getting the best possible treatment. I think we can put up with the repercussions," she said.

"We did the right thing. Definitely."
She nodded, but then grinned, mischievously.

"Doesn't mean we can't have some fun though. I reckon the two of us could be quite a handful."
Now it was my turn to grin, wondering what antics we'd get up to next.

__Angel__

It was a strange feeling, sitting opposite JC at breakfast, knowing that he was probably looking at me differently. He'd been *officially* allowed to see me naked and we'd very nearly taken things a stage or two further. It was bloody difficult to be normal again while we ate – my body was still tingling, despite having had a cold shower. I wanted to rip his clothes off right there and shag him senseless!

A day out at the Iguazu Falls was just the distraction we needed and it was a gorgeous day outside the air conditioned hotel. The sun was blazing hot, but without the humidity and regular downpours of the jungle.

We walked hand in hand to the bus station, accompanied by Simon and the reporters, who tried to engage us in conversation. JC ignored them, speaking only to remind them of the promised three days of peace to recuperate before we'd be available for interviews. They were probably still getting some film footage of us though so presumably their paymasters were happy enough.

JC resumed his usual running commentary, describing the lavish hotels that lined the road to the Falls and his first glimpse of the raging waters and spray as we approached the entrance. I could hear the roar of the water as we wandered into the park, the power of nature in full flow. I felt JC stop and turn back towards the entrance.

"Fantastic! Don't you just love rules," he said.

"Why? What's going on?"

He laughed.

"Apparently they need some sort of professional permit to film in here. Let's get a head start, it probably won't hold them up for long…"

We hurried on, knowing that they'd catch up with us eventually. I squeezed his hand and trotted alongside, feeling a light spray drift over me as the roar of rushing water grew louder.

"Wow!"

JC slowed us to a stop.

"Angel, this is amazing. Can you feel the spray? There must be twenty or thirty individual waterfalls, all curved at different angles, with several tiers stepping down to the river below. It's absolutely fantastic…"

"I know, I can hear it, feel the rushing water. It's like we've stepped into a movie set!" I said, grinning at the sensations.

JC

I've seen pictures of the Niagara and Victoria Falls, but this was a world apart. There were loads of walkways that allowed us to get really close to the millions of gallons of water constantly thundering over the edge of the staggered cliffs above us. It was so stunning it couldn't possibly be real. Multiple waterfalls cascaded all around us, surrounded by lush green trees and exotic scrubs, spray hanging in the air, providing a welcome cooling shower.

We carried on walking right to the end of the walkway, getting wetter and wetter as we neared the viewing platform, only a few metres from the cascading water. Far below, two speedboats zoomed upstream, taking passengers right up to the edge of the waterfall, almost disappearing from view in the mist, which created a beautiful rainbow. It was one of the most amazing sights and sensations I have ever experienced.

I glanced across at Angel, saw her grinning too. Like me, her shorts and tee-shirt were getting saturated from the spray.

"Are you okay with this, it's pretty wet..."

"Hell yes, I love it!" she shouted back against the roar of the water, squeezing my hand.

I stood there rooted to the spot, less self-conscious now about looking at her, drinking in her curves, getting turned on watching her soaking clothing cling erotically to her body. I reached forward. I had to kiss her. She responded as her pert wet body clung to mine, sending my hormones rocketing.

"I need you JC," she whispered in a throaty voice as we parted.

"Oh God yeah. Later is not soon enough!"

A cheer went up from our fellow tourists, prompting us to pull back, but not for long.

The sun was even hotter now, much like my state of mind. I needed to cool off or I wouldn't make it through the rest of the day. Earlier, I'd noticed a small passenger ferry crossing to a central island, where there was an area marked out for swimming in the Iguazu River. We didn't have any swimming costumes or towels, but I figured we could probably get away with our underwear, our clothes were sopping wet now anyway, so what difference would it make? Angel didn't hesitate when I suggested it, but I never thought she would.

We caught the boat across to the small pebble beach where we stripped off and waded into the gorgeous cool water, sinking in up to our shoulders, our bodies magnetically drawn together. Angel slipped her arms around my neck and we kissed, tentatively and gently at first, then with more intensity and passion.

"I've been thinking…" she said between kisses, "there's a way to escape Simon and the others without becoming a media freak show…"

"There is?"

"Mmm. Means being a bit naughty though…" she said, slipping her hand down my stomach and inside my pants.

"Jesus Angel, you turn me on!"

"Shut your eyes," she said.

"But I love looking at you," I said, reaching out for her, running my hands over her breasts, feeling her shudder.

She started to pull my boxer shorts down over my thighs, sending my heart racing even faster. I dropped my hand to stop her.

"We can't…"

"Close your eyes, experience this with me, just by touch. Lose those inhibitions…"

"It's too public,"

"That's the point! Let go of everything you know…"

I hesitated, then released her hand, kissed her again and unclipped her bra. I traced the outline of her skin down from her breasts until I felt the material of her underwear. My breathing was erratic now, I moaned as she cast my boxers aside and wrapped her fingers around my erection, encouraging me to pull her panties aside and slip my fingers inside her, feeling her heat…

"Have you got your eyes shut JC?" she said, almost panting.

"Yes… it's erotic because it's daylight and I know there are people but I can't see them…"

"Shh… No other people, just us."

I felt her body shudder as I slipped my fingers deeper inside. She lifted herself up, wrapping her legs around my back as she guided me in, pulling our bodies close, hips touching, rhythmically grinding together. We kissed deeply, her fingernails clenched into my skin, pert bare breasts pressed against my chest, the cool water tingling around our hot bodies. I remember being totally absorbed in our lovemaking, eyes clenched tightly shut, oblivious to everything else.

She was right, we could have been anywhere. There was no one else here, just us. I carried our pulsating bodies back towards the shallower water, where I lay her back on the beach, pushing deeply inside.

I heard her whimper and cling to me even tighter, as I felt myself start to let go.

"Bloody hell! I'm going to cum…" she gasped, moaning as our rhythm increased, pelvises flexing in and out, both building towards a pulsating orgasm that clamped us together, weeks of pent-up sexual tension exploding. I tensed up, held her tightly, lost in the ecstasy of the moment. Gradually I felt my muscles relax as I sank into her embrace, kissing her, completely absorbed in the moment.

We lay there for a few moments on the beach, water lapping against us, our bodies as one, engrossed in a relaxed feeling of satisfaction and fulfilment.

And then the cheering, wolf-whistles and clapping began!
Blink.

I forced my eyes open, already cringing, wondering how badly we'd messed up, hoping against hope it was just a couple of people.

Oh bloody FUCK!!

I glanced around, disbelief draining me of all the passion I'd just been revelling in. There must have been fifty people on the beach. But the worst of it was, at least three of them had video cameras trained on us! And advancing through the cheering crowd were two members of the park's security staff!

Beneath me, I felt Angel start to giggle.

"How bad is it?" she said, laughing out loud as I dropped my head into her neck, burying my head in shame.

"I think we've just become stars of a Brazilian porno movie," I said, not knowing whether to laugh or grab our clothes and run.

Angel whooped out loud and slapped my arse hard.
YEOOWW!!

"Stay for a bit, we should enjoy this moment. Let's walk away from this with dignity…"

"Dignity?! We've just shagged in front of fifty people, and been filmed! I think dignity is the least of our worries!"

"I don't see fifty people," she said, actually managing to sound indignant. There was nothing else for it, I laughed. What else could I do?

One of the park's staff stripped off his tee shirt and offered it to Angel to shield her important bits from the many eyes and cameras that were fixed on us. Under the supervision of the security staff, we were escorted to our clothes where we got dressed and were then frog-marched out of the park.

Despite the deep shit we were in, I had a stupid grin plastered across my face. So did Angel.

"Let's put it down to stress relief, after our time in the jungle," she said.

It turned out the Brazilian authorities had a slightly different interpretation of our being *a bit naughty* and we were escorted into a police van, past Simon and the film crew, who had been waiting in the shade playing cards. I watched their confused expressions as we sped away, and I couldn't help giving them a cheeky wave. I turned back to face Angel, who was sitting back against the side of the van, still grinning.

"So," she said, playfully.

"So. We made it to the end."

"The end?" she said, surprise creeping into her voice.

"Of the trip. We outlasted my expectations."

"Hmm. Um, I'm wondering where we go from here JC…"

"Home to the cold, probably. A big roast dinner. Followed by a cool beer or two. Then I'm going to start planning my next adventure. I've got a taste for travelling. Thank you Angel. It's been… an eye-opener!"

I leant forwards, kissed her on the cheek, then sat back and watched the emotional roller coaster of expressions flash across her face.

"That's it? We're done?"

"We broke our pact Angel, we got sexually involved. Sure, we had a few laughs along the way, but honestly, us? Nah."

Angel sat frozen opposite me, in complete shock.

"But I want to see you again!" she blurted out, overcoming her temporary rigor mortis to reach out, touch my knee.

"Oh, you will. Just make sure you put in the highest bid…"

"Highest bid?"

"Yup. I'm going to do another auction, try out the next Kate Thornly. I reckon what with the fumble on the beach and being an international celebrity now, I should get a few takers."

Angel

I sat there completely dumbfounded. I felt my bottom lip start to quiver. He couldn't be serious? After everything we'd been through. What a bastard! I shook my head and opened my mouth to speak, but no words came.

Then I felt him run his fingers through my hair and he gently pushed my jaw back up, snapping me out of my daze.

"Gotcha!"

Forty Five

Angel

The worst bit about the next two days was being apart from JC. But I had all the memories of our romp on the beach to help ward off the boredom while we waited for the powers that be to decide what to do with us. In the end, I think they took the easy option and deported us, which is what I'd hoped would happen when I first had that crazy, naughty idea.

Was it worth it, the stigma and all the extra attention we'd heaped on ourselves? Absolutely! It was a moment of mad, reckless fun that I'll never forget. Paris Hilton, a comfy hotel room, with no live audience, pah!

And that's how we found ourselves sitting on a plane home, our South American adventure over. But we'd had a pretty good run, I had no complaints. It was mid December and only two weeks shy of the full three months. The Brazilian Authorities had been pleasant enough, even mildly amused, but they were at a loss as to what the right course of action should be. They had to do something and so a crusty old judge cautioned us and sent us packing. Justin and the TV crew were furious, but as far as I'm concerned, we'd kept our end of the bargain.

Flying out of Rio airport was something else. As we were escorted into the terminal, a huge cheer went up. I could hear hundreds of people waiting to see us off, many of them wearing printed tee shirts of us cavorting naked on the beach. Under the picture was a caption in Portuguese that apparently said something like; *From Iguazu to Eternity – fucking English!* Maria would be proud!

JC

The departure gate was bonkers! There were people everywhere wearing those crazy tee shirts. So this is what being a celebrity is like, I thought, as we were escorted through the barrage of flash photography and cheering crowds. We were famous!

But the real adventure for us was just beginning. It was this thought above all the other experiences we'd had travelling together that made me smile the most. Our future was unwritten. How would we get on together back home?
How would we cope as a *family?*

I was both nervous and excited to find out the answers, but I knew that whatever happened, life would never be boring again.

I was roused from my thoughts by a stewardess finishing her announcement; we'd be landing at Heathrow in a few hours. Angel squeezed my hand and leant towards me, whispering mischievously in my ear.

"Hey Superman, fancy joining the Mile High Club?"

*

This book is dedicated to the anonymous blind girl who, on Wednesday 31st October 2007, made me blink back tears as she walked the Inca Trail on the arm of her Peruvian guide. You are my inspiration and the real hero of this book.

*

For more information about me and my other writing projects, please look me up at: www.markdavidgreen.co.uk

Printed in Great Britain
by Amazon.co.uk, Ltd.,
Marston Gate.